A Blackmailer in Bermuda

An Elspeth Duff Mystery

D1707483

Ann Crew

The Bermuda Biological Station for Research changed its name in 2006, shortly after this book was written, and is now called the Bermuda Institute of Ocean Sciences or BIOS.

Also by Ann Crew

[In Order of Publication}

A Murder in Malta

A Scandal in Stresa

A Secret in Singapore

A Crisis in Cyprus

A Gamble in Gozo

A Deception in Denmark

Praise for *A Murder in Malta:*

"Each main character has a rich backstory with enough skeletons in cupboards to provide grist for a number of future novels.

An often compelling . . . excursion through exotic locales featuring unusual, complex characters."
—*Kirkus Review*

To Sally Roberts
who is an inspiration to all her friends

Part 1

The Guests at the Bungalow

Prologue

"Fire, of course, is one of the most dreaded occurrences at any hotel. It destroys property and endangers lives, but equally, a substantial fire can single-handedly shut down a hotel by demonstrating negligence by its owners."

Elspeth Duff, rather than paying attention to the head of security's words, was thinking ahead to dinner with Richard, who would be arriving in London from Malta at any minute, and had promised to ring her once he reached Gatwick.

"Our buildings are designed with the latest fire prevention devices to prevent any . . ."

Elspeth could almost recite the words, as could every other member of the Kennington hotels security staff, whether they were permanently stationed at one of the Kennington hotels around the world or were roving security advisors, which was the case for her. They all were required to attend this same lecture every six months. It varied little, but over her eight years of employment with the Kennington Organisation, Elspeth paid less and less attention, just as she seldom listened to flight attendants' instructions on fastening one's seat belt and putting on one's oxygen mask before helping someone else. She travelled too extensively to pay heed, or so she thought. She ran her hand over the sleeve of her new silk blouse, hoping her husband Richard would like the colour, and brushed a fleck of lint off her skirt, part of a new suit that was smart and classically cut by her French dressmaker from a tropical weight gabardine. She had left the jacket back at her desk, as London was baking hot for early October, and even in the air-conditioned areas of the skyscraper that housed the Kennington Organisation in the City of London, the climate felt oppressive.

The head of security introduced the local fire chief, whom Elspeth recognised. He was dressed in his uniform and began his practiced speech, one he had given many times before. Elspeth stifled a yawn and tried to keep her eyes open. And then, totally without warning, smoke filled the room and spread so quickly that any chance of seeing more than a few inches beyond one's face became impossible. Elspeth gagged and began to cough, but the lectures over the years must have made an impact because she automatically fell to her knees. She groped for her Maltese lace-trimmed handkerchief, a present from Richard, but unfortunately, it was in her suit jacket pocket several rooms away. By instinct she covered her nose and mouth and crawled on hands and knees towards the door of the room, silently cursing the sealed windows of modern office buildings, which, if operable, could have let in relieving air. On her way towards the door she collided with other staff members, who obviously had also heard the fire chief's lecture on emergency procedures before. As she approached the door, however, the entrances to the room were flung open and several firemen brought in large suction fans to dissipate the smoke.

The fire chief called to them all to resume their places. "That woke you all up, I see. Most of you were not listening and the rest only half-heartedly so. The smoke bombs I've just set off are totally harmless, but had it been smoke from a fire, you very well could have suffocated. And not only you, but the guests in the hotel as well. Don't ever forget that! When a fire happens, you are the ones who are responsible for the lives of the guests. Remember it is their lives and health that are important, not their possessions. Possessions can be replaced; lives cannot."

Afterwards, Elspeth called Richard and said she would change their dinner booking at the restaurant where they were to meet to a later hour, and asked him to come instead to their flat in Kensington. She needed to change her clothes and wash her hair, both still tainted with the smell of smoke, benign though it was.

She had little idea that this dramatic presentation by the fire chief would become so profoundly important in her next assignment, and the consequences of such would ultimately lead to her arrest for murder.

1

It was not as if Elspeth Duff had never met royalty before or dealt with them professionally. She had, both in her role as security advisor to the owner of the Kennington hotels, and more recently, as wife of a senior member of the diplomatic corps. But, she never had been asked before, as Lord Kennington had just done, to be in charge of security for members of the royal family who presently had plans to visit the new Kennington Bermuda resort hotel, and therefore she would, by necessity, be in daily, if not hourly, contact with them over the course of their stay. To step in when security problems arose at any of the worldwide Kennington boutique hotels was one thing; to attend to the comfort and safety of a prince and a princess and their entourage was quite another. She could remember the correct forms of address and proper protocol over short periods of time, but how long could she sustain this without making a gaffe? She was not at all sure, and wondered why Lord Kennington had chosen her above the others in the Kennington Organisation who had more experience with this sort of thing. Did Eric Kennington think the assignment in Bermuda was a lure to keep her under his wing after her marriage, that she would see the job as some sort of plum? Did he think that during the tempestuous weeks before her wedding, when she almost broke off her relationship with Richard, she would return to her job, crawling to his lordship and asking him to send her to a far-off place so as to forget? Or, did he think after the blissful time of their wedding, in whose arrangements he had lent an extensive hand, she would give herself over to her husband and resign her position with the Kennington hotel chain altogether? He had tested her in Denmark and not found her wanting. Or, did he think this new assignment was a prize to be given to one of his favourite employees, while she saw its potential for disaster? Despite Elspeth's dedication to her job, which she had every intention of keeping, and despite the change in her marital status, she felt she had gained a bit of an upper hand over Eric Kennington after the successful ending of her assignment in Copenhagen. He did have a tendency to bully his employees. When negotiating the new terms for her continued employment, Elspeth had insisted that Richard could visit her while she was on a long assignment. Lord Kennington, when he wished, could be manipulated but only if he achieved the result he had hoped for in the first place. In any case, he always seemed to be amused when Elspeth made demands which he had already decided to agree to, and he usually told her so.

With these thoughts playing on her mind, Elspeth had boarded the plane for Bermuda after explaining to Richard that this would be the longest time they had been apart after their wedding trip to California four months before, and the brief hiatus towards the end of their honeymoon in Copenhagen. Before they were married, he had promised to respect her career, and, since he was frequently away from London so as to fulfil his diplomatic responsibilities in Malta, she was comforted by his immediate acquiescence to her new assignment and his willingness to coach her on royal protocol. While Richard had never disguised his strong royalist tendencies, Elspeth had spent over a third of her life in America and considered British royalty a necessity to promote British trade and tourism, but little more. Like the rest of the world, she had followed the foibles of the royal children and respected the British queen for her graciousness through it all, but Elspeth's interest was limited to reading the lurid press headlines when waiting in a queue at the supermarket or in airport shops while looking for something to read during her long flights.

Elspeth, however, was not well-versed in the other royal families of Europe. Therefore, when assigned to Bermuda, she invited her closest friend, who was coincidentally Lord Kennington's business partner, to dinner at her Kensington flat, and used the occasion to pick Pamela Crumm's brain.

Pamela, despite being a shrewd business-woman, was a romantic at heart. She filled her in on all the details of the royal couple. As Elspeth tossed the salad left ready for serving by her housekeeper, Pamela rolled the lineage of both the prince and princess off her tongue as easily as reciting the alphabet. Elspeth only listened partially, as, other than knowing that most of the royal families in Europe had some tie to Queen Victoria and her nine children, she took little interest in the comings and goings of the British royal family's continental relatives. Unlike Pamela, she found the stories in the sensational press superficial and was inclined to believe they were only partially true. Too much of Elspeth's job involved diverting the press from taking any interest in the guests who stayed at the Kennington hotels. She had cultivated the skills necessary to persuade reporters and photographers that any guest at the hotels was beyond reproach or, when pressed, she would simply deny their existence. She had succeeded, with a few rare exceptions, but her opinion of the paparazzi could be rated in the freezing temperatures.

The prince and princess, Pamela confided, had been married for over twenty years, despite the prince's family's initial objection to his marriage to a commoner whose titled German grandfather had been a member of the National Socialist Party and an industrial supplier to the Nazi war machine during the expansion of the German empire in the 1930s. Although he had later denounced the regime and fled to North America, her family was tarred with a past that continued to nag them when the royal prince's nuptial ambitions were announced. The princess, who was Canadian by birth, had been educated in England and Switzerland, spoke German, French and English fluently and, despite all the criticism in the prince's country of origin, always appeared in public with such a sincere smile that in the end, she could not fail to capture the hearts of the prince's countrymen. Even the king was captivated and finally blessed his brother's marriage. At least, Elspeth thought, as Pamela rattled on, I won't have to communicate in my limited French or almost non-existent German. The prince and princess had only one child, a daughter in her twenties, who tended to be as wild and selfish as her mother was restrained and selfless. Pamela explained that the daughter was currently on a cruise in the Caribbean with one of the more notorious Turkish playboys. At least, Elspeth thought, my assignment had some consolations.

The flight attendant cleared away Elspeth's meal, and Elspeth took out her notes to review once more the members of the royal party and affix their names and titles to her mind. Prince Michael and Princess Honorée led the list. The prince's private secretary, Harald Wade, held a British passport but his address matched that of the prince and princess. The princess's lady-in-waiting was noted as Baroness Greta von Fricken. Her husband, Baron Klaus von Fricken would be at the hotel as well. The von Frickens were described as Swiss citizens, despite their seemingly German titles, and like Mr Wade, they lived with the prince and princess. A couple called Mr and Mrs Francis Tilden and their daughter Miss Mary Tilden, whom

Elspeth assumed were friends of the prince and princess, were Canadian, but were traveling from the West Indies to join the royal party. The list seemed benign enough, and Elspeth assumed most of the guests were at least middle-aged, except perhaps Miss Mary Tilden and Mr Harald Wade. Even Mr Wade could well be older. Certainly no one on the list sounded threatening, making Elspeth wonder why Eric Kennington had given her this assignment. Was there some dark secret lurking in the shadows that he had not told her, or was there a danger to the party from other guests at the hotel? Or, perhaps Eric Kennington had a suspicion that something was amiss, and he wanted Elspeth to take care of it. Damn, Elspeth said silently to herself, I hate going into a job without set parameters. What did Eric have in mind? He had specifically instructed her that he, not Pamela, would supervise her actions.

The taxi from the airport swept up a narrow drive lined with a profusion of lush plants. Elspeth recognised the palm trees but was amazed at their different varieties and heights, some squat and spreading, and some with long, bearded trunks towering into the sky. Hibiscus hedges were interspersed between broad-leaved plantings and bird-of-paradise bushes which displayed their orange and white spikey flowers. The driver, in her soft Bermudian accent, gave the names of the other plants, most of which Elspeth did not recognise. As they mounted the hill which led up to the hotel, she saw small decorative ponds lined with low growing succulents placed among the extensive lawns. No wonder Bermuda was described in guidebooks as a gardener's heaven.

Pamela had told Elspeth that the Kennington hotel was housed in one of the old estates in one of the parishes of the island chain. The main house was built on the top of the hill, and bungalows and small outbuildings clustered nearby, sloping down towards more gardens, the pink sand beach, and the turquoise and navy ocean beyond. Had she not been on assignment, she could envision relaxing on one of the chaise longues she saw on the beach in the distance.

If the colours of the houses she had seen during her ride to the hotel were any indication, she had expected the hotel's exterior to be painted coral or a soft pastel colour, but Lord Kennington's designers had chosen a stark white set off by the white limestone roof tiles, which were ubiquitous on all the buildings they had passed on the way from the airport. Dark louvred shutters hung from the tops of the long windows. With black lanterns on stanchions and more palm trees marking the entrance to the hotel, she felt like she had arrived in an enchanted world.

The hotel manager met her and showed her to her rooms, which were situated in one of the courtyards by the main building. The porter brought her cases, and she quickly changed into less heavy clothing, even though the temperature was mild, rather than oppressively hot. She was now ready to meet the royal family.

2

"Perhaps, Ms Duff," Prince Michael said, "I should first apologise for bringing you to Bermuda under what you may have perceived as feeble pretences. I asked Lord Kennington to keep the purpose of your visit under wraps until you arrived. You see, the circumstance of our stay here has deep implications for my family, and there could be no hint of any impropriety before I could talk to you in person. Eric assures me you are the best person for the job and the very soul of discretion."

Elspeth did not know what she expected the prince to look like in person despite having seen a newspaper photograph of him in royal attire, but any image that she might have had did not correspond with the man who summoned her into the small sitting room near the door of the royals' bungalow, which lay below the main building and offered a spectacular view of the ocean. The length of the prince's legs emphasized his height as they stretched out from the checked fabric of his Bermuda shorts. He was shod in casual leather sandals, and he wore a short-sleeved open-necked white shirt revealing sinuous arms and a tuft of blondish hair at the throat. Only his face, long, thin, and dignified, betrayed a long history of privilege and exalted ancestry.

Elspeth had taken a seat in one of the rattan chairs opposite the prince and had accepted a cup of tea. She acknowledged his words with what she hoped was a concerned expression, but inside she smiled to herself. How like Eric to keep her in the dark and let her muse on the significance, or lack of it, of the assignment he had given her. She should have suspected something more was afoot.

The prince continued, "I wanted to talk to you before you meet the other members of our party, so that you would understand the importance of our being here."

"I'll do anything I can to help, Your Highness," Elspeth said, "and you may rest assured that I'll keep any request you make of me in strict confidence."

The prince looked at her discerningly, and finally said, "Yes, I think I can trust you." He rose and shut the door to the hallway. "I'm not certain the island architecture offers as much security as the heavy walls and sturdy doors of our family's palace, but I've asked to be left alone while I speak to you. Have you heard of my daughter, Ms Duff?"

"Our London office gave me a brief background rundown." She almost added 'would you like to fill me in?' but stopped short of doing so as she was uncertain if it was proper for one to make direct requests of the brother of a ruling monarch.

"Then let me tell you more," he said, as if reading her thoughts. "My brother, the king, has been blessed with only one child, a son, who unfortunately has never been in the best of health as he was born with an irregularity in his heart. This malady has never been revealed to the public, but it's of deep concern to the whole family. After my brother's death, which we all hope will not occur for a long time in the future, his son will succeed him, but if anything happens to him, I'm to be next in line. I have no desire to inherit the throne, our lives being simple ones, but the possibility does exist. My brother's son seems to have no inclination to marry, as he is absorbed in his studies of palaeontology and leads the life of a recluse, only performing his royal duties when forced to by his father. My wife and I have one child, our daughter, the Princess Christiana, who is fourth in line to the throne. She's always been a rebel, defying me and her mother from her earliest years. We thought she would grow out of this, but unfortunately, even with her strict education, she has bucked our control and has become fodder for the tabloids ever since leaving school five years ago. Our country is noted for its openness towards the monarchy, and, unlike your queen, we are treated as ordinary citizens, but most our people expect us to act with a sufficient degree of decorum to justify our continued constitutional role. Christiana laughs at this when we confront her. No threat seems to change her ways.

Until now we have been able to exert a certain amount of control over the press, but her recent escapades with a Turkish playboy, who calls himself Ali Ayan, have brought us to a point where we need to challenge her directly. A week ago she announced she was going to marry Ayan and convert to Islam. I don't need to tell you the ramifications of her doing so for both our family and for our nation. I'm sure you can imagine."

Elspeth turned her eyes from the prince and quietly blew out her breath. Because of the history of long-established European royalty who had carried on the Christian legacy since the early saints had come north from Rome or east from Ireland, one would hardly expect the ever-consuming friction between Muslims and Christians of the modern world could ever touch their hallowed traditions, let alone the line of succession. Even the affair between the Princess of Wales and the son of a prominent Egyptian entrepreneur did not reach these proportions, as in that case the accession to the throne was not an issue.

Elspeth paused before speaking. "How are you proposing to deal with this? I assume that is the purpose of your visit?"

"I've brought together here all the people in my

household and family who are closest to Christiana. I'm sure Eric has acquainted you with their names, but I requested that he not tell you their roles in our lives. If you had known, you might have assumed we simply were on holiday and that our party was here for rest and recreation, as they say, and not for a serious purpose. I expect you wondered why you were sent here at all?"

"I did," she conceded.

"We were not aware of Christiana's intentions until she visited my wife's sister, whose name is Hope, and her husband Francis Tilden at the Canadian High Commission in Antigua and Barbuda. At this time Christiana was already on a cruise with Ali. Francis is the Canadian High Commissioner there, and both he and my sister-in-law are close to Christiana. In fact, Christiana often confided more in Hope than her own mother. It was my wife's suggestion that if Francis and Hope were here, along with their daughter Mary, who is Christiana's confidant, we all could talk sense into Christiana."

"Will she listen?" Elspeth asked.

"It's the best we can hope for." The prince's tone sounded none too hopeful. "Have you ever been a part of a family confrontation, Ms Duff? I hear in the cases of alcoholics and drug addicts they can be highly effective."

"I never have," Elspeth admitted, "but I've heard the same thing."

"I asked Eric to send you here because we need absolute secrecy when we challenge Christiana about her behaviour. She can't be seen entering the hotel or leaving it for fear the press could follow her."

"Of course," Elspeth said. She had dealt with similar issues in the past.

The prince cleared his throat. "This will be particularly important since she will be brought here against her will and therefore may try to make a scene.

That would be very like her." He sounded bitter.

"How, Your Highness, do you plan to get her to Bermuda?"

He lifted his face and looked down his long nose. "We have a detective who is going to abduct her the next time she sets foot off Ali's yacht." He said this with utter confidence, as if his order would be carried out without being questioned.

Elspeth swallowed. Throughout her career with the Kennington Organisation she had been instructed to overlook certain breaches in the law, but abduction had never been one of them.

She tried to keep her voice neutral. "When is this to happen?"

"Hopefully today."

"How will she be brought to Bermuda?"

"On my private yacht. She should be here in about four days' time. In the meantime I hope you will become acquainted with my family and other members of our party. In doing so, you'll have time to ask them about their feelings towards Christiana."

Elspeth left the royals' bungalow filled with misgivings. Her immediate instinct was to call Pamela Crumm and get further information on the people in the royal party, but she considered that this might be a breach of her agreement with Lord Kennington. While Princess Christiana was en route from the Caribbean, Elspeth thought, it might be best to take time to make her own assessment.

She had no sooner started to cross the garden that separated the bungalow from the main part of the hotel, when a voice called out to her. "Ms Duff, may I have a word?"

Elspeth turned and saw Princess Honorée, whom she recognised from her photographs in the press, motioning her to return to the bungalow. The princess was tall like her husband but dressed less casually. Her linen trousers and loose-fitting blouse were unwrinkled, and she wore gold earrings, a gaggle of long gold necklaces and a large diamond by her wedding ring. She was coiffed in the way of many older European royals with long hair, pulled up and sufficiently lacquered so that it could not become disarrayed by the wind. Knowing of the princess's Canadian roots, Elspeth expected to hear a North American accent but was surprised when the princess spoke in the tones of the British aristocracy.

Because the princess had affected her accent flawlessly, Elspeth was taken back when the princess addressed her without formality.

"Prince Michael, I know, has told you our reason for being here. I don't completely agree with his methods, but the situation is such that I can't conceive of a gentler way of handling our daughter, and I can't dismiss her actions as merely another foolish attempt to annoy her parents. If she were to carry out her threat, the consequences would be dire for my adopted country."

"I understand," Elspeth said.

"It was I who convinced the prince to come to Bermuda rather than rushing off to the Caribbean and taking charge of things himself. Although normally a man who considers things carefully, he's always been angered by Christiana's more outrageous doings. Since Christiana was a child, I've often played the role of peacemaker between them, although any effect has often been short-lived. Perhaps because of my early childhood summers in western Canada, where I was given free range to do as I pleased, I can feel some sympathy for a girl who is expected to lead an exemplary life. Michael doesn't tolerate Christiana's free spirit, which often exacerbates the already difficult relationship between them, but this time even I think she has gone too far."

"Your Highness, it's my duty to do everything I

can to help you. In fact, Lord Kennington has insisted I do so. I work for him directly and not for the hotel, so I have greater license to act than the staff here. I don't know how I can help, other than assuring the privacy of your family here."

"I want you to meet us all without the others becoming aware of what Michael and I may ask you to do in the future. Will you join us for a private supper in the bungalow this evening? I've arranged for a buffet but asked that there be no wait staff in attendance, so that we can talk freely. It will be informal and only members of our party will be there."

"It will be my pleasure."

"Shall we say seven for drinks first?" With these words, the princess dismissed Elspeth and returned to the interior of the bungalow.

Elspeth returned to her room feeling somewhat ambivalent as to how to proceed. As the afternoon lingered on, the heat persisted, and she closed her windows and turned on the air conditioning, not so much that she wanted to cut off the cooling breezes that usually rose later in the day, but because she wanted to make a private call to Eric Kennington. Elspeth pulled out her Blackberry and punched in her password. She scrolled down until she found what she wanted and then entered another code, one she used only in emergencies or when she needed to talk directly to Eric Kennington. She found the phone number she was looking for, one that would connect her directly to Lord Kennington's private phone console, bypassing both the main reception desk of the Kennington Organisation and that of the administrative assistant who kept guard over the lobby leading to Eric Kennington and Pamela Crumm's executive suite. In the many times she had visited his private office, Elspeth had seen his emergency line blink only once. He had answered it immediately and without explanation, dismissing everyone, including Pamela, who had been in the room with them.

"Kennington here," he snapped.

"Eric, Elspeth Duff. I've just talked with both of your high-ranking guests. There's more here than perhaps you anticipated. Have they told you their plans?"

"Of course." His voice edged on being annoyed.

Elspeth was not to be put off. "How many of the details?"

"The details are up to you, Elspeth. I've let them know you are the best person for the job and you will not fail them. Why are you ringing me? Didn't I make everything clear before you left London?"

"Yes, but how far can I go with this? Surely our laws or similar ones apply in a British overseas territory such as Bermuda. Do you know if they have diplomatic immunity?"

The irritation left Lord Kennington's voice. "Are you implying that they are about to break the law?"

"I'm not sure, but they possibly could. Thus my question. How far do you want me to go with this?"

"I want you personally to stay within the law, but I can't vouch for our guests. Keep me apprised whenever you think you may need to make an exception to my rule." With that ambiguous piece of advice, he rang off.

In different circumstances, Elspeth would have contacted Pamela Crumm for advice and solace after Eric Kennington's harsh words, but she knew she could not do so in this case, both because of her promise to the prince of confidentiality and her specific instructions from Eric that he would handle the case directly and she was not to rely on Pamela. Elspeth supposed this was a mark of Eric's faith in her abilities, but right now she wished he had given her less individual responsibility for the success of the royals' stay in Bermuda. On most jobs she had the backup of Pamela and the Kennington Organisation security department if she needed it. Eric had forbidden her to rely on them this time, telling her that she would have to use her own resources because of the sensitivity of the identity and activities of the guests.

She rang the housekeeper and began attending to her clothing. Normally she chose her wardrobe carefully when travelling so she could carry at the most two suitcases, but because she had no idea what would be required of her in the presence of the royals, she had shipped overnight two large FedEx boxes with appropriate apparel to Bermuda. She unpacked these and handed the wrinkled items from the boxes along with the clothes which lay crumpled in her carry-on bag to the housekeeper and asked that her garments be pressed out and put in her wardrobe before evening. She then lay on the sofa in her sitting room and took a long, hard look at her situation. The prince might be plotting to abduct his daughter in the West Indies, but would transporting her to Bermuda under duress actually be a crime? Did he plan to tell the authorities when his daughter had entered Bermuda, or would he smuggle her into the Kennington hotel without respecting the proper immigration procedures? Or, would he have the captain of his yacht present the princess's passport to the customs and immigration officials, assuming she would have it with her? Had the prince thought through this detail and instructed the detectives who were going to snatch the princess to be certain that they brought her papers in an intact enough form so as to make her arrival in Bermuda legal? Elspeth would have to wait and see. In the meantime, the entire royal party would have to wait for the princess's arrival. Many frayed nerves could well fester over that time. Elspeth decided she could do little to calm these, but if she kept in close contact with them, she might be able to learn their patterns of behaviour towards each other. Elspeth's interaction with Princess Honorée earlier had given her a glimpse into the dynamics of the couple's relationship and so she consequently sensed it had not always been a smooth one, particularly concerning their daughter. Supper tonight would be a start for Elspeth to untangle this web. She was not certain whether she was looking forward to it or not.

3

Stretched on a sofa and busily texting a message to her husband in Malta to see what time he would be available to talk, Elspeth was interrupted by a knock at her door. She rose, crossed the sitting room of her suite and opened the door where Kit Lord, the head of security for the Kennington Bermuda hotel, was standing. Elspeth had met Kit a fortnight earlier when he was in London, but at the time she did not know she soon would be coming to Bermuda.

"May I come in?" he asked. His face looked worried. "I'm afraid something has come up that may be of concern to our guests in the bungalow." Kit had not been told the details of Elspeth's assignment, but he did know the identities of the royal guests and that they were to be kept confidential at all costs.

"Certainly, Kit. I have about twenty minutes before I need to dress for supper," Elspeth said. She hoped that he would not be offended by the caftan she had hastily thrown on after showering. The robe was handsomely made from a heavily embroidered, stiff fabric stitched with brightly coloured thread. Elspeth had bought it in Morocco because she could quickly put it on when needed day or night. She currently wore little under it and had bare feet. To her relief, he seemed not to notice.

"Elspeth," he said, "one of our guests has spotted the princess."

She raised her eyebrows and shook her head. "That's not good news. Tell me who and let's see if we can deal with it, is it him or her?"

"Her. A Mrs Lilianne Balfour who says she is the wife of General William Balfour, commander of one of the American divisions in Iraq, I believe. Citing her husband's position, she has been quite demanding, much to the annoyance of the staff, particularly the concierges."

"One of those," Elspeth said with a short groan. In her experience, people in positions of power were seldom demanding and often grateful for the cosseting given them in the Kennington hotels, but their spouses, perhaps because they were less comfortable with their authority, often caused trouble. "What did she say?"

"She gushed," Kit said, screwing up his face in disgust.

"Gushed?"

"Gushed."

"Oh. What did she say when she gushed?" Elspeth asked.

"That she knew the-Kennington-hotels-hosted-some-of-the-best-people-in-the-world-and-for-the-prices-you-charge-you-would-hope-so-but-she-had-never-expected-to-be-in-the-same-hotel-with-royalty. She said it all in one breath."

"I see, one breath. Did she identify which member of royalty she had seen?"

"Yes, Princess Honorée."

"But how, Kit? The royal party was escorted with great secrecy to the bungalow, and it's surrounded by a fence high enough to block anyone's view. I hardly think the princess would come out from behind the barrier. Did you ask Mrs Balfour when she had seen the princess?"

"I did. She said last night she saw the princess 'tripping', that was her word not mine, across the lawn towards the kitchens. It seems Mrs Balfour is a great reader of *Hello* and *Royalty* magazines and was positive in her identification."

"Unbelievable," said Elspeth, almost to herself. "How could this have happened?"

Kit shook his head but did not answer.

"Do you want me to speak to Mrs Balfour?" Elspeth asked.

"I was hoping you would."

"I can't come now, but tell her I'll see her in the morning. In the meantime warn her that she must keep everything hush-hush. And wink at her."

"Wink?" Kit said as if he had been asked to do something indecent. He was sufficiently new to his job to want to uphold the dignity of his position.

"Have her come to your office in the morning. Let's say half past nine, and have coffee and the chef's best breakfast delicacies brought there. Before then I'll think of some way to placate her," she assured him.

But after he left, she frowned because she knew she would have to confront the princess with this information. Elspeth's initial plan had been to gather the members of the royal party together in the morning and brief them on the security the Kennington Organisation had planned for their visit. Elspeth had put this off too long already. She would broach the subject at supper and set the meeting for as early as possible. They had all come from Europe, except the Tildens, and more than likely would be up early on their first full morning in Bermuda.

Elspeth knew that her first opportunity to evaluate everyone would be during supper. She had long before learned how to 'circulate', even at affairs where one was seated. Tonight would be no exception. She chose her wardrobe carefully, striking a balance between casual and a nod to her position as a professional in the employ of Lord Kennington. She never wanted them to think of her as a friend or social acquaintance, which might happen if she let down her guard. To be subtly overdressed would suggest she was not ready to relax in their company. Her clothes were informal but handsomely tailored. She chose several finely-tooled gold bracelets and a pair of earrings that she had bought in Florence. As she left the room, she realised she had never finished her text message to Richard and that by now it was too late in Malta to expect him to ring her after she returned from her supper with the royal party. She deleted the half-formed message and simply send one that read, "Tlk 2 U Tmrw. Lv. E." Richard disliked short text messages and when on the rare occasion he replied to them in kind, he always included all the vowels, used both upper- and lower-case letters and did not abbreviate phrases.

The sun had set, twilight crossing the grass lawn between the main hotel building and the bungalow, and an evening breeze touched Elspeth's beautifully cut hair. She took in a deep breath of the fragrant air, filled with the aroma of the flowers in the garden and the balminess of the sea, and wished herself luck.

The gate to the bungalow was locked, causing Elspeth to reach in her handbag and extract the master key card for the hotel. As she did so, she saw a figure in the distance who might have been watching her, or might only be out for a walk in the gardens which were open to all guests. The light was elusive enough that she could not make out if the figure were a man or a woman. She thought of Lilianne Balfour but did not have time to linger to see who was there. Elspeth unlocked the gate, and when she was through it, drew it shut, carefully making sure the lock was secure. She crossed the bungalow's private garden and knocked at the tall, eight-panel, and probably old wooden door.

The door was opened by an unknown hand to reveal an interior filled with lighting carefully arranged by Lord Kennington's interior designers to give a sense of warmth and hospitality. The woman who opened the door grinned openly at Elspeth, who stood back, momentarily confused. It was not the princess, but it was.

The woman extended her hand and said in a definitively North American voice, "Ms Duff? I'm Hope Tilden, and, yes, we are twins. Come in and meet the rest of us."

Hope ushered Elspeth into the large sitting room that dominated the main portion of the bungalow. The French doors were opened out to the patio, and the room's occupants were seated on rattan chairs gathered around a hearth filled with flowers.

A black man rose and came towards Elspeth. She took in her breath. He was one of the most distinguished looking men she had ever encountered, her husband included. He was extremely tall, perhaps six feet three or four, and slender, fit without being muscular, and he wore his clothes as if he had just stepped from a men's fashion magazine. His dark skin covered an exquisite bone structure that plastic surgeons would have fought to duplicate. He approached Elspeth and took her hand in his, his grip firm but warm. His eyes held Elspeth's, and she saw both intelligence and humour in his gaze.

"Welcome, Ms Duff. I'm Francis Tilden," he said in basso tones. "These are our family and friends." Elspeth had seldom felt more welcome.

Hope came up to her husband and drew her arm through his. Elspeth watched them exchange a look that bared the depth of feelings between them: love, respect, and caring. It was unmistakable but brief.

Elspeth quickly surveyed the room, remembering who should be there. Prince Michael and Princess Honorée were not among them. She caught the eye of a round-faced, merry looking woman of middle age and medium height, who rose from her chair and bustled across the room to where Elspeth was standing.

She was dressed in several layers of clothing, giving the impression that the heat bothered her but she did not wish to give in to less covering.

"Ms Duff, I am Greta von Fricken."

"Baroness," Elspeth said.

"Let me introduce you to Klaus, my husband."

Klaus von Fricken was at the sideboard dispensing drinks. He turned towards Elspeth, his face mirroring his wife's roundness and merriment, although his head was almost completely bald, in contrast with his wife's curly blonde hair, which she had obviously struggled to contain under several hair combs.

"Ms Duff, Elspeth, let me offer you a drink," he said, his guttural accent more pronounced than his wife's.

Elspeth accepted a gin and tonic, although she preferred sherry, and turned to the last occupant of the room. Mary Tilden unfolded herself from her chair as a mime artist might rise from a lotus. Each part of her body extended itself, and she finally stood fully erect, showing that she was almost as tall as her father, but she was definitely completely feminine. Her body was scantily clad in a diaphanous dress that covered her sufficiently enough for polite society but accented the beauty of her lithe body. She had her father's bone structure but the same soft beauty that Elspeth had seen in Hope Tilden. Mary smiled genuinely and shook Elspeth's hand.

"Mary Tilden," she said, as if the introduction were necessary.

Elspeth felt suddenly at ease. These were people to whom she could relate and with whom she could mix easily. The members of the royal party became real people.

She had no sooner accepted her drink from Klaus von Fricken than the prince and princess came through a side door, a young man behind them, obviously in attendance.

Elspeth felt the atmosphere shift. Hope went up to her sister and led her into the room, chatting frivolously. Prince Michael walked in stiffly by himself. He nodded slightly towards Elspeth and went to shake Francis Tilden's hand. The gesture was formal, which made Elspeth only guess as to its meaning. Prince Michael's country was known for its tolerance, but did this translate to the members of his wife's family? Elspeth was determined to find out. After all, someone had created this group to confront the miscreant Princess Christiana, and Elspeth suspected it might have been Francis Tilden.

The young man with the prince and princess stood dutifully at the side of the room until Mary Tilden went over to him, took his arm and pulled him over to where Elspeth was standing. He blushed. Colour rose through the pale skin of his neck and face and settled at the roots of his fair hair, which verged on white. What had caused the blush, Elspeth wondered, his shyness or Mary Tilden's touch?

"Ms Duff, let me introduce Harald Wade, my uncle's private secretary," Mary said in a rich alto voice. "I'm afraid the prince finds him indispensable, and he'll have to bear with all of us while we are here."

Harald Wade spoke appropriate words of greeting, glancing up at Elspeth, but his eyes dropped to Mary's hand on his arm. Mary looked askance at Elspeth, her eyes twinkling. Was she baiting Harald Wade or was she keen on him? Elspeth was not sure. The dynamics in the room had suddenly become more complex. Klaus von Fricken broke the momentary tension by offering Mary and Harald gin and tonics. Mary accepted; Harald asked for tonic alone.

Sensing that neither Mary nor Harald had much to say to her, Elspeth turned back to the other people in the room. Prince Michael and Francis Tilden spoke together quietly, the prince occasionally shaking his head and Francis nodding his head in assurance. They could have either been discussing the days ahead or the cricket scores; their body language did not tell. Feeling this was a private conversation, Elspeth turned towards the twin sisters. The princess laughed briefly, tapped her sister's arm and came towards Elspeth.

"Ms Duff, you must think us very rude ignoring you, but I see Klaus has already given you a drink. Come and join me and Hope. I'm certain we'll get to know each other better over the coming days, perhaps more for business than pleasure, but tonight I hope we all can relax and enjoy our simple meal."

Elspeth knew the meal, if prepared by the Kennington kitchen, might appear simple but would be the result of arduous hours of menu planning in the central culinary department of the Kennington Organisation in London and had been approved by Lord Kennington's main chef, who insisted in tasting every dish served at the Kennington hotels world-wide, even the local specialities.

The princess suggested, or rather gently commanded, that they all gather together by the hearth. She gestured where each of them was to sit with a practiced air of social authority. Elspeth looked at Hope Tilden, who winked at her playfully. What was her message, amusement at her sister's unspoken control, or distain for her underlying pompousness? Or something else?

The conversation that followed was banal and was thankfully interrupted when Greta von Fricken, who had left her seat five minutes earlier, entered the room and announced that dinner was ready to be served.

The dining room of the bungalow combined indoor dining with the experience of the outdoors. Both ends of the room had French doors which with the warmth of the evening had been left open and caught the evening breeze. The table was laid with an array of colourful linens and silver cutlery, and on a long side table lay a buffet so opulent that Elspeth doubted a party double their size could make an appreciable dent in it. The princess dictated the order in which they should serve themselves and then directed them to their seats at the table. Elspeth, as the only guest, was seated to the right of the prince; Hope Tilden was to his left. Conversation at first was stilted, centring mostly on the food, but soon the prince, who apparently was a noted raconteur, launched into a tale of his recent fishing trip to Scotland. Everyone chuckled at the end, which they might have done whatever his story, but he had been sufficiently amusing to make the laughter genuine.

"You're a Scotswoman, aren't you, Ms Duff? Surely you're a fisherwoman as well?"

"No, Your Highness. I left Scotland when I was eighteen and only return for family events or to see my parents. As a girl I preferred rambling on the moors or in the forests rather than fishing in the lochs."

The prince nodded politely but seemed uninterested. Instead he began discussing a recent play he had seen in London. The prince's domination of conversation gave Elspeth time to survey the other diners. The princess sat at the far end of the table and was conversing quietly with Francis. Their words were polite, but the two of them did not seem intimate. Greta von Fricken made an occasional comment to Mary Tilden, who was only listening superficially to the prince's discourse. She seemed to have retreated into her own thoughts, smiling now and then as if finding a happy memory. Klaus von Tilden ate his meal with gusto and made sure that the wine was circulated whenever a glass was almost empty. Harald Wade sat silently, stirring his food around his plate, eating little, and keeping his eyes averted from Mary.

The supper guests presented interesting dynamics, Elspeth thought, far different from the prevailing family warmth that always surrounded her trips home to Perthshire. Was it the royal party's reason for being in Bermuda that had affected their behaviour, or was it more? If she were to ensure the security of these people and that of the hotel, Elspeth would need to know. She had not yet formulated a way to do so.

The prince gave her the opportunity. Having finished his dessert, he motioned to the princess, who rose from the table. All the others followed, except Greta who stayed behind to fuss over what was left of the meal. Hope brought the coffee tray from the sideboard into the sitting room and set it on the large table that dominated the seating area, but it was the princess who poured.

When all had accepted, or in Harald's case rejected, their coffee, the prince stood up and proceeded to the mantelpiece, where he laid his cup.

"I've made special arrangements," he said, "with Lord Kennington in London to bring Ms Duff here. He's assured me that she's the best security person in his employ and will offer us good advice when we need it. I feel it would be best if each of you spoke with her privately over the next few days, as I'm sure she would like to understand the exact nature of our concerns. I asked Honorée to invite her here this evening so that we all could meet her, but I hope you understand that she has a job to do, one that will be very important over the coming days, and she's not here as a guest, despite any ease you may feel with her. I'm asking you to be direct with her, but not rely on her to provide services other than for those involving our security. Lord Kennington assures me that you may trust her."

Heads turned towards Elspeth, who in turn looked up at the prince. He had made her position clear and for that she was grateful.

"Ms Duff, how would you like to begin?"

Elspeth smiled and acknowledged the prince's words. "Perhaps, Your Highness, the best way to start is for me to speak to you one-on-one over the next day or two. I'm used to irregular hours and therefore anytime would suit me. It would be best if I see everyone here in the bungalow out of sight of the other hotel guests. Your Highness, may I use the small sitting room where we met this morning?"

"Of course," he said, "and everyone should respect Ms Duff's privacy. Honorée, I'll leave it to you to arrange with Ms Duff the best times." He then added, "It's been a long day and therefore I shall say good night to you. Ms Duff, Hope will show you out."

Elspeth knew she had been dismissed and walked to the front door with Hope. Unexpectedly, Hope came through the door and walked with Elspeth to the gate.

She bid Elspeth good night and then added, "Michael is such a pompous ass. You would think his position counted in the world. I don't know how my sister stands him." She spun round and left Elspeth standing alone. Elspeth watched her walk back towards the bungalow and then turned her attention to the keypad on the gate.

As she crossed the garden to her suite, Elspeth thought how odd it was that throughout the evening no one had mentioned Princess Christiana, although she was the main reason they all were there.

4

Her mobile phone was flashing when Elspeth returned to her suite. Hoping it would be a call from her husband, she listened to her voice mail messages and heard his loving baritone voice inviting her to call Malta no matter what time she returned. Warmth flooded her body. Dear Dickie. Four months had passed since she had married him, and she still had not shed the happiness of their wedding day in Gozo or at their wedding trip to her retreat in California, despite its disastrous end. She often berated herself for her giddiness, more appropriate for a teenaged girl than a middle-aged woman who had been married before, but delighted in it nonetheless. She returned his call immediately.

Well into their conversation he asked, "So how are the distinguished guests?"

"Dicey. Dickie, they certainly have more family problems than me and thee."

"Making your job harder," he said.

"Definitely. The tension at dinner tonight with them was unmistakable, but I haven't yet discovered the source of it. It will be a challenge to keep on track and not get entwined in their web. Wish me wisdom over the next few days."

He did so, with the disclaimer that she probably did not need wisdom as much as the ability to set boundaries.

Later, just before Richard rang off, he said, "There's the slightest chance I may be able to get away for a few days. I've a report to write, which can be done anywhere with internet access. I know you're involved there but could you do with a companion at night at least?"

"Dickie, how completely splendid! I'll make arrangements here at the hotel. When you arrive, have them come and get me wherever I am. I can't promise you a great deal of time, but even Eric does allow me to rest occasionally. The time will pass quickly if I have an agreeable partner waiting for me to ease me into sleep."

"How many agreeable partners do you have?"

"On recent count only one, but I expect a lot from him."

Richard chuckled. "I'll try to meet expectations. Even a few moments together with you will make the trip worthwhile. I'll give you as much notice as I can."

Early the next morning, as Elspeth was finishing dressing, a call came from Greta von Fricken.

"Ms Duff, Elspeth, the princess asked me to set up an interview schedule for you, but so far everyone is not yet about except the Tildens. Would you mind seeing them first? They should be finished with their breakfast in about twenty minutes and could meet you then."

"Can we make it half an hour? I haven't eaten and will be in a much more cheerful mood if I do."

Elspeth could almost see Greta's face brighten. "Come and have breakfast here. There's far too much food, and we have good strong coffee as well as tea."

"Give me the twenty minutes then," Elspeth said.

Breakfast had been laid out on a side table in the sitting room, and Elspeth found Hope and Francis Tilden with their coffee reading the morning newspaper. Greta was dispensing coffee, which Elspeth accepted gratefully, and then she suggested that she and the Tildens retire to the small sitting room. Greta piled a plate high with rolls, muffins, and pastries, and Hope carried it and a flask of hot coffee in with them.

The morning sunlight filled the room and cast zebra-striped shadows from the shutters across the room. Elspeth made a quick inspection of the space and suggested that the Tildens take seats facing the windows. Therefore Elspeth had the advantage of seeing their faces more clearly than had they been silhouetted against the light. She also suggested they turn on several of the lamps to lessen the striations of the sun's rays.

Hope poured coffee and Elspeth selected a croissant, which she hoped would not make her fingers sticky. She would have preferred other food but was glad that she could speak with the Tildens first as they seemed to be more direct than the others.

Elspeth did not expect Hope to take the lead, but she did.

"Lord Kennington has put you in a difficult situation, hasn't he?" she said.

Elspeth cocked her head and smiled. "That's all part of my job, and he expects me to succeed in whatever assignment he gives me."

Francis Tilden laughed. "I told you, Hope, that Ms Duff would probably prove her worth despite all."

"What is 'all', Mr Tilden?" Elspeth challenged.

"You have walked into a family maelstrom," he said.

"You mean Princess Christiana?" Elspeth asked.

"No," Hope replied. "A major disagreement between my sister and her husband."

"You must understand that I'm here to protect you, but I'm a security person rather than a family counsellor," Elspeth said with a grin.

Francis turned to his wife. "You might explain."

"Ms Duff . . ."

"If we are to be involved in confidences, perhaps we should use our given names," Elspeth suggested.

"All right then," Hope said. "Elspeth, the

33

situation that's coming to a head here in Bermuda has been brewing for a long time. As I told you last night, Honor, that's her real name, not Honorée, and I are twins, but our lives almost from birth, went different ways. Hope and Honor. I was the first and Honor came twenty minutes later. I don't know if our names determined who we are now, but I've always wanted fairness and equality among people. Honor, on the other hand, wanted to repair our family's reputation in the world. Hope for humanity; Honor for the family. Do I sound cryptic?"

"A bit," Elspeth admitted.

"Our grandfather made machine parts for Hitler's army in the 1930s and became enormously rich, but when Hitler went into Czechoslovakia, my grandfather saw what his climb to wealth was doing to Europe. He was a wise man and had sent a great deal of his wealth to Switzerland and consequently, he and our immediate family were able to escape from the Third Reich and to emigrate to Canada before the beginning of the Second World War. My grandfather left behind a vast industrial empire that the Nazi thugs immediately commandeered. As a result he was never again trusted by either side. Canada took him in and used his knowledge for their own arms development, but I think they never fully believed he had changed allegiance. After the war, the family moved west. Grandfather became involved in uranium mining and amassed a new fortune. My mother and my uncle were raised as Canadians although they had been born in Germany, and Honor and I didn't know about our grandfather's involvement in the war until we were well into our teens. I was ashamed by what my grandfather had done. Honor, to the contrary, always defended Grandfather and said he had acted bravely in finally standing up to Hitler and emigrating to Canada. I think I'd have been more sympathetic had Grandfather not hidden the gains from his war profiteering in Switzerland and used them to establish our family and his business in Canada. Can you see Honor and my differing points of view?"

"You both seem aptly named," Elspeth said.

Hope continued, "As we grew up the differences between us were magnified. Honor asked to be schooled in Europe, first in England, and later in Switzerland. She learned all the social graces and ways of the aristocracy and made sure she was included whenever nobility or minor royalty were invited by her friends. That's how she met the prince. I stayed in Canada, took two degrees in psychology at McGill University and in the process married Francis. I may sound smug, but I'm happy with my life and, although she'll not admit it, she's miserable. It seems fitting that she changed her name to Honorée, meaning one to be honoured, from Honor, which has a straightforward English meaning."

Elspeth glanced at Francis to see his reaction to Hope's words.

He was leaning back in his chair, as if bearing witness but not wanting to participate in the conversation. As Elspeth turned to him, he sat up and said, "When Hope and I were married thirty years ago, racially mixed marriages were much more unusual than they are today. To someone with Honor's ambitions, our marriage became an anathema, and she broke off contact with us. As different as they are from each other, the rift was hugely hurtful to Hope. We married for love and those feelings have never lessened or failed us. We have a child whom we adore and who adores us. She may look like a supermodel, but her greatest ambition is to be a marine biologist and study the ancient micro-organisms that live in the depths of the Pacific Ocean. Contrast this to Honor's life. I've never seen a sign of affection pass between her and the prince, whether because the royal family discourages any public show of emotion or because their romance, if there ever was one, eroded quickly. The prince has no fortune and Honor does, but it's my suspicion he controls the proverbial purse strings, although the money is rightfully hers. I've no idea how either Michael or Honor feels about their daughter, as they've never told us, not even when she was a baby, but Christiana, as you may have heard, is wilful and selfish and plays the two of them like a harp. Poor kid."

Elspeth appreciated the Tilden's candidness. She had yet to determine whether their perception was correct or not, but she sensed their warmth and underlying concern.

An awkward moment ensued, and to fill it Hope offered more coffee, which Elspeth accepted gratefully. She declined another croissant, but in the length of time that these acts took, she had decided how to proceed.

"Hope, or Francis," she said, "I'm not sure how this affects the problem of the moment. Obviously the prince and princess have invited you here, and therefore there must have been some reconciliation between you all."

They exchanged glances. By some signal not visible to Elspeth, it was Hope who responded. "I love my sister," she said, "and despite her attempts to break away from me, I wouldn't let it happen. It took fifteen years, but I never gave up. During that time, I suffered many setbacks and heartbreaks. Francis and I were not invited to the royal wedding. My father died and Honor did not come to the funeral, although there was a large array of flowers from the royal palace with a stiff note of condolence, but it was not personally written by my sister. My mother became ill and I helped nurse her back to health. A cheque arrived from the palace every month to help defray the expenses of her home care, but it came without a card or letter. But I know Honor is a good person underneath all this, but I've always felt she was trapped by her own ambitions. Francis and I have lived all over the world, but Honor and the Prince have never found time to visit us. Eventually Francis held high enough posts to allow him to sponsor a royal visit, but the palace, when we invited them, always replied that they were busy with other more pressing obligations. That hurt, but I don't give up that easily." Hope lifted her head in pride, and then wiped the moisture from one of her eyes as if bothered by the light.

"This has nothing to do with my reason for being here, so forgive me if I'm stepping out of line. What eventually reconciled you?" Elspeth asked.

Francis answered simply. "Our daughter Mary."

"Mary? But how?"

"You have met Mary. She's truly beautiful and not even the most racially prejudiced individual could deny it," Hope said. "Even as a child, people would stop on the street and admire her. When Mary was thirteen, she saw a picture of Honor in a tabloid and asked if she were related to me, since Honor and I look so much alike. I'd never spoken of Honor to Mary, but at that age Mary envisioned princes and princesses as fairy tale figures and their lives the ultimate fantasy. We never lied to Mary, although there were things we hadn't told her. Mary was elated that her aunt was a princess, and, without Francis and me knowing, she wrote to Honor and enclosed a family photograph. Even then Mary believed in researching her topic and had discovered she had a first cousin called Christiana, who was a princess as well. Mary straightforwardly asked Honor if she could come and visit them."

"How did Princess Honorée answer?" Elspeth was intrigued, as her own daughter had similar types of fantasies at that age, but Elspeth had been able to produce little more than her cousin Johnnie Tay, a little-known Scottish earl who had no castle or fortune but did have a fun-loving heart. Elspeth's daughter had laughed, as her cousin Johnnie would always play raucously with her when they visited Scotland, but he did not fit a teenager's vision of a fairy-tale existence.

"Honor didn't answer at first," Hope said, "but Christiana somehow found the letter and responded to Mary. Over the next few years they became great pen pals without either Michael or Honor's knowledge. I never read their letters, but I always expected that Christiana shared secrets with Mary that her parents would have preferred to remain untold. Francis and I, of course, were aware of their correspondence, as many of the letters came in the diplomatic bag and were franked by the palace.

We didn't press Mary about them, but sometimes I longed to use the two girls' connection as a channel to re-establish my relationship with Honor. When she was seventeen, Mary finally came to me and asked if Christiana could come and visit us. Francis was then a deputy head of mission at our high commission in Los Angeles, a location where one could easily visit Hollywood, which would appeal to any teenager. I spent three weeks composing the letter to Honor, and then sent it by FedEx, receipt of delivery required. The confirmation came back the next day. Then I waited. I think my heart pounded more rapidly than it ever had done before when I received Honor's letter a week later. It was not what I expected; it was a hidden appeal for help."

Elspeth was surprised. "Help? With what?"

"With Christiana, or Christie, as Mary calls her. 'Christiana' makes one think of a snow queen, but 'Christie' doesn't. Far from it, she was a girl filled with passion and fun, and, when she arrived in Los Angeles, she and Mary had become inseparable over the time she spent with us. Honor's letter was stiff, saying that she would come to Los Angeles a week after Christiana's arrival to take her daughter back to Europe because she feared a summer in California might have spoiled her for the realities and requirements of the royal palace, where she belonged. But at the end of the letter, this time in her own handwriting, she asked if, when she was in Los Angeles, she and I could talk about Christiana." No longer making any pretence of wiping the sun from her eyes, Hope took out a tissue and blew her nose.

As his wife was composing herself, Francis said, "Honor arrived with two security escorts, 'goons' we called them, but I convinced her that a better way to connect with Christiana was to send the goons to stay at their consulate in Los Angeles and let Honor have time alone with her sister. I knew their consul general, who was not aware of Honor's trip before I telephoned him, and I called in a favour, which he was happy to grant." Francis smiled, "I'd sheltered a certain lady friend from Canada for him when her presence was not desirable in his diplomatic circle."

Elspeth could imagine this as Richard had told of similar events in his career.

Hope smiled at this recollection. "She actually was quite charming and grew up near my family's ranch in Alberta."

"How did Princess Honorée act when she arrived?" Elspeth asked, knowing she was probing into an area beyond her need to know.

"She was tired from her trip, of course, so I made her take a long shower, wash the lacquer from her hair, and shed her European clothes. I made her put on a pair of my jeans and a tee shirt saying 'Hollywood or Bust' across the front. Somehow this amused her, and we fell laughing into each other's arms. Then she began to weep, the kind of crying that one stores up for years. I held her for a long time. Do you know the feeling?"

Elspeth swallowed hard, remembering when she had done the same in Richard's arms when she had discovered who had murdered her fiancé at Cambridge many years before. "I know the feeling," she said with a catch in her throat but without giving an explanation.

"Francis was in the middle of a visit from some high-ranking visitors from Ottawa, so I appealed to a friend who had a cabin in the Sierra Nevada mountains, and I took Honor, Christiana, and Mary up there. We spent four days living on our own, cooking meals from the limited supply of supplies at the local general store, building our own fires in the barbeque pit at night and talking almost non-stop, either one-on-one or all four of us together. We were women bonding in a way that daily life doesn't normally allow. I think for the first time Honor saw her daughter as a human being, a young woman who had her own feelings and ideas. It lasted until we returned to Los Angeles."

"What happened then?" Elspeth asked.

"The goons were waiting when Honor and Christie came back," Francis said. "They had a message from the royal palace that their return was immediately required. Honor went back to her hairspray, and Christiana sank into a shell we had not seen before."

Hope nodded. "The four of them, Honor, Christiana, and the two security men, left the next day. Honor had assumed her cloak of superiority, and Christiana looked as miserable as any teenager could look, which, as you know, is very miserable indeed. But as the car came to get them, Honor wrapped her arms around me and said in a whisper, "Let's stay in touch." We have done ever since, at first by letter and now by e-mail. Sometimes months pass when our messages are completely superficial, but every now and then I see the old spark that was Honor before she decided to become Honorée."

"And Mary and Christiana?"

"They continued e-mailing as well and later sent text messages. The bond between them has never been broken," Hope said. "Christiana wrote how she longed to be free, to live in Canada or the States, where no one knew her, and to go to university the way Mary had, rather than finishing school in Switzerland with 'acceptable' classmates, whose social status rather than intelligence and interest in life defined their existence."

Unlike her friend and employer Pamela Crumm, Elspeth knew little of the children of the European aristocracy, but she imagined that many of the old, nineteenth century manners appealed to the world's established elite or those who wished to be accepted by it. Elspeth's own life had been one of non-conformity despite her roots in the Scottish gentry, and she attributed her freedom to her parents who had always allowed her to make her own choices, whether they were wise or otherwise. They had been both. Elspeth could feel deeply the longings of a girl more restricted than she had been when young and who was bound by tradition on one side and ambition on the other. To Christiana, Mary Tilden must have seemed the spirit of freedom.

"So you can see," Hope said, interrupting Elspeth's thoughts, "when we learned of Christiana's most current form of defying her parents, I contacted Honor and appealed to her to choose a neutral place to allow us all to get together to discuss the problem."

Francis reached over and took his wife's hand. "Hope always believes that confronting something head-on is best. Her insistence hasn't always made for comfortable domestic relations, but, on the whole, it has saved our small family many times, particularly when Mary was a teenager. Mary learned that she could always trust us to be open with her even when she wanted to prove us wrong. We always listened to her, and occasionally she had a valid point to make. It made us all better people, although there were times when we laid down the law. Mary respected us enough to know we did not do so lightly."

5

Elspeth left her interview with the Tildens with feelings of uncertainty. Did Lord Kennington know the extent of the prince's intentions and, if so, what did he want her to do? Elspeth felt that her employer had a hidden agenda that he had not yet told her about. When giving her assignments, he always accompanied it by his standard lecture to keep the hotels and their guests' activities out of the eyes of the press, but Elspeth was convinced there was more to this assignment than that alone. She wondered how much Pamela Crumm knew about her current mission. Elspeth could, of course, call Pamela on her secure line, but something was different this time. Pamela normally instructed Elspeth before she went out to the field to do a sensitive task, yet this time Eric had seen Elspeth alone in his office and asked for strict confidentiality. He had specifically said she should not rely on Pamela for assistance. He and Pamela had built the Kennington Organisation together, and its success was the direct result of their opposite but vital talents at running their ever-increasing number of high-end hotels.

As she walked back across the grass towards the main building of the hotel, Elspeth considered her options. She could call Eric directly and ask him, or she could ring Pamela and ask obliquely. She had not decided on which approach to take when she saw Kit Lord coming across the garden toward her.

He was not smiling when he greeted her. "Elspeth, I'm so glad I've found you. I suspected you had gone to the bungalow, so didn't want to distract you, but something has occurred that I think you ought to know about. Will you come into the security office with me?" His face was anxious.

"Is it Mrs Balfour again?"

"No, worse luck. She's probably harmless. I would prefer to speak where no one else can hear us."

Kennington hotels had always maintained the highest level of security for their guests, but Eric Kennington insisted they should have no inkling of this. Each hotel in the Kennington chain had its own security offices as well as equipment to monitor every public space in the hotels and the grounds as well. The staff was trained to be discreet and, when there was trouble, had been instructed to keep it out of the public eye. In addition, the staff, whether they are those who were stationed in the lobby, those who made up the rooms, or those who worked in the dining rooms, were instructed to be vigilant about anything that might appear out of the ordinary. Usually this diligence on their part averted any difficulty before it came to the attention of other guests. Kit Lord, like his counterparts at other Kennington hotels, was well-educated, personally presentable, and well-spoken. If required, he could blend in with the guests without appearing out of place. He also was proficient in the martial arts and was extremely fit physically. Because of the high cost of staying at a Kennington hotel and the generally exalted station of its patrons in the social, political or commercial world, the problems that developed seldom required him to use these skills. The Kennington Organisation in London also chose carefully when recruiting the hotel security staff, and their competence was rewarded by generous year-end bonuses for detecting and defusing any disruptions at their hotels.

Elspeth's position fell outside of this hierarchy. She and a few others like her worked directly for Eric

Kennington, although their work entailed close cooperation with the security department in London and the staff at each hotel. She operated independently and took direction only from the top. She was seldom called into a situation unless Eric or Pamela felt her presence was warranted because the local staff could not cope with both the daily running of the hotel and the special requirements brought about by any unusual event. Elspeth had worked for the Kennington Organisation for eight years and had never once thought that she had been assigned to a matter frivolously. She had learned over that time to work in tandem with the local security staff and only exert her authority when absolutely necessary. Consequently, her reputation in the field allowed her to come into a hotel without being seen as threat, and to work comfortably with people like Kit Lord. She took great care to keep her good name intact.

Kit Lord was one of the youngest members of the security department to have been given the position of security manager at one of the Kennington hotels. The Kennington Bermuda was small by comparison to the hotels in some of the larger cities. Lord Kennington, however, was counting on it prospering as he branched out into resort settings following his earlier successes with urban hotels. He hoped his clientele who would have previously had the Kennington 'experience' while on business would respond to the appeal of a Kennington resort hotel for their holidays. He had told Elspeth that he thought his new venture was somewhat risky, but he wanted his resorts to be as seamlessly efficient as all his other hotels. Security at this new type of hotel had to be as tight or perhaps even tighter, as his guests would probably be more relaxed and less vigilant about both their possessions and personal safety.

Knowing these things, Elspeth entered the inner offices of the Kennington Bermuda cautiously. Because Kit Lord was new at his job, she did not want to use her position to downplay his obvious concern.

The security office was in what must have once been the servants' quarters of the estate that Lord Kennington had converted into his hotel. The building stood alone and offered none of the amenities of the larger buildings and outbuildings, such as the bungalow where the royal party was staying. As Elspeth and Kit entered his private office, she saw the panel of monitoring screens, and a young woman diligently scanning them there. Kit did not introduce Elspeth, but she suspected the woman already knew who she was. Kit's office was small, but the thickness of the walls and the high windows gave the impression of privacy. He motioned Elspeth to a chair by a low table at one side of the room and took a seat opposite her.

Kit seemed anxious, and Elspeth decided to put him at ease. "What's the problem, Kit? Nothing I hope that can't be managed easily."

"London has instructed us to send the list of our guests to their central computer each day. I understand that this is for a variety of reasons, but as you know it also flags any guest who has been difficult in the past. I seldom get any warnings from London, but yesterday one of our guests came up with a red flag next to his name. Do you know the name 'Martin Hagen'?"

Elspeth faintly recognised the name, but nothing concrete came to mind. "Tell me about him."

"You personally tagged him as a possible problem seven years ago. Normally we would deal with questionable guests routinely, but since you were here and you must have had some dealings with him in the past, I thought I should alert you."

Elspeth's memory was usually acute, but other than a tickle of recollection at the name, she drew a blank. "Fill me in."

"You wrote a report when you were on assignment at the Kennington Mayfair in 1999, saying that you suspected him of, I think your term was 'preying on unattached women of a certain age'. Do you remember?"

Lord Kennington had recruited her to work for him shortly after she had discovered a crime being committed at the Kennington Beverley Hills, where she was a guest shortly after leaving her first husband. A friend had given her the gift of a week's stay at the hotel, but Elspeth, with her restless nature could not simply quietly luxuriate in the hotel's opulence and had uncovered a money laundering scheme which could have affected the hotel's reputation drastically. Lord Kennington had noticed and hired her shortly afterwards. She always suspected it was not for her prowess alone but also because she was British, Cambridge-educated, had a habit of dressing well, and carried herself with the demeanour only French women of the highest class could ever assume, an art her Maltese aunt had insisted she acquire before she entered Girton College at Cambridge. The report to which Kit alluded must have been written during her first year of employment with the Kennington Organisation.

"Do you have a photograph," she asked, hoping that her visual memory was better than her recollection of names.

He stood and went over to his computer's flat screen, which he rotated so that Elspeth could see. The face meant nothing more than the name.

"And you are telling me that this Martin Hagen has checked in to the hotel?"

"Two days ago. I thought you ought to know since the flag on the report was yours."

Elspeth's responsibilities with the Kennington Organisation had evolved over time as Lord Kennington and Pamela Crumm had grown to trust her. Whatever Elspeth might have done seven years before, noting the activities of a dubious male guest of the Kennington

Mayfair, had become a distant memory.

"Kit, I suggest you watch Mr Hagen. He may remember my encounter with him more clearly than I do, which means he will either try to avoid me or to approach me. I would prefer that you deflect any contact he tries to make with me, since I don't want to be distracted from dealing with matters at the bungalow. Let me know if this becomes difficult."

Kit relaxed a bit. "I thought you might let us handle it, but I wanted to make sure," he said

"Thanks. I appreciate your warning me. There's one other matter, however, I would like you to handle as well. Mrs Balfour's insistence that she saw Princess Honorée going into the kitchen last night concerns me. I want to you to take Mrs Balfour under your wing and stress that you never disclose the identity of guests, but that the person she saw was not the princess. You could emphasise how important people's privacy is, including her own, and that a guest who might look like a celebrity but was not, would not like to be singled out. In the meantime I want to see whether either the princess or her sister did go to the kitchen yesterday evening."

"I can check with the kitchen staff, if you like," Kit offered. "But on your instructions, only our two most senior waiters, both who have had a long career with the Kennington Organisation, take food to the bungalow, although they don't know of its residents' identity. As far as I know, no other person in the kitchen has seen them."

"May I speak with the two waiters? Will you call them here?"

Kit picked up his phone and spoke into it. Several minutes later the waiters appeared, but, as it was between meals, both were in casual clothing, as they were only required to dress formally whilst on duty. Elspeth recognised them both, one from London who was called Ken, and one from Oslo called Lars. Both were in their forties, Elspeth guessed, and both in the course of their new position had developed deep tans, undoubtedly a reaction to their many years living and working in more northerly climates. The transformation looked better on Lars, who had fair skin but dark hair, than it did on Ken, who had numerous freckles.

Elspeth rose and shook both of their hands, a gesture of recognition of their longevity at the Kennington hotels and for her current need of their services.

"As you both know, Lord Kennington has asked that the identities of the people staying in the bungalow be kept away from the other guests and from the public. Because you have both dealt with situations like this before, I want you to tell me how the kitchen handles the orders for food from the occupants of the bungalow and how you carry it to the bungalow when it is prepared."

"I go round to the bungalow in the morning," Ken said, "There's a kitchen there, a small one meant mainly for guests to get morning coffee if they rise early, but there is a cooker, microwave, fridge, sink, and dishwasher there. Normally guests would cross the garden and eat in the one of the dining rooms, but we were instructed that the people now in the bungalow would take all their meals there. Each morning when I go over, the cheerful woman with the round face, who seems to be in charge of the food arrangements, meets me. I don't know her name."

Elspeth nodded at this information but did not supply the Baroness's name or title.

"I take over the menus from all the restaurants, and she picks out the meals for the day, although I offer suggestions, particularly if what she selects is not suitable for a buffet. Shortly before the meal is to be served, Lars and I pack it up in the kitchen and carry it to the bungalow. The cheerful lady helps us set it out in the dining room or sitting room, and we leave before the other people in the bungalow make an appearance."

Elspeth suspected the security office in London had set up this procedure. "Have you seen any of other people there, other than the round-faced lady and, if so, did you recognise them?' she asked.

Both waiters shook their heads.

"Has any member of the party come to the kitchen, perhaps after dark?"

Both denied any knowledge of this happening.

She complimented them on their good work, and, although it was not necessary, urged them to keep silent about their duties at the bungalow even if prodded by the other staff. After they had left, she turned to Kit. "How do you suppose Mrs Balfour saw the princess?"

Elspeth stayed in Kit's office for several more minutes, again going over the arrangements made for the royal party. She decided to return to her suite to call London. The shortest path for her to take was through the lobby. Absorbed in deciding whether she should call Eric or Pamela, she did not see that she was on a collision course with a heavy set, middle-aged woman, who was converging on her like a naval fleet.

"Ahoy," this woman called. At first Elspeth did not realise that this call to attention was directed at her. She stopped, and the woman blocked her passage.

"Ahoy," the woman said again, this time less loudly and more teasingly. "I just had to come up to you and tell how much I admire your clothes." The voice came out of the American south.

"Thank you," Elspeth murmured and tried to pass.

"I believe that women of our age," she said, winking at Elspeth, "should dress to their best advantage." Elspeth looked at the woman, who obviously had taken a long time applying a great deal of makeup, but not a long enough time to see that the orange dress she was wearing made her look rather like a large pumpkin. "I couldn't help noticing the fineness of your suit yesterday and the excellent cut and fabric of your slacks and blouse today."

Elspeth smiled and tried once again to dodge her assailant.

"I'm Lilianne Balfour, Mrs William Balfour," the woman said, "wife of General Bill Balfour."

"Hello." Elspeth did not offer her name.

"Are you and your husband staying here?"

Elspeth realised that Mrs Balfour had caught sight of her wedding band and the ruby ring Richard had given her shortly before their wedding. Politeness, a Kennington hotel policy, dictated that Elspeth should answer, at least briefly.

"No. He's on business elsewhere."

"You are an American!" Lilianne pronounced.

Elspeth cursed herself. She had lived in America for over twenty years and could speak Standard American English, which she considered a foreign language, without anyone being able to detect her British roots. The habit of addressing Americans in their own language was so ingrained in her that she had switched without thinking. Elspeth did not want to engage with Mrs Balfour further, but nonetheless was being dragged into a conversation with her, almost against her will.

"I lived in Southern California for many years," she said without further explanation.

"Then you must tell me where you buy your clothes. In Hollywood?"

"Sometimes," Elspeth lied. "Here and there." Her French dressmaker in London would have cringed, and she silently asked him to forgive her and would not complain at his price increases the next time she saw him.

"I think we shall become friends, but you haven't told me your name yet."

Elspeth had hoped she could avoid giving it but saw there was no courteous way she could avoid doing so. "Elspeth Duff," she mumbled as if she had marbles in her mouth, hoping Mrs Balfour would not be rude enough to ask Elspeth to repeat what she had said. Lilianne's hearing proved too sharp.

"Why, Mrs Duff, the pleasure is all mine. Will you join me for dinner tonight since your husband is elsewhere?"

"You're very kind, but I have other plans." Elspeth mentally noted that, if she were not invited to the bungalow to join the royal party for dinner, she would find something on the room service menu to her liking.

"Well, you tell that husband of yours that he should not leave you alone her in Bermuda. The tropical winds can lead to all sorts of romance. The general and I are here for our twenty-fifth wedding anniversary, and our romance has never died." She winked again.

By this time Elspeth was more entertained than put off. "I'll tell him," she said, omitting that Richard would undoubtedly be amused when she told him of her encounter with Mrs Balfour. Elspeth also hoped that the general and his belle would have left the hotel by the time Richard arrived.

"Toodle-oo, Mrs Duff. Until later."

"Goodbye, Mrs Balfour."

She got to her suite without further interference and sat a long time before picking up her satellite phone. She remained equivocal on whom to call in London, and finally decided she would wait before making a decision. Instead she dragged out her laptop and began typing her notes from her earlier conversation with Hope and Francis Tilden.

6

Elspeth worked on compiling her notes well into her lunch hour, and finally rang room service to get a sandwich on a toasted roll and some coffee. She set up files for each member of the royal party, and then typed in individual comments about them. At such an early stage in her assignment, she did not attempt to make any evaluations. As she rose to take her sandwich out to her private patio, the phone rang. Greta van Fricken told her the princess would be free at two and would 'receive' Elspeth at the bungalow then. From Greta's tone it was clear it was a royal command. Now twenty minutes to two, Elspeth bolted down her sandwich and wished she had chosen something less difficult to chew and swallow. She gave up on the idea of sipping her hot coffee.

Princess Honorée was waiting in the bungalow's garden. She had chosen a seat on a long teak bench near the wall, and in the warmth of midday looked coolly aloof. The spot was shaded by banana trees and embellished with orchids hanging from pots suspended from the almost invisible shade structure above. She motioned Elspeth to sit in a chair opposite her.

"Your Highness." Elspeth dipped her head in acknowledgement of the princess's offer of a seat, but purposely kept the gesture brief so that it would not seem to be too acquiescent.

The princess did not seem to notice. "I thought we could talk more freely here. The walls of the small sitting room are thin, and I find it hard to believe they are completely soundproof. At least if we sit here, we can see someone coming, and the breeze is cooling, don't you think? I trust that everything we speak about this afternoon will remain just between the two of us. I must stress that none of what we say to get back to either my husband or my sister."

Elspeth nodded in agreement, although the exclusion of two of the people closest to the princess was puzzling. She sat up a bit straighter. "I'll certainly respect your wishes."

The princess shifted her position on the bench. Her posture became studied. It was in stark contrast to her sister's relaxed bearing earlier in the day.

The princess looked down at her manicured fingers, laden with several large rings whose workmanship and value were easily recognisable. "I'm sure this morning my sister made a very moving case for her own happiness and for the lack of mine. I also suspect that she told you how pleased with life Christiana was when she visited them in Los Angeles, and how the prince and I dragged her back to Europe, unwilling to allow her to lead a 'normal life'."

The princess waved her hand in the air, dismissing her sister's opinions as she would have brushed off a troublesome fly. "You have to understand that Hope believes that if everyone were equal, the world would be a place without strife. We have argued about this many times. She doesn't seem to understand that there are people born to higher positions who have responsibilities to others and cannot simply do as they wish. Our daughter is one of them. When Christiana spent time in Los Angeles with the Tildens, both Hope and Mary tried to convince her that she is an ordinary person. Of course she isn't. She's third in line to the throne and needs to act accordingly. Our country may be small, but we have a Christian monarchy that goes back to the fourteenth century without a break in succession, and, like so many of the European kingdoms, some of our monarchs have been women. The thought of Christiana ignoring her heritage is appalling to both the prince and myself. I directly attribute Christiana's current behaviour to the Tildens's influence when she was with them."

Elspeth was confused by this. The prince had told her that Christiana had been wilful ever since she was a child. The princess also had earlier mentioned Christiana's free spirit and the prince's lack of tolerance of it. Hope had mentioned the days in the Sierra Nevadas where the four women had stayed in what sounded like casual bliss. Why the princess's sudden turnaround, and this insistence that Christiana conform to over seven centuries of strict religious and regal tradition? Perhaps it was caused by Christiana's threat to become a Muslim, at least nominally. Or, was it something else, something that had changed since the bonding weekend or even after Christiana's semi-nude picture had appeared in the popular press? The exact moment of Princess Honorée's change of attitude did not matter as much as the hardening of her position did now. Elspeth made a quick decision, speculating that winning the princess's trust was more important than exploring the intricacies of her shifting mind.

"Your Highness, the next few days do appear to be critical. I'm here to support you, and can do so more effectively if you let me know what you want me to do to assure you will be safe, from both media scrutiny and that of the outside world, although not specifically to help you and the prince find some sort of reconciliation with your daughter."

The princess said nothing but looked at Elspeth so intently that she became uncomfortable, but she kept her chin raised and eyes focused on the princess. She was completely surprised at the princess's next question.

"How long have you worked for Lord Kennington?"

"Eight years."

"Do you enjoy your job?'

"Usually. It would be dishonest to say always. Sometimes I have to deal with disagreeable people, some with criminal intent, but it's part of my job to treat them politely, even if sometimes firmly. It's not something I like doing."

"What do you enjoy most?"

"Dealing with people I like personally. This happens far more frequently, and of course, the travel; I've seen a great deal of the world."

"I see you are married. Does your husband object to your job?"

Elspeth did not want to share the true nature of her bargain with Richard before she married him and remembered their disagreement in Copenhagen several months before. "He works abroad; we accommodate each other's schedule and find our times together are enhanced by our absences."

"Then you are a very lucky woman."

Elspeth could not help smiling. "I know."

"Do you have children?"

"Yes, a son and a daughter, but they are now adults who lead their own lives."

"Did they ever cause you trouble?"

Elspeth considered why Princess Honorée might be asking all this. There had been times when Elspeth had worried about her children, but they had been raised to be independent and to take responsibility for their own actions. Often Elspeth had wished they had confided in her more, but could also appreciate that the slow and quiet dissolution of her first marriage when her children were about Christiana's age had bothered her children more than they were able to admit, and that they might have withdrawn from her to protect themselves. She had since re-established close contact and was grateful that the time of their separation from her had passed, although she was still unsure whether they accepted her recent marriage to Richard.

"A bit of trouble occasionally," Elspeth responded. "Luckily we've all grown out of it."

"And how does your husband interact with your children?"

Elspeth thought she detected pleading in the princess's eyes and wanted to be tactful. "Their father, my first husband, stays close to them I believe." Then she grinned. "I'm never very sure how my current husband regards them, or they him. He's always discreet, as are they."

The princess's reserve broke. "Ms Duff, I find your openness refreshing. I hope I'm one of the people you like."

Without knowing exactly why, Elspeth did like the princess. She was undoubtedly a complex person who had chosen a life with many responsibilities and strictures over one of ease, which she might have done considering her family fortune. Certainly she enjoyed the privileges of a royal life but must have realised early in her marriage that they did not come without a price. Elspeth wanted to ask her if the cost was worth the rewards, but she knew that would be rude, as well as unprofessional. Instead she returned to the problem of the moment.

"Your Highness, I'm here to assist you in any way I can. I realise that your situation with Princess Christiana is complicated by the public nature of your lives and the need to uphold the name of your husband's family and country. Perhaps that's where I can help most."

The princess looked down and pinched the bridge of her nose. When she looked back up, Elspeth saw her unexpected tears. "Do you always inspire such trust?" she asked, choking on her own words.

"It would be ungracious to say that it is just part

of my job. Over a good number of years I've worked with people who needed re-assurance in the face of many different kinds of troubles. I've always thought that the skill to do so comes from me being able to put myself in the other person's position and to try to understand what they were experiencing. Their feelings run the whole gamut of raw human emotions: fear, outrage, hatred, or a sense of being personally violated physically or mentally. Underneath, however, there's always the sense of needing to be cared for when a situation has reached a point where they can no longer cope alone."

"Do you like doing that?"

"For the most part. Each time it's a new sort of challenge. Even in a place like a Kennington hotel, each person I deal with is unique, and every problem is distinct. Some of them are easier to solve than others, but Lord Kennington prefers that I deal with the more complex ones, ones that his onsite staff have neither the time nor the experience to handle internally."

Had she said too much or touted her own skill more than the situation merited? She had intended to assure the princess rather than provide a justification for her own career. Richard had more than once accused her of diving into her assignments without fearing the consequences of trying to meet Lord Kennington's high expectations of her. It was not in Elspeth's nature to expect failure, except perhaps in her previous personal relationships with men. She hoped that her marriage with Richard had put that problem behind her, but it did bother her at odd moments. Could her marriage truly be as happy as it seemed to be most of the time? Focus, she told herself, not on your own life but that of the princess. In the past her thoughts had not wandered as frequently as it did after she knew she had fallen in love with Richard. She drew her mind back to the garden and the princess. She could not foresee any personal risk in dealing with the prince and princess and their party. Looking back at the princess, she could see a look of acceptance in her expression.

"Thank you, Ms Duff. You have given me a sense of hope I didn't have before."

Elspeth saw before her a woman who had taken on a task far more formidable than normal mortals would have ever considered. The fairy tale vision of becoming a princess in fiction always ended in the assumption that she would live happily ever after. No one considered the demands of the royal court, any rebellious children who were to follow, or the devastating effect of always being in the eye of the popular press.

"Let me do what I can." Elspeth had used these words frequently in the course of her work. Their effect varied, and therefore she was not surprised by the princess's reaction.

"Help me, please, help me rescue Christie." Christie, not Christiana.

Who was she really, this calm and disciplined woman who sat across from her in the garden? Princess Honorée, wife of Prince Michael and a staunch member of the royal court of an old but respected kingdom, mother of the third in line to the throne, or Honor, Hope's twin sister, a mother who on a chance four-day retreat to a cabin in the California mountains had discovered her daughter to be a child in need of affection?

On an impulse, Elspeth reached out to the princess, taking both of her hands in hers. Elspeth was sure that Richard would not have approved, but at the moment the gesture was so genuine that she did not think the princess would object.

"Please trust me," Elspeth said.

The princess's hands clasped hers eagerly, to the point of pain.

"You have no idea . . .." The princess's voice was constricted.

"Trust me," Elspeth said again.

The princess withdrew her hands. "Yes, I think you're my last hope. Shall we go out and walk on the beach where we can't be heard?"

Elspeth considered the security of this. She had walked out on the private beach below the hotel several times since her arrival in Bermuda and had never met another soul. She was almost certain that there was no physical barrier to stop intruders except the rocks separating the beachfront of the hotel from public access to the beach, but she had not gone beyond the perimeters of the hotel property to make sure.

"Princess," she said, "do you have a hat and dark glasses? I worry that you might be recognised." Elspeth thought of Mrs Balfour's assertion that she had seen the princess crossing the garden.

"Yes, inside. I'll fetch them."

"Shall we meet back here in five minutes? I'd like to get a hat as well, as at my age I'm much more conscious of the ravages of the sun than I was when I was younger." Elspeth thought of the many hours she had sat by the pool or on the beaches of Southern California and watched her children play in the sun, after only the lightest application of sunscreen.

"Hope has probably filled your mind with the idea that I set out to find an aristocratic husband. God knows she has often accused me of this to my face, but that's simply not the case."

They were walking along the sand, both protected from the sun and from prying eyes. Elspeth felt a growing connection with the princess as they had kicked off their sandals and carried them dangling from their hands. Waking barefoot with someone had a levelling force somehow.

"Our mother was Canadian with a Scottish

background, but our father was German by birth. Mother always drilled into us that we should make no apologies for our roots. The von Alteberg family was one of the most respected Prussian families in the nineteenth century. My family's home was filled with the nobility, artists, musicians and philosophers. Guests came from all over Europe to stay at our home, a rather hideous neo-Gothic building that was as expansive as it was garish. Even the Kaiser came on several occasions, although family myth has it that he was rather boorish each time he visited. Hope has conveniently forgotten all this. She takes after the dour highlanders of our past, all good works and social responsibility. Unlike Hope, I'm not ashamed of my German family. Germany went through terrible political and social upheaval during the twentieth century, but I can't reject what we once were. Hope opted to stay in Canada and to defy the heritage of her forbearers by marrying Francis. No one can deny that she has made a great success of her life and that the marriage has prospered, despite the many people who found their marriage unacceptable and said so openly. Francis is too charming and too brilliant for this criticism to last. Hope told me this when I came to get Christiana in California. I'd not known about it before, but certainly should have."

They walked along in silence. Princess Honorée seemed to be gathering her thoughts.

"Mary," she finally said, "is an incredible child; no, she is a woman now. All the best parts of her multiracial background seem to have coalesced into a beautiful, intelligent young woman who is completely comfortable with who she is. I give Hope credit for that. But isn't it odd that Christiana, who had all the advantages of birth, position and wealth, is not? When I asked my parents to go to Europe for school, I envisioned re-establishing the von Alteberg name to its former position of patron of the arts and humanities, of an aristocratic status that would once again raise the consciousness of Europe and perhaps even North America towards the intellectual greatness that Germany held before Kaiser Wilhelm decided to make war on his cousins in 1914. Isn't it strange that that was over ninety years ago, but that the impact is still profound? In many minds the Germans are characterized as fat, crude and violent. My family name was brought down by my grandfather's misguided patriotism in the early days of the Third Reich, but he also was a von Alteberg.

"Ms Duff, I assume from your name you are a Scotswoman, but the Scottish heritage of intellectualism dims in contrast to what Germany was before its political missteps between 1914 and 1945. Thirty-one short years in the history of a proud and cultivated people. I asked to be educated in Europe and not Canada because I wanted to rediscover my German roots. I didn't set out, as Hope perhaps implied, to snag a member of European royalty for my husband. Hope has never reconciled that I, just as much as she, want to reform the current troubles of the world. She wants to establish something new and good; I want to restore something old and equally good. As much as we may seem opposites, we are actually very much the same. It's just that our focus is different."

Elspeth allowed the princess to talk without interrupting. Her thoughts tumbled out as if she had suppressed them for a long time.

"How did you meet the prince?" Elspeth asked, hoping to hear the princess's side of the story.

Princess Honorée smiled, the first genuinely relaxed expression Elspeth had seen on her face since their interview started. "He was opening a new cultural centre and cutting the ribbon. There were objects in the exhibition which came from my family's ancestral home, so I'd been invited to attend. Just as he was about to use the large pair of shears to cut the ribbon, I tripped over a cobblestone and in turning to see what had happened, he brushed the shears across my arm. The damage was slight, but it did draw blood."

Elspeth laughed. "And the rest is history?"

The twinkle in the princess's eyes was discernible even under her dark glasses. "Yes, the rest is history. I'm not the conniving woman Hope makes me out to be."

For most of her life Elspeth had assumed that royal marriages, particularly on the continent of Europe, were conveniently arranged. As the Victorians were so fond of saying, if love happened at all, it often happened after marriage. Hope had suggested that Honor had made herself conveniently available. Certainly, her fortune was as attractive as it was vast, but it was strange that in her criticism of her twin, Hope had never mentioned the fact that her own fortune was equally as large Princess Honorée's or the effects it had had when she married Francis Tilden. For all Hope's egalitarian sentiments, the topic of money must still have loomed large. The lifestyles of the granddaughters of Graf von Alteberg posed an interesting juxtaposition that they needed to be sorted out. Elspeth suspected that she had not yet heard all that there was on this subject.

"Tell me, Your Highness, what the rest of history turned out to be?"

They found a bench carefully placed so that a cluster of broad-leafed palms shaded them from the mid-afternoon sun.

"Michael is older than me, by ten years. We were married when I was twenty and had been thoroughly vetted by the royal family, the country and the media. Christiana came three years later. It was a difficult birth and afterwards the doctors told me and Michael there would be no more children. We've never told this to anyone. A prince had not yet been born, and

Christiana was the hope of the next generation. She became everyone's darling, particularly Michael's. She was cosseted and pampered. Soon she learned she could manipulate almost anyone with her fair looks and impish smile. She was given everything she wanted and never told no."

Elspeth detected that the princess did not approve of this upbringing, but said nothing except "And?"

"It certainly wasn't Christiana's fault how she turned out, but in some ways I blame myself. In retrospect, I was devastated at not being able to have more children, even though no one in the family, other than Michael, knew. When we were out in public, I could see people looking at me to see if there were signs of another child on the way. Like Michael, I should have had high hopes for Christiana, but inside I felt she had ripped my fecundity from me. I've never mentioned it to anyone before, but I see myself as the root cause of what is happening now. My own drowning in self-pity left me feeling bitter inside, and I know it affected my feelings towards both Michael and Christiana. She was so overindulged that I never thought she needed me or loved me." The princess lifted her dark glasses and wiped a tear from the corner of one of her eyes. "Why am I telling you this?"

"Because you know I'll keep everything you say in strict confidence and that when you leave here I'll no longer be a part of your life or your world. It happens all the time. Rather like sharing a private story with a stranger on a train." Elspeth wondered why in the past train travel was more conducive to strangers sharing secrets than on present day plane flights. Was it that there was more privacy between people in the old-fashioned carriages, where one was not being pestered with another meal, or where one's seat companion was not wearing earphones?

The princess drew a handkerchief from her pocket and blew her nose.

"One would have thought," she continued, "that as Christiana entered her teenage years, she would have all the confidence in the world. She had grown tall early, had position and wealth and was as attractive as any young teenager can be. I should have seen beyond her external appearance, but I didn't. That's why it came as such a shock to me when I discovered Christiana had been corresponding with Mary Tilden behind our backs. Michael had seldom been angry with Christiana before, but he was obviously upset with her when she announced that she was going to California to stay with her aunt, uncle, and cousin and that no one could stop her. Of course we had the power to prevent her and she knew it. Hope and I had broken off our relationship when I announced I was taking the von Alteberg name and going to Europe. You've already heard the reasons for this. When Hope wrote to me about re-establishing contact, I was too absorbed in my own angst to reply.

"Twins are supposed to have a special bond, aren't they? But the words that we exchanged before I left Canada to go to school in Switzerland were cutting and angry, and their scar was too deep for me to deal with it and Christiana at the same time. Through all this Michael and I continued to present ourselves to the royal family and the public as a loving couple with an ideal daughter. To allow Christiana to go to Los Angeles meant I'd have to admit to the world that I had a twin sister who had chosen to defy social convention through her marriage to Francis, and from whom I had broken away, having carefully concealed this since the time of my marriage to Michael. Not only could I not produce any more children, but I'd also be portrayed as self-serving and intolerant, qualities that both his family and our country would find appalling, particularly as I had kept the secret for so many years. I finally convinced

Michael to let Christiana go, just for a week or two week, but as an ordinary citizen, as 'Christie Alteberg', not Princess Christiana. The excuse would be that she was spending part of her summer holidays with a school friend and her family. But those few days changed the relationship between me and Michael. You see I'd never told him about Hope, Francis, or Mary. Whether the omission was intentional or not I've never been sure. Ever since then I've mulled over in my mind why I feel the way I do. I've never come up with satisfactory answers. Do you think less of me for that, Ms Duff?"

"No," Elspeth said. "We all have Gordian knots that are difficult to cut and are all haunted by our inability to do so."

"Have you?"

Elspeth thought of her complicated history after the murder of her fiancé at Cambridge.

"Oh yes." Elspeth's tone was so honest that the princess seemed taken aback. "We all do, I think, even those who won't admit it."

Silence fell between them. Princess Honorée could have been regretting telling Elspeth as much as she had, and Elspeth respected her for that.

"I think we should go in now," the princess said. "Michael will wonder where I am. "

7

The Princess left Elspeth at the back gate to the bungalow. Elspeth, feeling unsettled, walked back down the beach and found a seat among the rocks that led out to a point that delineated the hotel's property from that of its neighbour. She sat there thinking about parents who only had one child. Princess Honorée seemed to find shame at her inability to have more and anger at her daughter for having caused this. Hope Tilden, however, seemed unconcerned at having only Mary. Elspeth wondered if Hope and Francis Tilden had chosen to have only one for some good world cause such as overpopulation. That would be like Hope.

Elspeth's thoughts turned to her own parents, robust eighty-plus year olds who lived in the Highlands of Scotland and refused to be old in their ways. Had they ever wanted more than one child? Elspeth had never considered this, nor had they ever mentioned it in her hearing. Or was this something that no child needed to know, a quiet secret that stays locked away between a husband and wife for their entire lives?

Elspeth picked up a shell at her feet and looked at it absently, when she heard someone approach. Turning, she saw Greta von Fricken, dressed in the multiple layers of clothes that seemed to be her fashion statement. Her round face had lost its cheerfulness, and she drew up her hand to tame her hair, which was being ruffled by the wind now coming off the ocean. Elspeth rose and waved at the baroness. Greta plodded towards Elspeth, and they arrived together midpoint.

"Baroness, are you all right?"

"No. What have you done to upset her?" Greta's distress was plain.

Elspeth was surprised. "Nothing I'm aware of."

"Then why did she go into her room and bolt the door behind her, saying she didn't want to be disturbed. Even the prince can't get her to unlock the door. He's quite annoyed with you, Ms Duff."

"With me? I can't think of anything I said that might upset the princess. She wanted to talk about her background, and I simply listened."

"Don't believe all she said."

"I don't understand."

"Honorée sometimes makes things up."

"Makes things up?" she asked, frowning. The princess had seemed perfectly straightforward to her.

"Ever since Princess Christiana was born, Princess Honorée has suffered from depression. Most women grow out of this if it happens, but the princess never has. I've been Honorée's friend since we were in school together in Switzerland. My family is as old as hers, but we lost everything in the First World War, as we backed the Prussian regime. My father was with the Kaiser when he died in the Netherlands, and afterwards we settled in Switzerland. Due in part to our common background, Honorée and I became friends at school. When she married Prince Michael, she offered me the position of lady-in-waiting; I've been with her ever since. I tell you this because you need to know the closeness between us, and the number of years we have lived side by side. From the very first I knew that she had great dreams, dreams of restoring her family's reputation and dreams of having sons who would carry on the family lineage. When Princess Christiana was born, she told me of her disappointment but vowed there would be sons. In the German tradition, the children of a nobleman, both boys and girls, inherit the title of their father. At school Honorée called herself Graffin von Alteberg, after he grandfather, Graf or Count von Alteberg, who had fled from Hitler in 1938 and emigrated to western Canada. I was the only one at school whom she told that she was a Canadian and her real name was Honor. She did it one night when she came home from a party where she had too much drink and where she had gone without the school's permission. She didn't remember telling me in the morning. All the years before Hope and Mary Tilden appeared in her life, I've hidden from her that I knew about her childhood. She only told me the truth again when she was going out to California to bring Christiana back from her stay with the Tildens."

None of what Greta von Fricken told her directly contradicted what the Princess had said, except the part about the sons, and therefore Elspeth did not understand why Greta said Honorée had lied.

Greta seemed determined to blurt out more of the truth. Elspeth was concerned that the heat would soon cause great harm to them both, so led her to a small gazebo that the Kennington Organisation landscape architect had placed nearby. Greta seemed relieved by the shade and bench provided, and lowered her large body onto the teakwood slats circling the interior of the structure. Elspeth seated herself near Greta.

"You see," Greta continued, "Honorée has always seen the world as grander than it actually is. She set her sights on Prince Michael from the beginning, getting herself invited to the ribbon opening on a slim pretext and thrusting herself at him when he opened the ribbon cutting scissors. She will deny this, of course, but I was there. I've been her friend and lady-in-waiting for a long time. Did she tell you she couldn't have any more children? Truthfully, there's no reason physically why she can't, but Prince Michael was worried about her mental state. He didn't want her to suffer again from the depression of her first pregnancy and childbirth. He told me this six months after Christiana was born, when the doctors confirmed her post-partum depression. Afterwards we kept her under close observation. Does this surprise you after what I believe she just told you?"

Elspeth listened to Greta without revealing anything Honorée had said earlier. Elspeth had learned long before to listen to guests but not to tell others what she had heard. At the same time, she felt that Greta was telling her less of the truth than the princess had. The princess, Elspeth believed, had spoken from a deep place in her heart. Despite her earnestness, Greta was unconvincing. Could this be because of her concern for Princess Honorée's wellbeing, or did she have some other reason to want Elspeth to distrust her conversation with the princess? Where did the truth lie among the people who had shared their thoughts that day with her?

"Baroness, tell me about Christiana. I still have no sense of who she is and why she's acting the way she is now."

"Christiana," Greta said, "is spoiled, unruly, and not very likeable."

"Harsh words." After she said this, Elspeth was sorry she had.

"Not harsh if you know her. Christiana has never thought of anyone but herself, and everyone in her family has constantly encouraged that."

"Both her mother and her father?"

"And all the others too."

Greta's once cheerful face, which Elspeth had first assumed reflected her outlook on life, was subsumed in bitterness. Did she have children? Considering her place in the royal household, it seemed unlikely. Had Christiana's existence been a sore point for the princess's school friend, who because of her position wasn't able to have a child of her own? Elspeth could not know.

"Christiana has always taken pleasure in splitting her parents. Her father gave her everything she wanted. Honorée argued with him about this, but in the end she gave way."

"What about the days in California with the Tildens'?"

"Honorée refused to tell me what happened there, but her attitude towards Christiana changed. I see her sometimes watching her daughter. I don't know what she's thinking, but I could see a quality of softness in Honorée's face that had never been there before. Once or twice I saw Christiana come up to her mother and touch her cheek. Honorée's eyes would glisten every time Christiana did this. Those gestures were the only times I have seen any affection between them."

"Then something must have happened in California."

"It didn't last," Greta said.

Elspeth could not guess the cause of the acrimony in Greta's voice, but she resolved that she would try to find out whatever it was.

"Baroness, you've known Princess Christiana for all her life and Princess Honorée for a good portion of hers. I can see that you're a woman who sees things clearly. Can you tell me what's going on now? Is Princess Christiana serious about marrying Ali Ayan or is she baiting her parents?"

Greta looked up at Elspeth. She seemed to be composing her answer, but she came up short.

"You will have to ask her," Greta said.

"Will she tell me?"

"She will tell you something, but be careful before you believe her. She is a sly one, our little princess is."

"Has she ever spoken against you to Princess

Honorée?"

"Ach! So many times I cannot count."

"Why?"

"Because I tell her mother the truth about her."

"What truth?"

"About all the things she has done to hurt her parents."

"Why would she want to do those things? You just told me they overindulge her. Why would she want to hurt them?"

"When I was growing up, we didn't speak against our parents."

"Unfortunately in the modern world that's no longer the case. One can only hope that eventually children will be mature enough to see their parents as human and fallible, but wise in their own way."

"Do you have children, Ms Duff?"

"I have two."

"Do they find you human, fallible and wise in your own way?"

"I hope so."

"But you're not sure?"

"No, but I try to see their points of view as well as my own. We couldn't love each other if we didn't."

"Is that a common English sentiment?"

Elspeth tried to be polite, but always inwardly bristled at when people assumed she was English. "My family is Scottish, and the Scots believe strongly in their family ties." Elspeth said. She gave her best smile and Greta grinned back, the cheer returning to her face.

"My apologies," the baroness said. "I forgot that the British are sensitive about which part of the UK they come from."

"No matter," Elspeth said, although it did matter to her.

"I have spoken out of my concern for Princess Honorée and hope you can help to reduce her anxiety," the baroness said.

"I don't know what I can do to lessen the stress my conversation with the Princess has caused her. In no way did I offer advice. I simply listened. My assignment here is to make the prince and princess, and indeed all of your party, feel safe in the hotel environment. If you can think of other ways that I might do this, I would appreciate it if you would tell me. I can't necessarily understand all that's happening among you all, but I want you to know that I'm available at all times to help any one of you."

Greta twisted her head and looked at Elspeth. "We've been taking advantage of you, haven't we?"

Elspeth shook her head. "No, I just hope you don't think I can solve the issues that exist in Princess Honorée's family. I'm simply here to protect you from the outside world, not from yourselves."

"We all hope someone could save us from ourselves," Greta said enigmatically. She rose as if to leave.

"Baroness, would it be possible for me to speak with the prince again, tonight or perhaps first thing tomorrow morning?"

"It would be better in the morning. I'll call you."

Greta took her departure, leaving Elspeth sitting alone in the gazebo and feeling apprehensive. She took her sandals up from where she had laid them on the bench, and slowly climbed up the hill towards her rooms. She was puzzled by the different stories she had heard, none of which helped her in her stated aim of protecting the royal party. Her presence had splintered them, she thought, but, then again, it sounded as if they already had complicated their own relationships, and she had only become the latest lightning rod for the expression of their feelings. More than anything, she wanted to have a long shower and consider what her next course of action should be.

She put her key card in the lock, went into her suite and leaned against the door after she closed it. The light on her room phone was blinking mercilessly. Lord Kennington's voice message waiting for her was abrupt. "Call me on your secure line the minute you get in. And, why don't you have your phone with you?"

8

Because, Elspeth thought with her jaw clenched, I have been working all day with only ten minutes for lunch and I didn't think it appropriate to have my mobile on while interviewing people. Her words to Lord Kennington had quite a different tone.

"I rang as soon as I got your message. What is it, Eric?"

"Have you read the *Evening Standard* tonight?"

"No, I prefer *The Times*, as you might expect, but what does the *Evening Standard* say that I should know about? I doubt it has been delivered here yet."

"Go online," he barked.

Elspeth booted up her laptop as she listened to Lord Kennington. When she read the screaming headlines on the newspaper's website, she saw why her employer was not happy.

'PRINCESS DISAPPEARS FROM ALI'S YACHT. Not seen since early yesterday morning."

Elspeth abhorred bad syntax, but readers of the *Evening Standard* were less finicky. She assumed it was the princess and not the yacht that had not been seen since the previous morning.

"Did you have any intimation that this was going to happen? If you were with them all day, they must have told you."

"I suspect they don't know about the press article."

"Damn it, Elspeth, what did you talk about?"

Elspeth wanted to say 'female bonding' and

'women with only children' but that sounded impertinent, even though it was true. She knew Eric Kennington well enough to recognise that deep concern lay beneath his badgering.

"I seem to have become their father, or rather mother, confessor. I've heard a great deal about how various people in the party feel about each other. I hoped by doing so I would get some insight into who they are and how I might protect them."

"Have you?"

"Obtained some insight or protected them?"

"The latter is your charge, not the former."

"As I well know." Elspeth grinned as she said this and was glad that she was not on a video link.

"Elspeth, I want you to find out everything you can about the reaction of your party to the news in the *Evening Standard,* and I want you to get back to me within the hour."

Elspeth swallowed. "I'll do my best."

"Not just your best. I want to know what is happening whether it is your best or better than your best. I'll be here expecting your call, no matter how late."

He hung up abruptly.

Elspeth felt the person she needed to talk to most was the prince. After all, it was he who had talked about Christiana's 'abduction'. Greta had indicated he would not consent to an interview until the morning, but this newest information prompted Elspeth to devise a way to see him immediately. She called Kit Taylor.

"Do you have a direct line to Harald Wade's room?" she asked him.

"Harald Wade?"

"Prince Michael's secretary."

Kit had an answer for her in seconds. "Room B6."

Elspeth picked up the house phone in her room and dialled the number.

"Wade here," a sleepy voice answered. His grogginess confused Elspeth. Surely if a family crisis was going on, the prince's secretary would be at his side.

"It's Elspeth Duff. I need to speak to the prince immediately on a matter of extreme importance. Please tell him that I'll be at the bungalow in about five minutes. We need to speak privately."

"But Ms Duff, I can't . . ."

Elspeth had perfected an authoritarian voice, which she seldom used, but which had an impact that only the most arrogant people could ignore. Harald Wade was not one of them. "Yes, you can," she said. "If he wants to meet me in the bungalow's small sitting room, I'll be there. Or we can meet in the garden outside. I'll let myself in."

The prince was waiting just inside the gate when Elspeth unlatched it.

"Harald tells me you won't be put off," he said. Elspeth could not tell if he was annoyed or amused at her insistence on seeing him.

Elspeth didn't offer any explanation. "Tell me about Christiana."

"What about her?"

"Your Highness, I've just had a call from Lord Kennington, who tells me that the London evening press is blaring your daughter's disappearance across their front pages. You told me earlier that you were arranging for this, but no one I spoke to today seemed to be aware of anything about it. I can't protect you and your party unless I know the truth."

"I think, Ms Duff, that I've already told you too much."

Elspeth was not satisfied with his dismissive tone. "You Highness, I'm not here to assess the legality of your actions towards your daughter. I don't know the laws of the sea, and I don't want to exercise moral judgment on what could have happened yesterday morning. My job is to see to the well-being of you, your group, and the other people staying at the Kennington Bermuda. My first loyalty is to Lord Kennington, who has carefully developed and guards the reputation of his hotels as places that respect assiduously the privacy of his guests. Every one of us on Lord Kennington's staff is trained in the absolute need for discretion in dealing with all our guests. There are times, such as this one, when he sends out members of his staff who personally report to him, I being one of them, to help facilitate the comfort and safety of guests who may require special attention, but I can't help you unless you're forthcoming with me. If your daughter is indeed on her way here, I'll need to set up special provisions to safeguard her presence here. Do you find that so onerous that you can't tell me more? If you need to talk to Lord Kennington about my credentials, you are most certainly welcome to do so. I spoke to him not ten minutes ago, and he's waiting in his office in London for word from me. I can patch you through on my secure phone if you wish to speak to him and not to me."

Elspeth's speech was longer and more direct than she had intended. At first the prince looked away from her haughtily, but gradually he turned back to her.

"I can see why Lord Kennington has confidence in you. You won't take no for an answer, will you?"

"Not when I need information but am having difficulty in obtaining it, even if it's from a member of a royal family. In any case, I don't want to incur the wrath of my employer because I happen to like my job." Elspeth said this with the slightest hint of a smile and challenge in her eyes.

The prince held back his head and laughed. "All right, Ms Duff, I believe you."

Elspeth relaxed slightly. She felt she had finally broken through the prince's defences.

"I told you yesterday that I planned to have my

daughter, what was the word I used, 'abducted' from Ali Ayan's yacht. She's already in my detectives' care and aboard my own yacht. I spoke with the captain earlier today, and they have set course for Bermuda. If they make good progress, I expect them to arrive the day after tomorrow, in the evening, or possibly the following morning."

"Which, of course, effects what I must do for you in the meantime. Lord Kennington will want to know."

"I would prefer that you don't tell him this." The politeness of the prince's words glossed over his obvious command.

"Why, may I ask?'

"Because as much as I'm learning to respect you, I don't want this information to go beyond our bungalow. I suggest you tell your employer that you have the situation fully in hand, and also have my full cooperation. Lord Kennington will have to trust you, and me as well. If he doesn't, I assure you my assistance to you will come to an end."

Elspeth drew back, raised her head and looked into his eyes. She found their pale blue colour icy; their focus was directed at some distant object. She had dealt with this sort of resistance from others before and had always struggled with it. She seemed to have the ability to win the confidence of people, although she often felt it was a misplaced reaction to her looks and demeanour. She could not hide her intelligence, nor had she any desire to change the way she dressed, spoke or carried herself. All were a part of who she was, and, to some degree, the measure of her success. She knew the power of these attributes and used them without the slightest embarrassment.

When Elspeth returned to her room, she kicked off her sandals, flopping down on one of the two sofas in her sitting room, and blew out a long breath. She felt no further argument would budge the prince, and therefore she now had to cross a dangerous line with Eric Kennington, because she knew he could be belligerent when defied. She fumbled in the pocket of her jacket for her mobile. It suddenly took on the aspect of an instrument of medieval torture, and its imminent use would cause her psychological if not physical distress.

He answered almost before the call went through.

"And what did you learn?"

"That the prince is a stubborn man."

"Is that all? Surely, Elspeth, I don't pay you far too high a salary for you to return with such a feeble excuse. Get on with it, woman!"

Eric Kennington always became abrasive when he was worried, but the day had been a long and irritating one for Elspeth. She wanted to snap at him, matching his tone, but instead she bit the edges of her tongue so hard that they hurt for a long time afterwards.

"If you must know, Eric, he said that you should rely on me to handle the matter without me telling you any details."

There was a long silence on the London end of the call.

"If I do and you fail, Elspeth, then . . ." He did not finish the sentence.

Elspeth did not like working alone. She was skilled at what she did, but she was not comfortable taking full responsibility for a difficult problem without support from Eric Kennington, or from Pamela Crumm. The prince's demand had set her adrift.

"Elspeth, I've told you multiple times not to endanger yourself physically. As you have so well proven in the past, you haven't always listened to me and have suffered the consequences. I don't want to see a repeat performance of what happened to you in Singapore or Cyprus. I'm going to gamble on you handling this without further assistance. The prince is being recalcitrant and, at least for the moment, you're to pay lip service to him, but remember that in the end you work for me. Now I'm already late for the opera." He rang off abruptly.

Elspeth had feared worse treatment, but she knew that Eric Kennington well enough that in the long run he was a fair and rational person.

After the warning from Eric, Elspeth wanted to stop to gather her wits, then pour herself a glass of wine and settle down with a good book. Realising she had finished the best-selling novel she had bought at the airport in London, she sighed and ventured out of her room to find the small shop, which was usually hidden away discreetly in all Kennington hotels, and which sold toiletries, magazines, books and small high-quality gifts. The shops did not sell souvenirs but always had a corner devoted to cut flowers and handmade chocolates. Elspeth found a copy of a Jane Austen novel that had recently been serialised on the BBC, and tried to remember when she last had read it, probably before she had entered Girton. She was clutching the book like an old friend as she emerged from the shop and relished thoughts of a quiet evening ahead. She headed towards the reception desk to let them know that Richard would be arriving later in the week, when a voice interrupted her introspection.

"I finally worked out where I know you from. You're Elizabeth Foxworthy's mother, aren't you?"

Elspeth turned to find a woman of about her own age addressing her. Like many of the guests who stayed at the Kennington hotels, the woman was handsomely dressed, wore jewellery that was real, and was fashionably coiffed. She stood slightly taller than Elspeth and her appearance shouted her status as a member of the 'county set'. The woman looked vaguely familiar.

"I am," Elspeth said. "Please do tell me your name."

"Dorothy Ayers. My daughter and your Elizabeth are in a mothers' group in East Sussex. I remember that the last time we met we were all playing charades at a dinner party your daughter was hosting on Boxing Day. That must have been almost two years ago."

Elspeth recalled the Christmas far too well. At the time she had been in the midst of trying to find Malcolm Buchanan's murderer. She and Richard had had a row over this, and they had not spoken for several weeks, nor had they exchanged even superficial Christmas greetings. Elspeth had not been in a state to remember later the names of Lizzie's friends' parents with whom she had played childish word games. There had been much laughter, but Elspeth had not felt a part of it.

"I remember you well. When we were introduced, I though your name sounded like a heroine from a Scottish novel who bound her family together in the face of great adversity."

Elspeth laughed. "I hope you didn't tell Lizzie that. She will be expecting a lot more from me. Tell me, Mrs Ayers . . . "

"Dorothy, please. If we have romped together in front of our children in a silly game, the least we can be is on a Christian name basis."

Mrs Ayers was a person who obviously enjoyed life and exuded enthusiasm. Elspeth was not immune.

"All right, Dorothy. Are you here alone? Would you join me for drinks in my suite and fill me in on what is transpiring in East Sussex? I've not seen Lizzie for over a month and the twins for longer than that. As you can see, I'm not really the heroine who binds the family together, but rather a mother and grandmother who is all too often too far away from the UK to see my daughter and her family with any frequency."

"There're no bad feelings, I hope."

"Oh, absolutely none. Lizzie and I lead rather separate lives, but we love each other nonetheless."

"To answer your questions, yes, I'm alone, and, yes, I'd love to join you for drinks. Let me freshen up first as I've been raiding the better shops in Hamilton and feel in the need of a wash."

"Shall we say seven?" This agreed upon, and Elspeth having given her suite number, Dorothy Ayers and her many bags of purchases bustled from the corridor outside the shop and up the stairs to her room.

Dorothy Ayers made Elspeth laugh, which provided her with a relief more satisfying than Miss Austen's heroine could possibly have done. Dorothy gave Elspeth news of her daughter and family and regaled her with tales of her own life.

"I was Stafford's trophy wife, you see. He was thirty years older than me, and I was already a bit long in the tooth when we had Olivia. I suffered the brunt of many jokes, but it really didn't matter because I loved Stafford and had more than enough money of my own to counteract the usual comments about being a 'gold-digger', a horrid phrase I always thought. Stafford died ten years ago, and every year around the time of our wedding anniversary I try to visit one of the hotels where we had stayed when we travelled together. It keeps his memory alive for me. But, tell me, Elspeth, did you recover from your injury? Elizabeth told me you had suffered massive head trauma."

Elspeth did not like to talk about her health, much less the circumstances that lead to her brutal beating in Singapore a year and a half before. She decided to make light of it.

"I'm fully recovered, except for the occasional headache, which might have more to do with my work than my injury. The worst part was having my head shaved. I never have liked that look on woman, although I know it's quite popular now. Only a woman with the finest bone structure can carry it off."

"Elizabeth told me that you travel for your work. I'm glad they do give you a holiday occasionally. You must be enjoying a suite at a Kennington hotel."

Elspeth laughed. "It comes as part of my job," she said. "I'm here on business, not on holiday. I work for the Kennington Organisation, but, please will you keep that under wraps. I've been dreading eating another room service dinner by myself, but want to avoid someone I might possibly meet in the dining room. Would you mind joining me for dinner, perhaps at the patio grill? I'll see that Lord Kennington pays for it if you will pretend we had prearranged our dinner together."

"I should be delighted and will, if approached, assure one and all that we are old friends and set up our meeting weeks ago. I do love a good conspiracy."

9

Richard's forthcoming arrival nor arranged for him to be given a key card to her suite. She scribbled a note on the pad of hotel stationery to remind herself to do so. She had lingered longer than she had expected over dinner with Dorothy Ayers, whose chatty manner and amusing stories of life in the 'counties' had been diverting, and cleared her mind of the more taxing parts of the day. Elspeth had a bath, slipped into silk pyjamas and finally curled up to enjoy the societal dilemmas of Miss Austen's heroine, but she soon nodded off and fell into a dreamless sleep. The persistent buzzing of the phone next to her bed brought her back to full consciousness. The silver LCD numbers on the clock beside her bed informed her it was 11:37.

The call came from the reception desk. "Ms Duff, there is someone here asking for you. He said you would not mind being disturbed. His name is Richard Munro."

Elspeth's heart jumped in her chest and she sprang from bed.

"Yes, tell him I'll be right there!" She hoped her voice sounded professional, but she could not hide her excitement.

Throwing on her caftan and fumbling about for the slippers that matched them, she half-ran and half-skipped towards the lobby in a most undignified manner, but it did not matter as no one was in the garden. He was standing there, tall and distinguished, with his angular face and thin nose, and his long fingers that she had stroked so many times in both moments of trouble and of love. He was chatting amiably with the receptionist, who seemed to be in his thrall. Elspeth stopped as she rounded the corner to make sure it was Richard. He looked around, and on seeing her, a smile spread across his face. She wanted to rush to him but slowed her pace and walked with composure towards him. Her eyes met his, their hazel-green twinkling at her.

"Oh, Dickie," she said, unable to pretend any longer, and ran to him before noticing the receptionist's curious look.

"I was able to leave Malta earlier than I expected." He folded his arms around her shoulders and brushed her tousled hair with his lips.

"Oh, Dickie," she said again, "I'm so glad." Then she drew back. "I've been remiss in telling the hotel you were coming. I meant to earlier." She turned to the receptionist. "You are Cecily, aren't you? This is my husband, Sir Richard Munro. He will be staying with me for the next few days. Will you have someone take his case to my rooms, please. I'll come around in the morning to make the final arrangements."

Taking Richard's arm, she led him through the garden and down to the beach beyond. The moon was playing with the clouds and brushing the crest of the waves with its intermittent beams. They stopped by the gazebo, and he took her into his arms, holding her lovingly.

"Dearest Elspeth, I've missed you so. I couldn't stay away. Am I being terribly intrusive?"

She answered without words, but the meaning was clear that he was not.

They lingered in the gazebo, exchanging words too banal to be repeated if not spoken to a lover, and interrupted them with kisses more passionate than decorous. Finally, using her key card, which fortunately she had slipped in her pocket, she drew him from the beach and up through the patio gate up to her rooms.

She had become accustomed to him being beside her at night and lay listening to what she called his 'night noises'. She loved the resonance of his deep breathing when he fell off to sleep, the small grunts he expelled from time to time as he shifted position, and his random murmurings when she knew he was dreaming. Elspeth lay awake, resting beside him, but did not touch him for fear of waking him. Her two hours of deep sleep before Richard's arrival had left her restless, and she slipped into thoughts that bothered her more frequently than she wished. She loved her husband in a way a woman does who had been surprised by love, had tried in every way to avoid it, and then who finally had given in to it because it was stronger than her will. The intensity of her emotions frightened her as much as they sustained her. Richard had told her often that he had loved her from the day he met her, during his summer between his first and second year at Oxford, when he was eighteen and she fifteen. He was already dignified and serious, while she was a brainy but an unrepentant tomboy, and he had loved her over forty years, despite their marrying others and leading vastly diverse lives.

Then they had met unexpectedly two and a half years ago, when she was on assignment in Malta, and at fifty-five, not fifteen, she found herself plunging into love with him although she could not reconcile doing so with her chosen independence after her divorce. Her ambivalence had made her keep him at bay for two years. She had often treated him shabbily, making demands, while at the same time skirting acknowledgement of his unflinching and unwavering love for her. Even up until three weeks before their wedding, she had confronted him with her indecisiveness, no, more her fear that if she gave herself to him, she would lose herself. She had made demands of him; he had accepted them, asking only that she not doubt his love. Now her doubts were not about his love, that was too apparent every time they were together, but about what she had done at the end of their honeymoon. Would her insistence that she continue in her job, that she keep her own name, and that she asked to be free from performing the duties of his diplomatic wife, eventually lead to her losing him? Elspeth hated the persistence of these thoughts, but they came too often after they had made love and he had fallen off to sleep. She wanted to roll over to him, nestle against his body, have him reassure her, as he had so many times, that all her demands were agreeable to him. But were they, or did he merely say so?

"You're awake, aren't you?" he whispered in her ear. In her brooding she had not heard his breathing change. "And fretting."

"Dear Dickie," she said in a small voice. "I'm always so afraid you will go away if I act badly."

He came to her and held her. "I know I did in Copenhagen, but I never will again," he said. "For all your worrying about such things, you give me everything I have ever desired. I don't want you to be anything other than you are, Elspeth. Sometimes I find you vexing, certainly, and I know there are times when we disagree, but we've always been able to work things out. What we have is so precious I never would give it away."

"Are you sure?"

"What do you think?" he chuckled and showed her it was so. Afterwards she slept soundly, but not after wondering if such love would last if they were together all the time and with all the proper manners her grandmother had taught her, she was dispensing tea at the High Commission in Malta to yet another trade delegation.

Elspeth shut the outer door of their suite quietly, hoping not to wake Richard, who had not stirred when she rose and dressed. She would let him sleep. She had taped a note in her large hand on the shaving mirror in the bath to let him know she would be occupied for the morning but hoped they might have lunch together, if she could free herself of her obligations.

First, she went to the hotel manager's office and completed the arrangements for Richard's visit. That being settled, she made her way into the breakfast room and, after serving herself from the buffet, found a quiet corner where she could read the morning's paper and drink her coffee in peace.

She had barely read the front page and noticed the stop press item in the lower corner that informed readers that Princess Christiana had still not been located, when the effervescent voice of Lilianne Balfour alerted Elspeth to the fact that the tabloid size of the newspaper, despite its seriousness, had failed to keep her out of sight. Elspeth lowered the paper and smiled at the American. Then she raised her paper again.

Lilianne was obviously not going to be put off. "And how are y'all this morning? The general is sleeping late this morning. May I join you? Did y'all enjoy your timeout last night?"

Elspeth considered quickly. Her coffee cup was empty, although she was thinking of having another, and she had eaten most of her light breakfast.

"Forgive me," Elspeth said with the sweetest of smiles, "but I was just finishing and am meeting someone shortly."

"Are y'all going out shopping? I found some wonderful stores yesterday that I must tell you about."

Elspeth felt that Lilianne and Bill Balfour's anniversary trip must be lacking the pleasure Elspeth and Richard had found together the night before. Had Elspeth not been on business, she would have lingered in their room and not be forced to be courteous to strangers. Many people, she knew, enjoyed making new acquaintances while travelling, but Elspeth had neither the time nor the desire to get to know Mrs General William 'Bill' Balfour better. However, being an employee of the Kennington Organisation, she had to be polite.

Elspeth started to make the motions of rising from the table, when she was stopped by Lilianne's next words.

"I saw her again last night," Mrs Balfour whispered. "You know, the princess."

Elspeth was alarmed but responded neutrally. "Oh, really?"

"She was tiptoeing across the lawn toward the kitchen, just like the last time. In the moonlight I saw her plain as day. I haven't told a soul but you."

Not yet, though Elspeth, but undoubtedly the next person Lilianne met would also be privy to this juicy titbit of gossip. Elspeth must stop her, but she wanted to do so without revealing her position in the Kennington Organisation.

"Mrs Balfour, perhaps you can appreciate that many of the guests here wish to have their identities protected. I'm sure that you and the general are among them. It would do no good for the press to learn that the general is here. Think of the security issues. If the person you saw was a princess, which I doubt, wouldn't she want privacy too?"

Lilianne looked at Elspeth and winked. "Well now, I guess she would. My lips are sealed, and I promise not to tell who I saw y'all with late last night on the beach."

Elspeth gulped inwardly, covering her reaction with another sweet smile. "Thank you," she said. "I would appreciate that."

Elspeth was not certain why she had refrained from telling Lilianne who Richard was. What had started out as dissuading this indomitable woman from sharing secrets that might identify the princess as a guest had ended with her insistence that Elspeth admit to a clandestine relationship the night before with a man who might not be her husband.

"I really won't tell, honey, I promise. Y'all know at our age we have to get all the happiness we can, and you're still an attractive woman." Lilianne once again winked one of her heavily mascara-laden eyelashes.

Elspeth excused herself as quickly as she could and carefully took her newspaper with her, hoping Mrs Balfour was not inclined to read the daily newspapers or the stop press about Christiana. But why would Princess Honorée have left the safety of the bungalow grounds and gone to the kitchen? It made no sense because there was a small kitchen in the bungalow with a significant amount of food and drink available, and Greta von Fricken or any other member of the royal party could have called room service, which was available throughout the night.

10

The person Elspeth wanted to talk to most was not Princess Honorée but her niece, Mary. After all, Mary had been in contact with Christiana when she was on Ali Ayan's yacht and had persuaded Christiana to come for a brief meeting with the Tildens at the Canadian High Commission in Antigua and Barbuda. The mysterious appearance of the princess in the garden by the kitchen for the two nights before could wait, as either Lilianne Balfour had an overly active imagination or there could be some logical explanation that at the moment escaped Elspeth.

Elspeth carefully surveyed the lobby and assured herself that Lilianne was still at breakfast and out of sight. Elspeth made her way to Kit Lord's office and got the number for the phone in the corridor of the bungalow. She let it ring five times and was almost ready to hang up when Hope Tilden answered.

"Mary has gone out for a swim and took her snorkel and fins with her, so I don't know how long she will be. The others are all still asleep, but come over and have coffee with me. I could do with some company other than the family. One could go easily crazy with the silences here, and the tension."

Elspeth decided to take a more circuitous route to the bungalow rather than crossing the garden because Lilianne Balfour might be watching. Elspeth hoped that General William 'Bill' Balfour would rise soon or that his lady would decide to stop waiting for him and go out into Hamilton to spend more of his hardship duty pay. Elspeth walked under the arcade that surrounded the interior courtyard of the main hotel and hurried down the last few yards to the gate leading into the bungalow. Hope Tilden was waiting for her as she had been two nights before.

"Mary just came back and is showering. I told her you were coming, and she's willing to talk to you if she can do so in confidence. I'll leave the two of you here alone in the dining room. Please feel free to have breakfast with her if you haven't already eaten."

Elspeth was glad she had not had a second cup of coffee earlier and that she had eaten lightly. A large urn of coffee was on the sideboard of the dining room, and she was pouring a cup for herself when Mary entered. Her hair still wet from her swim, she was wearing shorts and a tee shirt and was glowing with the health of the well-exercised.

"My mother told me you wanted to talk to me, and I assume it's about Christie."

"Yes. You seem to be closer to her than the rest of the family. I don't want you to tell me any secrets you have with her. That would be unfair of me to ask, but if I understood more about Princess Christiana and what her arrival here may mean to you all, I would feel my ability to help you would be greatly improved. Your mother and father have been forthcoming as has your aunt, but I still have very little grasp of who Princess Christiana is and if the recent press reports about her bear any credence."

Mary helped herself to some fruit from a large bowl and took a piece of toast from the rack. She skirted the coffee urn and the tea dispenser, finding some juice instead and filling a glass with it. She took a place at the table opposite Elspeth.

"Christie can be a chameleon. It depends who she's with," Mary said.

"Is that true when she is with you?"

"Yes and no. That isn't an answer, is it?"

"An answer, yes, but an ambiguous one."

"There are times when I feel Christie's being completely open with me. Usually this happens when we are alone and she lets down her guard, but if others are around, particularly her parents, it's almost as if I don't exist."

"Do you have contact with her often? Your mother and father told me you text the princess frequently."

"Only when she wants to. We can be in touch several times over a day and then not at all for weeks."

"When was the last time you were alone together for any length of time?"

Mary took a long drink of her juice before replying. "Before our return to Antigua and Barbuda and her joining Ali's yacht—about two months ago, maybe three. I was in London doing some research for my thesis. My aunt and uncle have a home in Mayfair, and I was staying with them. Christie came in for the weekend, saying she wanted to see me. We talked for hours, walked in Hyde Park, rode the London Eye, went to the movies and had tea at the Ritz. The prince and princess seemed delighted, although they never asked what we were talking about."

"Which was?"

"Her anger with her parents."

"Over what?"

"Over them not allowing her to marry someone she had fallen in love with. Her parents found him quite unsuitable."

"Is he?"

"That depends on what you call unsuitable. He has no title and no money, but he is well-educated and presents himself well. You've met him."

Elspeth frowned.

"Harald Wade, my uncle's secretary."

Elspeth thought of the shy man who had sat silently during drinks and dinner two nights before.

"Does Mr Wade know that Princess Christiana confided in you?"

"Absolutely," Mary said. "Didn't you notice the other night how he wouldn't make eye contact with me?"

"I wondered about that. I thought perhaps he found you attractive."

"Hardly." A shade of bitterness filled Mary's voice. Elspeth could not determine what caused it, but she sensed that Mary, for all her beauty, had feelings about her family and background, which allowed her to relax with North Americans but more difficult to interact with Europeans.

"Harald, according to Christie, could be the saviour of her life. He's asked her to go to Oxford with him. He's finishing a doctorate there and supports himself by working for my uncle. Harald assured her that they could live happily there, and Christie could get her degree. I've never been sure if this is what she really wants, but because her parents won't let her attend university, she's always said she wanted to. Christie is a living contradiction. One moment she wants something, particularly if her parents say no, and the next, if they give in, she doesn't want it at all."

"Do a university degree and Harald Wade fit in this formula?"

"Who knows?" Mary said with a slight shrug

Elspeth bit the corner of her lip, which she did when thinking. "Harald Wade seems too shy to have openly expressed his feelings to the princess."

"Exactly," Mary said. "I think the whole idea was really Christie's. You haven't met her, Ms Duff, but she oozes charm, if she wants to."

"Is it genuine?"

"With Christie, you never know. She can manipulate almost anyone."

"Do you think she's happy doing so?"

"Honestly, no. Can I trust you not to tell my family any of this?"

"You can."

"I think the best thing in the world for her would be to live incognito for several years, to go to university if she wants, to become Christie MacAdam, our grandmother's maiden name, or use whatever name she wants, to have a limited allowance so that she has to budget herself, to have to work to achieve something, and most of all to be away from the money, power and position that her family and title give her. She has told me so herself."

"Then why this affair with Ali Ayan?"

"She didn't say, but I think she wants to so outrage her parents that they'll finally see her as a young woman and not a royal figure who must continue to uphold an anachronistic position in the twenty-first century."

"You are an egalitarian I can tell."

"You have met my parents," Mary said with a laugh. "What would you expect?"

"Nothing less. Does Princess Christiana agree with you?"

"On her better days."

"Or, is she simply being the chameleon you accuse her of being? Do you think she really loves Harald Wade?"

Mary cocked her head. "Perhaps, and it might work."

"That doesn't exactly answer my question."

"Since she was a young teenager, Harald has been the closest man she has ever met who is anywhere near normal. He has many good points: intelligence, good looks, and dedication to his work, which by the way is the history of the thirteenth century in Western Europe, particularly in the smaller monarchic states. His scholarship is solid; I've checked. He can be serious but also at times, when out of the view of my aunt and uncle, very entertaining. He is devoted to Christie, and I think she finds his quiet affection for her completely different from the public adoration she's used to."

"Mr Wade has attributes that are not readily apparent."

"Many of them," Mary agreed.

"Do you truly believe that he and Princess Christiana could make a relationship work? It wouldn't be an easy thing."

"Given half the chance, I think so. At least they should be given the opportunity. It certainly would be better than her marrying Ali Ayan."

"Do you really think Princess Christiana could drop out of the royal life and become the wife of Harald Wade, Ph.D., Oxford don, or whatever he might become?"

"Honestly, Ms Duff, I think she would like nothing better in the world."

This surprised Elspeth, but before she could ask why, they were interrupted by the arrival of Harald Wade in person. His first reaction was to apologize for the intrusion.

Elspeth had not looked closely at Harald Wade before. He was the sort who faded away in a crowd but could be interesting if found alone. Mary was right in saying he was handsome. If one paid attention, one could definitely see the intelligence in his eyes. He was presentably dressed in long khaki trousers with a sharp crease and an open-necked knitted shirt which sported an embroidered designer logo, and he wore highly polished loafers. He stood tall, without slouching, and his apology was more out of politeness than humbleness. Why had this escaped Elspeth before?

Mary rose and excused herself, nodding to Elspeth conspiratorially. "I've finished," she said, indicating her empty plate. "Perhaps, Ms Duff, you would like to talk to Harald without my company. I need to get back to my computer and download the photographs I took this morning. There are one or two species of fish I didn't recognise."

After Mary was gone, Elspeth sat back in her chair and held out her cup. "Mr Wade, will you kindly pour me another cup of coffee?" She often used this way of pulling rank to establishing seniority over younger people, although she considered it a cheap trick. There had to be some benefits to being middle-aged.

He smiled at her graciously. "It will be my pleasure, Ms Duff. I assume Mary left so that you could question me in private."

Elspeth returned the smile. "I hadn't expected to meet you this morning, but, yes, I would like to speak to you. Do you mind I do it while you're eating breakfast?"

"Better to get it over with," he said, laying Elspeth's replenished cup in front of her and returning to the sideboard to choose his breakfast. From his selection, he was a hardy eater when he was not with the royal party, although his slender body belied this fact.

Elspeth sipped her coffee, which was hot and perfectly blended. She expected no less from the hotel kitchen.

"I'm finding all sorts of unexpected things in my discussions with you all."

"Did Mary tell you about me and Christiana?"

"Her version of it. Why don't you tell me yours? I still don't have any sense of who Christiana is, but Mary indicated that the two of you are close."

"Not close, Ms Duff. I love Christiana with every fibre of my being. Have you ever loved someone like that?"

"Fortunately, yes. My husband. I think I understand."

"Can you? Christiana is outside my reach. Obviously your husband is not, as you're married."

"Have you told her how you feel?"

"Many times."

"And how has she answered?"

"She said she loved me too. She said she would marry me, but then *they* found out."

"The prince and princess?"

"Who else?"

"And they forbad it?"

"Yes."

"Why?" It was a simple question, but it seemed to crush Harald Wade. He slumped down in his chair and pushed his breakfast away.

"I'm not grand enough," was his bitter reply. "I'm a mere mortal and an underling. At best a toad; not even a frog who will turn into a prince."

11

Elspeth was so absorbed in the implications of the conversations she had just had in the bungalow that when she reached the hotel's main lobby, it took her a moment to connect with the outside world. She stopped and faced the man who had just addressed her. He looked at her expectantly, as if she should recognise him. She did not.

"I'm Martin Hagen," he said. He was a man of medium height, with dark hair, which was slightly receding, and a clean-shaven nondescript face, and he wore a white short-sleeved shirt, blue jeans, and trainers. If he had been walking in the street, no one would have paid particular attention to him, and if questioned later by a witness to a crime, he would probably not be identified. Judging by his accent, he was a well-bred British man, whose voice was a reedy tenor and whose manner suggested modesty rather than cunning.

His name eluded Elspeth, although it sounded familiar, a name someone had mentioned recently but she could not recollect where.

"You don't remember me, do you?"

Elspeth could not decide if he said this with regret that she had meant something to him at one time but had faded from her memory, or that he was accustomed to being unrecognised by people who might recall others of grander stature.

She smiled at him as she so often did with guests. When she first started working for the Kennington Organisation, she had practiced this smile in the mirror so that it was warm but not familiar. "Forgive me. I meet many people in the course of my work.

Please tell me who you are."

"We met in London at the Kennington Mayfair in 1999."

"That was a long time ago. Should I remember?" Elspeth then made the connection. Kit Lord had told her about Martin Hagen and warned her that he was a current guest.

"You're more attractive now than you were then," he said.

Elspeth resented the reference to her appearance, but because she purposely dressed in professional chic clothing, she did not take immediate offense.

"Is it the man you were with last night?" he continued, this time more suggestively.

"I beg your pardon, Mr Hagen. Should this mean something to me?" She was a bit put off by his remark, as she heard a touch of malice in it.

"Perhaps you would prefer to speak in private," he suggested.

Without thinking she said, "If you wish. The garden has few guests at this time of day. Shall we find a bench outside?"

"No, Ms Duff, I mean a place where no one can overhear us. I'm sure that you would prefer it that way."

Her suspicion of his ill-intentions grew.

"I'm sure there's a small conference room available. It will take me a moment to arrange it. Will you meet me here in fifteen minutes?"

Securing his agreement, Elspeth left him and made her way to Kit Lord's office, where she found him on the phone. He indicated a seat, which she took, and soon he rang off.

"Tell me again about Martin Hagen. He has approached me just now with what sounds like a threat. What possibly could have brought that on? He couldn't have known about my report, when was it, seven years ago now?"

Kit went to his computer and quickly downloaded the report. Elspeth skimmed though it. It suggested Martin Hagen had pursued older women staying at the hotel, particularly a wealthy widow called Mrs Robert van Dorn from Cincinnati, but she had never come forward with a complaint. Elspeth's flag next to Martin Hagen's name came up every time he booked a room at a Kennington hotel, which was once or twice a year, but no other reports had been filed against him. Elspeth had been a new employee of the Kennington Organisation when she filed the report, and she may have been overly zealous in her observations, but from her encounter with him several minutes ago she was aware that he had not forgotten her, although for her he was a dim memory, if a memory at all. Elspeth knew it would be best to confront Martin Hagen before he could cause any harm to her or to the hotel.

"Do you have a room where I can meet him?"

"Do you feel comfortable meeting him alone?" Kit asked. "I can give you some backup if you like."

Elspeth made a quick judgment call. "No, that's not necessary. I don't think any threat he'll make will be physical. Let me talk to him alone, and if he does pose any danger, I'll let you know. Don't worry, Kit, I've handled harder cases."

Kit made two calls and then told Elspeth that one of the small, private breakfast rooms would not be used again until the next morning, and therefore was at her disposal. "I'll come by in half an hour just to make sure you're all right."

Appreciative of his concern, Elspeth thanked him and went to find Martin Hagen, who was lingering in the garden. She led him to the room, but she purposely had not ordered coffee and tea, although under different circumstances she would have.

Martin Hagen did not take a seat, so Elspeth

stood as well. He shifted from foot to foot before speaking.

"I see you are still employed by Lord Kennington," he said with a thin smile.

Elspeth nodded but said nothing.

He cleared his throat. "And I'm sure you like your employment."

Elspeth's curiosity was aroused at the man's interest in her job, but she had already decided not to answer any of his leading questions. She would wait until he revealed his reason for suggesting they meet alone.

"What is your point, Mr Hagen?" She moderated her voice so that it would show neither impatience nor hostility.

"I'm sure Lord Kennington would like to know if any of his employees, particularly those who work directly under him, had engaged in activities that might give the hotel a bad name."

"What are you suggesting?" She kept her voice light and questioning, rather than challenging.

"That you might want to arrange for my hotel bill to be cancelled."

"For what possible reason?" she said with a raised eyebrow.

"So that Lord Kennington will not hear about what you were doing last night in the gazebo."

"And what was that?" Her tone exuded innocence, although she was aware by now that he must had seen her and Richard together.

"Ms Duff, you're a very handsome woman, and I'm sure many men are attracted to you."

Elspeth said nothing.

He continued. "I'm sure hotel policy does not allow staff to fraternise, shall we say for lack of a more descriptive word, with the guests. What I saw last night leads me to believe you've violated that policy. The man with you in the gazebo obviously had your full attention on a most intimate level."

Elspeth raised her head and looked at him defiantly. She was not going to respond to his accusation, although she easily could have offered the truth and diffused the situation.

"I'll keep quiet in exchange for my hotel bill being taken care of."

"Are your suggesting that for your silence I'm to arrange for your bill to be cancelled?"

"Or paid."

"And if I don't?"

"I'm confident Lord Kennington would like to know what went on in the gazebo last night and perhaps later in your room as well. You were seen taking him there."

Elspeth drew herself up. "Mr, Hagen, I have the authority to ask any guest at the Kennington hotels to leave. Therefore I expect you will be gone tomorrow morning and that by then you will have paid your bill in full."

"Don't call my bluff, Ms Duff." He spoke in a voice that Elspeth could imagine Disney assigning to a weasel.

"I'm not calling your bluff," she said coolly. "I'll arrange with the management to see that a porter calls for your suitcases at half past eight in the morning, by which time you will have settled your bill, and I'll make sure a taxi will be waiting for you shortly afterwards. I have nothing else to say to you."

Martin Hagen seemed confused.

"You can't deny what you did."

Elspeth drew herself up. She was only an inch or two shorter than he, but she hoped her contempt would make her seem taller. "Mr Hagen, there's no need for any more conversation between us."

"My conditions are real, you know." He snarled

as he said this.

"I'm sure they are, as is my request that you leave the hotel. I think we have nothing more to discuss. Now please excuse me."

Under different circumstances this exchange with Martin Hagen might have filled Elspeth with distress, but once she left the room, she felt sullied but relieved. The better hotels in the world were meccas for those who sought to bleed the rich. To deter them was one of the many tasks Elspeth performed in the course of her normal duties. Martin Hagen presented less trouble than the worst of them, but blackmailers were never welcome in Kennington hotels and needed to be sent away as quickly as possible.

Being well after noon, Elspeth decided to have lunch with the person who had twice been cited as the object of her *affair de coeur*. She stopped by the kitchen to order a light meal to be brought to their room, and, in the process, encountered the waiter, Ken, who served at the bungalow. Elspeth asked him if any member of the party there had come to the kitchen the night before, and he replied in the negative.

She found Richard deeply absorbed in a monograph entitled 'The Correlation between Money Laundering and Illegal Immigration in Southern Europe'. He looked pleased to be interrupted. She pecked his forehead gently.

"I've ordered lunch, sandwiches, some fruit, and some lemonade, which is particularly good here. There's wine in the fridge if you would prefer it. I hope you don't mind simple fare."

Pleasure filled his face the way it often did when Elspeth entered the room. "I never have had a meal at a Kennington hotel that I would consider 'simple fare'. You always spoil me when I join you at the hotels.

"We have been the topic of much discussion this morning," she said as she sat down next to him and took his hand. "It seems we were seen last night when we went to the gazebo. I shouldn't have been so naïve as to think we were invisible."

"We are married, my dearest. I thought we no longer needed to be discreet, especially since we had stepped away from the main building of the hotel. Why the discussion?"

"Because both people who mentioned seeing us last night assumed we were not married. One practically congratulated me that at my age I could attract someone as distinguished as you; while the other tried to blackmail me." She said this dryly but the corners of her mouth twitched. "I shouldn't be amused, I suppose, but I did feel a wee bit flattered."

Richard frowned rather than laughed. "Blackmailed?"

"I admitted nothing. One shouldn't with a blackmailer, but I did have him thrown out of the hotel. Unfortunately if I am the object of one of his schemes, others probably have been too."

"Can you?'

"Can I what?"

"Tell people to leave the hotel."

"Absolutely. The little rat said he would call Lord Kennington directly and tell him what I was up to. Let him try to get through the banks of telephones protecting Eric. If he could do so, Eric would either snub him, or more likely laugh. He's already warned me that if I didn't use your name, people might talk when we stayed together. I'd hate to admit that after last night there's some validity to his argument. However, it's one he won't win."

"Elspeth, I still can't quite make out your relationship with Eric."

"He needs me, and I suppose I need him. If I dig in too deeply, Pamela usually saves me. He is insufferable at times, but he runs one of the best hotel chains in the world and does so brilliantly. Unfortunately he knows it too well."

"I think you are very fond of him."

"I am."

"Should I be jealous?"

She turned to him, kissed him and only broke away when the room service attendant knocked.

"What do you think?" she said as she rose to open the door.

Lord Kennington had perfected the art of room service in the same way he had with every other aspect of his hotels. He had instructed his interior designers to create a daily pattern for the linens, and he had commissioned Laura Ashley to design them. Today's colour was canary, and the napkins were dominantly yellow, supplemented with cream, apricot, yellow-green and a touch of pink. As always, the cutlery was real silver. The room service staff was instructed to note any missing items from the returned trolleys, and these were discretely placed on guests' bills. The sandwiches and fruit were laid on the tray with an artist's eye, complementing the texture and hues of the table linens. Elspeth marvelled that even after the trip from the kitchen the pitcher of lemonade and the accompanying glasses were still frosted. And, of course, the whole was crowned with flowers, Lord Kennington's signature, daffodils and freesias, spring flowers raised in the Kennington gardens in Morocco throughout the year.

Elspeth told the waiter that they wished to eat on the patio. The day was warm, and the louvred shutters were raised, and the palms outside had been planted to offer shade for much of the day. The waiter wheeled the trolley outside and went about arranging the table, laying the cloth and then, in memorised steps, the table settings.

Elspeth admired his handiwork and then told him that they wished to eat in private. He silently withdrew.

As they began eating, Elspeth regaled Richard with the full details of her encounters with both Lilianne Balfour and Martin Hagen. She hoped to entertain him but when she told of Martin Hagen's threat, he looked warily at her.

"He can't harm you, can he?"

"I don't see how. There's absolutely no truth to his threats, although I didn't tell him so."

"Why do you think he's here at the hotel?"

"Fishing."

"Fishing?"

"Looking for possible victims, probably so as to approach them in the future. One can only hope that he has the good sense not to cross me again." She scowled and then laughed. "Dickie, there's something I want to discuss with you that came up in my interviews this morning." She bit the side of her lip as she said it.

"But you are finding it hard to do so," he said, finishing her sentence.

"How do you know?"

He grinned. "You only bite your lip that way when you are finding something difficult to say. You have done so since you were fifteen."

"Am I that transparent? Well, nonetheless, let me plunge in."

She took in a long breath.

"Dickie, how did you feel when I turned down your proposals at Girton and in London afterwards?" These events had occurred over thirty-five years before. "I've always wanted to know because I must have caused you a great deal of pain, but I didn't love you then, and besides it wouldn't have worked out."

He looked across the table at her and set his mouth, as he did when taking care to choose his words. Elspeth was relieved that his eyes were thoughtful rather than saddened.

"I knew you would turn me down," he said," but I loved you, and I had to try. Elspeth, you're the only woman I ever truly loved. My marriage to Marjorie did work, as you know; we had many happy years together, but only as companions in a stated purpose, the success of my career. I loved her the way one loves a member of one's family, but the whole time I was married to her I loved you far differently; I loved you as a man loves a woman, even though I thought you were unattainable. I was disappointed when you turned me down, but I never gave up hope that someday I could win your heart. It took forty years."

Elspeth's averted her eyes, but she could not hide her uneasiness. "I was always aware of it, especially when you and Marjorie came to visit us in Hollywood."

"Is that why you never would allow yourself to be alone with me over the years?" he asked.

"Yes, I was a coward and afraid if no one else was present you might tell me what I already knew."

"You were right. I wanted to," he said.

"I couldn't let it happen. It wouldn't have been fair to Marjorie, and it wouldn't have been fair to me."

"Did you love Alistair?" Alistair was Elspeth's first husband, whom she had divorced eight years before.

"At first, perhaps, but not the way I love you now. He was more of an adventure, an escape, a way to put behind me the pain of Malcolm's death and the dreariness I was feeling about my life in London. He was exciting at first, and then there were the children. I always looked forward to your visits, but they confused me. I thought of you as my dearest friend, but there was always a barrier between us because of the way I knew you felt for me. I don't know if Marjorie knew, but I think she did. I had to keep a distance, Dickie, for all our sakes."

"You only thought of me as a friend? Was it ever anything more? I always wondered."

She pushed a strawberry around her plate. "I'm not really certain. It just wasn't possible. Neither one of us had the . . ." She fumbled for a word but could not find it. "It wouldn't have been right," she said finally.

"Until Malta."

"I didn't intend to fall in love with you in Malta. That just happened." She took a wedge of one of the sandwiches and bit into it fiercely.

Richard smiled at her so lovingly that she almost choked on the bit of chicken and tomato she had just swallowed. She had told him this many times, but they had never discussed the possibility that when she had fallen in love him two and a half years ago this was something that had incubated for a long time and was not a *coup de foudre*. She felt unsettled admitting this. She looked up again at her husband; he had not lowered his eyes nor had the love gone from them.

The conversation had taken an unwanted turn. To cover her conflicted inner thoughts, she said, "I wanted to talk about a conversation I had this morning. I promised confidentiality, and so I must be circumspect, but what does it feel like to love someone when you know you have no chance?"

Richard's smile changed to a grin. "I always thought I had a chance with you if I waited long enough."

She growled at him. "Dickie, you're shameless. No, tell me how it feels."

"One is filled with unhappiness but also hope, that is if you really love the person. The hope can't be easily extinguished; the love doesn't ever go away if that's what it truly is."

The rest of the lunch passed pleasantly, but Elspeth rose from the table with more things to ponder

than the love affair between Harald Wade and and
Princess Christiana.

12

After lunch Elspeth settled in to write up her notes from her morning conversations with the members of the royal party and write an e-mail to the Kennington Organisation's central booking office to advise them of her action towards Martin Hagen. Richard went back to his monograph, and the two of them worked comfortably across the sitting room from each other, glancing up occasionally and exchanging looks of pleasure. The call came from Greta von Fricken just as Elspeth had finished her report to London.

"The princess wants to see you and has asked that you two meet on the beach and not here in the bungalow. Can you be there in half an hour?"

"Have her meet me at the gazebo." The gazebo, Elspeth thought, was assuming massive proportions in her assignment, but it was convenient. The princess could not possibly know the complications that had arisen from Elspeth and Richard's tryst there the night before.

As she rose to prepare for her meeting at the beach, Richard returned to his monograph again after giving her a brief kiss on her hand as she passed him. She was not sure how the problem of money laundering and illegal immigration could be more fascinating than she was, but she acknowledged that he had come to Bermuda on the pretence of finding a quiet place to generate a report for his committee at the European Commission in Brussels. She went to the bedroom to wash her face and to restore her makeup after a certain amount of damage had been done to it both by her interactions with her husband and the consumption of lunch. She found her sun hat and left Richard to his paper.

She found the princess waiting for her. As on the previous day she was wearing a large hat and dark glasses, although behind them Elspeth could detect lines of tension in her face. The princess could not have been older than fifty, but her mouth was pulled down and her shoulders sagged in the way of the elderly. The gazebo caught the cooling wind off the ocean and provided shade, but Elspeth was well aware that it offered little privacy. Therefore she suggested that they walk along the beach.

"Ms Duff," the princess said, "you must know that you have been the topic of discussion among us all at the bungalow. Everyone who has talked with you has been impressed both by your professionalism and your promise of confidentiality."

Elspeth demurred. "Princess, that's why I am here. I'm glad that I've succeeded."

The princess stopped abruptly. She put down her head and began drawing circles with her toe in the wet sand at the shore's edge. She seemed to be considering whether to speak or not.

"Is there something I can help you with?" Elspeth asked after watching the pattern grow.

"I've debated a long time whether to approach you or not. It's a matter quite apart from the reason we're all here, a personal matter. I need some advice, and I don't know of anyone else to ask."

"I'll try to do what I can."

The princess continued her sand drawing. Elspeth could feel her ambivalence, and therefore stood silent and let the princess find her own words.

"I'm being blackmailed," she said almost so softly that Elspeth could not hear her voice above the sound of the waves hitting the beach and the wind in the palms. Elspeth jerked her head up. Of course! Martin Hagen was here on more than a fishing expedition, she thought. Corralling Elspeth had only been a minor diversion from his real pursuit.

"Have you ever been blackmailed?" the princess asked.

Elspeth drew in her breath. "Yes, once, but the blackmailer had no idea that what he was trying to threaten me with was totally untrue."

"I see. The problem, Ms Duff, is that the blackmailer does have information that's not only true but also that I need to keep hidden. He approached me in my own country, again in London and has now followed me to Bermuda."

"Is he Martin Hagen?"

"I don't know his name, but he is staying here at the hotel."

"Only until tomorrow morning."

"How do you know?"

"I personally told him to leave. I have that authority. No, I'm not clairvoyant. He tried to blackmail another person in the hotel, and I learned about it. The Kennington hotels from time to time have to deal sharply with people like him."

At Elspeth's words, the princess seemed to let down her guard.

"Then I might be able to relax, at least until he finds me somewhere else."

"Would you be willing to tell me why he is blackmailing you?"

The princess began her toe art once again. "I did something to cover for a crime my daughter committed. In the moment I thought nothing of it. I love Christiana, and I felt what she had done was foolish, but not criminal."

"Which was?"

"Christiana took a piece of crown jewellery from the safe

in my room in our London home without asking me. She sold it to a jeweller on Bond Street. The blackmailer now has it in his possession."

13

As Elspeth stepped into the dimmed light of the hotel lobby, she expected it to be deserted, as lobbies so frequently are in the early afternoon. She took off her hat and rubbed her eyes, waiting for them to adjust to the interior light. Across the room she could see the receptionist working on her computer, and one of the concierges standing idly at his desk reading a tour brochure. Everything seemed normal for a Kennington hotel at this time of day. The carpets were free of any dirt or litter and no dust appeared anywhere, as the cleaning staff was in constant but unseen attendance. Because no one seemed to be looking, she straightened her back to relieve the tension she was feeling and rolled her head about her shoulders. Therefore she was surprised when a voice spoke her name.

Ms Duff," the rich male voice said. She looked around and saw Francis Tilden, who had just entered the lobby himself. "Perhaps you can help me since you seem to know everything that goes on at this hotel. I thought I saw an old friend of mine by the name of Richard Munro in the garden earlier. We served together in Africa. I haven't seen him in years, but he's hard to mistake. Do you know if he's staying here?"

Elspeth's inclination was to smile, but instead she said simply, "You must know I'm not allowed to reveal the names of hotel guests to other guests. But if I were you, I would leave a note at the reception desk and, if he is here and wants to see you, they will see he gets the note. Using this system, we are sure our guests are not disturbed if they choose not to be. Surely you can understand."

Francis Tilden nodded. "I see. Is there somewhere around here where I can get some paper?"

"The Kennington hotels always have a writing room, a hangover from the days when people actually did write letters." Elspeth motioned to the concierge and related Francis's request.

The awkwardness that Elspeth experienced every time she met someone from Richard's diplomatic past swept over her once again. One of the terms of her marriage with Richard had been that she would not assume the role of his first wife, Lady Marjorie, because she knew she could not do it justice. Besides she preferred not to try. Her own need for independence, which had become so important to her after she had left her first marriage, could not be quashed no matter how much she loved Richard. She had somewhat untruthfully claimed that she did not know the proper way to behave in diplomatic circles, but her grandmother, the seventh Countess of Tay, had schooled her unruly granddaughter in the correct ways to behave 'as a member of the Scottish gentry', as she put it. Every day Elspeth dealt with the international public using skills that would have just as well served at the British High Commission in Malta, where Richard was currently posted, or at any other diplomatic post for that matter, but she could not, in good conscience, pretend to be what she was not. She knew that any attempt on her part to assume the role that Marjorie Munro had held for thirty years would only end in disaster. She loved Richard more for having accepted this, although he seemed less pleased when she had asked also she keep her own name after their marriage rather than assuming the title she had gained upon marrying Richard. On occasion she felt he still paused before introducing her.

No sooner had she dispatched the Canadian diplomat to the writing room than another voice called her name and made her turn from her intent to return to her room. This time it was Dorothy Ayers, parcels in tow.

"Elspeth, I'm so glad to have caught you. Look at all the money I've spent. Ah well, that's one of the advantages of being a rich widow I suppose," she said dropping her parcels on one of the sofas. She surveyed Elspeth, who felt ruffled by the wind off the beach, but Dorothy's expression registered approval, not criticism.

"I'm sure Elizabeth will be delighted to know I met you. I'll convey what a charming mother she has, but I suspect she already knows that. I hope we'll meet again the next time you are in East Sussex. Now do tell me, where did you get your hat? I could do with one in the garden at home."

Feeling embarrassed by Dorothy's compliment, Elspeth looked down at her floppy hat. "Actually I forgot to pack one but discovered that the hotel gift shop has a number of them in a variety of colours. You could stop by the shop if you want to buy one."

"I do indeed. I also wanted to tell you how much I enjoyed our dinner yesterday evening. I'm leaving in the morning and may not see you again. Do you have any messages for Elizabeth?"

"No. We e-mail frequently. Just tell her you met me."

The wealthy widow moved on, and Elspeth held her breath, hoping she could make it back to her rooms without being confronted by another guest. Fortunately, no one else was about.

When Elspeth let herself into her suite, Richard was not in evidence. He must have slipped out earlier, and Francis Tilden had seen him then. Yet Elspeth suspected he had not been out for long, perhaps just to stretch his legs before taking up another dry document. Listening carefully, she heard breathing in the bedroom, so she went and quietly closed the door so that Richard could finish his nap in peace. Moments later Francis

Tilden's message, encased in a Kennington hotel envelope, arrived with an unobtrusive knock at the door. The sound was enough to rouse Richard, who emerged from the bedroom in his dressing gown, wiping sleep from his eyes. Elspeth handed him the note without explanation.

Looking perplexed, Richard tore the envelope open and read its contents.

"Francis Tilden," he said, "A person from the past who is staying here and asks if we could get together for drinks and possibly dinner. He wants to know if my wife is here with me. Elspeth, you told me Francis's connection to the royal party, but obviously you haven't told them your relationship to me."

"Dickie, I'm here on business. I try not to share my personal life with the guests." This was a half-truth, considering her recent revelations about her children to almost all the guests in the bungalow.

"Shall I ring him and set up something?" Richard asked.

"It might be wise to suggest we meet away from the hotel. You must also know Hope Tilden. Unfortunately she looks like her sister despite the differences in their haircuts and wardrobe. I think it best that the Tildens, or at least Hope, not be seen in the main part of the hotel."

Richard came around to her and gently took her by the shoulders. "You are worried, aren't you?"

"Perhaps more than I should be, but this assignment has taken on aspects that I hadn't anticipated."

"Have you contacted Eric or Pamela?"

"I'm debating whether I should or not. I don't know if I want Eric to know what I learned this afternoon from the princess because I'm not sure I can re-word the information into a form he would understand. He hates speculation, but that's what I'm doing at the moment, trying to make sense of what the princess told me on the beach this afternoon. Why don't you call Francis and arrange for us to meet him tonight for drinks and dinner somewhere other than here? I could do with a break from the hotel and have a new dress to wear which you haven't seen yet."

Richard picked up the phone and dialled the extension Francis had given him. Elspeth could only hear Richard's side of the conversation.

"Francis, it's wonderful to hear from you."

"We'd love to."

"Yes, but I'm more here with her than she is here with me, but I will explain later. Do you have a suggestion of where we might meet?"

"I haven't heard of it but I'll take your suggestion. Shall we say seven o'clock. Give me the address. We'll see you there."

"Splendid." Then Richard smiled. "And don't seem surprised when you meet my new wife." He chuckled and rang off.

"Are you teasing him, Dickie?"

"No, preparing him for the reaction I get from all my colleagues when I introduce you. I love watching their faces that open up in total admiration of me, seeing that I could have married such a splendid woman. The only difference here is that he has already met my wife, but he just doesn't know it." Then he frowned. "Elspeth, most of my life I've resisted adopting your penchant for tomfoolery and deception, but somehow marriage to you has made me enjoy it more."

She grinned. "I always knew that underneath the pompous façade you were human."

He looked at her, picked up a pillow lying on the sofa and with the art of a skilful cricketer threw it at her. She caught it and burst into laughter. For the first time since rising that morning she let down her guard.

They took a taxi to what was described as one of the finest restaurants in Bermuda as noted in the Kennington hotel's local guide to fine dining. The building was situated near the ocean and was surrounded by palm trees, hibiscus bushes and a grassy park. Painted a dark pink, the restaurant's exterior set off its lush surroundings.

Francis and Hope Tilden were chatting pleasantly at their table when Richard and Elspeth approached them. They turned, and on seeing Elspeth, looked puzzled.

"Ms Duff, how nice of you to show Richard the way. Richard, wasn't your wife able to join us?"

Richard grinned broadly. "But she has. May I introduce her? Although I believe you have met before. Didn't I say that I was here with my wife and not the other way around?"

Elspeth lowered her eyes but could not hide her grin. "I've sorely deceived you, I'm afraid. Please don't tell the others. I'm on business here, as you know, and would like to stay on that footing until the problem at the hotel has been resolved, but for tonight, I'm Richard's wife, at least until we get back to the hotel."

"How totally delightful, Richard. You are a lucky man indeed," Francis said.

They ordered and settled back, enjoying their drinks. Francis, Hope and Richard related a series of amusing stories about their time serving together in Africa to the laughter of all. Elspeth had not heard most of these tales before, but all three of her dinner companions were able raconteurs and were gracious in including her in their happy memories. Still, her mind could not help thinking about Richard's past. He had not shared much of his life, despite her friendship with him and her acquaintance with Lady Marjorie over the years. What had their life been like? She was getting a glimpse of the lighter side of it, but Richard had not risen so quickly through the diplomatic ranks on Marjorie's influence alone. Even now Francis Tilden's respect for Richard could not be disguised.

Elspeth watched Hope Tilden, who, outside the bungalow, became a polished diplomatic wife both in dress and manner, rather than the sister of a princess who had for many years denied her existence. By her own account, Hope had sat on the verandas of Africa and socialised with Marjorie, but, unlike Marjorie, Hope had a North American freshness and openness that must have been in stark contrast to Marjorie's primness and propriety. How had Richard felt through all the time he was married to Marjorie? Elspeth watched him in a way she never had the chance to do so before. Part of her heart wanted to know when he had thought of her, the way he had confessed he had even when married to Marjorie.

Did the dark, velvety nights of sub-Saharan Africa bring Elspeth to mind or was he so absorbed in his friends and his wife that he only remembered Elspeth when he was close to sleep after Marjorie had retired to her own room? Elspeth knew she could not ask him, but the revelations of the evening, for all its humorous reminiscences, weighed on Elspeth's mind. By temperament she could not have led the life Richard and Marjorie had, with the slowness of the pace or the correctness of the life style. Particularly when she was younger, she felt she would have made multiple gaffes or made fun when seriousness was called for. She could almost hear Richard's censure. She watched Hope Tilden, a person so different in her outward aspect from Marjorie, but Elspeth knew instinctively that Hope was of the same cut as Marjorie—always appropriate.

After the main course, when Hope and Francis excused themselves briefly, Richard spoke quietly to Elspeth. "Have we bored you, my dearest? You seemed somewhere else just now."

She bit her lower lip and hoped she looked quizzical. "I was trying to imagine what it was like out there for you all."

He leaned down and whispered, "I was desperately lonely all the time without you, Elspeth." Suddenly her world turned right side up. Her face must have told him so, because he took her hand and brushed it with his lips in a gesture more filled with meaning than many of their more intimate exchanges in the past.

When dining out, Elspeth could not help but compare the service and quality of food with that of the Kennington hotels. Tonight she was pleasantly surprised. The fish she had ordered had probably been caught that morning, and the sauce that covered it was subtle but savoury. She should tell Lord Kennington to send out his spies for the recipe. The others said their choices were equally delicious, and Richard complimented Francis on his choice of restaurant. The conversation had shifted from memories to more general topics, and Elspeth joined in with relief. None of them could have contemplated the impending interruption.

"Why, I knew it was true!"

Elspeth was startled at the intrusion of a voice from the hotel, the dulcet and annoying tones of Mrs Lilianne Balfour.

"You are Princess Honorée! I know it. I saw you in the hotel."

Hope Tilden raised her head and smiled. "You are about the thousandth person who has told me so," she said in a broader Canadian accent than her customarily soft one. "But, sadly, no. I am Hope Tilden. Your mistake is a common one."

Elspeth admired Hope's warm composure. Hope was indeed a consummate diplomat's wife.

Lilianne looked deflated. Then she looked around the table. "Why, Ms Duff, are you here too?" The answer was obvious.

Hope stepped in. "Forgive me. You seem to know Elspeth but have you met her husband, Sir Richard Munro?" Elspeth noted that Hope had used Richard's title.

Lilianne flushed. "Husband? Sir?"

Elspeth smiled. Richard rose and extended his hand.

Lilianne blushed. "Are you really a lord?" she said.

Richard looked kindly at Lilianne. "No, I am a mere knight, recognised by the Queen for the most mundane of services."

Lilianne eyed him and said, "Are you joking with me?"

"No, fair lady. We British hold on to our old ways, but I can assure you I do not wear armour, do not have a lance, and have only once or twice rescued a lady in distress. My wife will attest to that, since she is the lady in question."

Elspeth gulped, unsure of how Mrs General William 'Bill' Balfour would react. What Richard said was indeed true, especially the part about having rescued her on several occasions, but the way he said it made the whole thing sound fanciful. Elspeth tried to hide her amusement, which would have been inappropriate towards a Kennington hotel guest. Richard was truly beginning to buy into the world of the absurd that often entered her mind, but she couldn't outwardly show how tickled she was by the way he was verbally playing with Lilianne Balfour.

Lilianne seemed disconcerted. "Why, I'm sure sorry that the general could not be here to meet you. He no sooner got here than he came down with one of those terrible diseases that the members of the army get when they're out in Iraq. He's resting, but I could not just sit in our hotel room and let an evening pass in Bermuda without enjoying it." Her plea sounded as if she wanted to join them for dinner. Elspeth exchanged glances with Hope.

"I think you will find the dinners here quite delectable," Hope said. "I recommend the seafood medley. Do order it if you like crayfish." Hope's tone was kind but clearly dismissive. "It has been a pleasure to meet you."

The two men rose as if orchestrated and shook hands with Lilianne. "A pleasure," they both said almost in unison.

After Lilianne left, Elspeth put her hand over her face to cover her amusement.

"Who was that?" Francis asked.

"A very common type of guest at the hotels, someone with too much money and too little. . ." Elspeth sought a kind word ". . . discretion," she concluded. Everyone at the table laughed.

"Elspeth," Hope said, "how do you tolerate it?"

"Tolerate what? In the hotel business, the guests are always right, whether they are or not. Can there be much difference in your world?"

"I suppose not. Richard, you have a true treasure of a wife. Thank you for 'introducing' her to us this evening."

Elspeth wondered if this was said as a compliment or as a comparison to Lady Marjorie, and then chastised herself for continuing to think that way. Richard smiled at Hope's words. "For all the years I have known Elspeth, which now exceed four decades, she has always been a breath of fresh air." He did not elaborate.

Part 2

The Murders

14

The bittersweet acridity of fire is unmistakable. It can either evoke childhood memories of comfort by an open hearth, or it can convey horror to anyone who has experienced its uncontrolled destruction. The incessant noise of the fire alarms woke Elspeth, but she must have smelled the smoke before the blaring of the bells penetrated the door of her rooms because she was dreaming peacefully of the drawing room of her childhood home in Perthshire, where a fire was kept almost continuously lit in the fireplace. The blaring sirens destroyed any illusions of home.

Elspeth had learned from an Interpol agent with whom she had worked in the past always to have clothing ready for night-time emergencies, and tonight was no exception. As she had shed her new dress and prepared for bed, she automatically checked to see that her emergency clothing was in place. Once in a moment of boredom one evening during a tedious assignment in Gibraltar, she had practiced changing into it, and with practice she had made it from her customary silk pyjamas into outside clothing within eighteen seconds. Tonight she beat that record.

Leaving Richard as he was emerging from sleep, she ran to the lobby and saw that the cacophony was causing pandemonium among the guests. The hour was well past midnight, and many bewildered residents of the hotel had poured out of their rooms in various states of dress or lack thereof. The men tended towards bare chests and pyjama bottoms; the women short or diaphanous nightgowns. All those in night dress looked sleepy and confused, and few seemed to notice their scant covering, but some of the older women seemed concerned that they were in a state of *deshabille* and had pulled on dressing gowns. Men with heavier beards looked unshaven, and more than one of the women's faces was covered with night cream. Several guests were still fully dressed.

No source of the fire was apparent other than the smell and the pounding alarms, which made the guests seemed confused as to where to go. Elspeth spotted the night manager trying to herd people down to the beach, but he was only marginally successful. Many of the younger guests, particularly the men, gravitated towards both the smell and the few ephemeral wisps of smoke that came from beyond the kitchens.

Elspeth's mind went spinning back to the training she had just received in London. "Possessions can be replaced; lives cannot." But here were guests who were more interested in the origin of the fire than their own safety or that of their possessions. Hoping to find Kit Lord or any other member of the security staff, Elspeth pushed through the crowd, but she found no one she recognised.

The fire engines arrived quickly, their loud sirens cutting through the night as they arrived at the hotel. Finally Elspeth saw Kit, urging people back as the firemen funnelled through the lobby and out into the garden. The guests parted like the Red Sea at the sight of the fully kitted-out men wearing helmets and masks. She saw Kit, who looked up at her for a fleeting moment and went back to his task of getting the guests out of the way of the emergency crew.

"Where is the fire?" she mouthed. "In the kitchen?"

He came within hearing range and shouted unnaturally loudly. "In the smokers' wing. Get over there if you can, and find out which room the fire is in. I need to stay here with the guests."

She nodded and let him go. She sprinted across the garden, following the firemen closely and, as she ran, she yelled to the guests there, "Stay back! Stay back! Let them through!" The urgency in her voice seemed to have some effect, and only a few of the younger men refused to obey.

Several confused seconds passed before she could find someone in charge. The fire brigade had stopped outside one of the rooms in the smokers' wing. Flames were clearly visible through the curtains in the window. Elspeth identified herself and asked why the firemen had not broken through the window or door.

"It's too dangerous. The fire is well advanced, and if we allow any air into the space, the fire will spread. If we contain the space, eventually the oxygen inside will be used up and the fire will go out."

"Can you tell if there are any people in the room?"

"If there are, there's little chance of saving them. The fire's too hot and the smoke too dense. No one could have survived it. We'll have to let it burn out before we go in."

"What happened to the fire sprinklers? We have them in all the rooms."

"They don't seem to have functioned. If they had, we wouldn't be seeing this degree of burn."

Taking note of the room number, Elspeth hastily rummaged in her pocket for her mobile and dialled the number for the reception desk. A harried voice answered. Elspeth could hear the continuing chaos in the background.

Giving her name, she asked, "Who is staying in Room 17?"

"Hold on, Ms Duff. It's rather mad here," the receptionist said. There was a pause. "Martin Hagen."

"Has anyone seen him this evening?"

"I don't know. I must go. So many people are calling in." Elspeth could hear desperation in his voice.

Martin Hagen! Damn! Still even someone as poisonous as he was should not have had to suffer the effects of the fire. Was he in the room when the fire started and was he still there? More worrying was that the sprinklers had not worked. She would not know why until the fire had been contained and had no idea of how long that would take.

It seemed like hours later when the firemen finished their work. Elspeth stayed with them and watched their attempts to douse the walls and roof of the burning room and then to soak down the interior. Once they were able to enter the room, she peered around them but could see that nothing in the room except the mattress with a burnt form on it and an easy chair, which was still smouldering. The fireman in charge would not let her into the room even after the flames had been contained.

"Excuse me, Miss, there's a body in there, and it's not a sight for a woman."

Elspeth did not know what to call him so she chose a rank that would flatter him. "Captain, unfortunately in my work I've seen several dead bodies. I never like the sight, but because of my position at the Kennington Organisation, I'll need to see the body and identify it if possible."

"Ma'am, no one will be able to identify the body by looking at it. I've called the police and asked for their pathologist to come and examine the body or what's left of it. For your own sake, let the professionals do their work. Only those accustomed to the extreme desecration of a human body would not be sickened by seeing the body in there."

Elspeth did not force her point. The fireman's description was enough to turn her away, but she lingered until the pathologist arrived and the body, in a trussed bag, was taken out through the hotel's delivery area to the police ambulance. Looking at her watch, she realised that it was past four o'clock in the morning. The firemen had sealed off the area of the fire and allowed no one, including Elspeth, even with all her credentials, to cross under the yellow and black warning tape and enter the burnt-out husk of the room. She saw Kit Lord in the distance and made her way toward him. He looked as exhausted as she felt. His white shirt was covered with black streaks and his face was drawn thin.

He spoke quickly. "I think the guests are satisfied that there will be no more danger. All but a few have returned to their rooms. I've relocated the guests who were near Room 17 to the other end of the smokers' wing. Luckily we had a few vacant rooms further along."

"Kit, let's talk later this morning. We'll need to report fully to London as soon as possible, but it's still early there and a few hours' sleep wouldn't harm either of us. Shall we meet in your offices at eight?" Having obtained his agreement, she let him go.

The lights in her suite were on when she let herself in, and Richard had propped himself up on the sofa where she found him asleep. She touched his arm.

He opened one eye and asked, "Crisis over? It was terribly lonely out on the beach without you." Then he stood and came to her. "My dearest, you do look a fright. Have you been near the fire?"

Elspeth turned to the mirror by the door and saw that her face was covered with black smudges and her hair was tousled and sooty. "It was quite awful," she said setting her jaw and swallowed hard. "Someone was in the room. They wouldn't let me see the body, but they said it was horribly unrecognisable. I think it must have been Martin Hagen."

"Martin Hagen?"

131

Elspeth realised she had not given a name to the blackmailer who had approached her the morning before, as by its insignificance it had seemed not worth mentioning. As much as she trusted her husband's discretion, she needed to keep the princess's confidences about Martin Hagen's trying to extract money from her.

"Martin Hagen was the guest in Room 17. I think it was he who died in the fire."

"Elspeth, you're not telling me everything."

"I can't. You can appreciate that."

He nodded. "Are you in danger?"

"Personally I think not, but I'm worried about our guests in the bungalow."

"What possible connection . . ."

"There could be one." Elspeth had thought this throughout the fire and its aftermath. "I can't discount the possibility."

"Surely the fire was caused by an electrical short, or perhaps a dropped cigarette. It was in the smokers' wing, wasn't it?"

"It was, but I'm concerned that the fire suppression system didn't kick in."

"What are you implying?"

"That someone disabled the sprinklers in Room 17, and then set the fire. The Kennington Organisation is obsessive about preventing fires. An entire section of Eric's design staff deals with fire prevention. Every room has fire sprinklers that are designed well beyond the normal standard to ensure fires will not spread, particularly in the smokers' wings. Eric hates smokers because of the smell they leave behind and the danger they pose if they fall asleep with a cigarette in their hand. He doesn't mince words about this problem, but he also knows he must cater to guests who come from countries where smoking is widespread. I suppose this could be considered some sort of discrimination, but in this instance I agree with Eric."

Richard frowned. "And you are suggesting that the fire could have been used as a means to murder this Martin Hagen?"

"There can't be any other explanation."

"Which complicates your assignment here."

"Yes." She bit her lower lip. "I suppose I'm struggling with our new relationship, Dickie. As my husband, you should be privy to everything I do, but so much of my job involves the secrets of others. I don't want to cut you out, but you do understand, don't you?" Her eyes beseeched his.

"My very dearest one, I deal in the world of confidentiality as well; it's one of the many parts of my job. Besides, I trust your judgement above all things. 'Our new relationship', as you call it, is not predicated on sharing the details of our jobs. Now let me help you get clean and then take you to bed, where for a few hours I can hold you in protective safety." The sentiment even from a knight was archaic, but Elspeth gave in without protest.

Elspeth left the room in advance of her meeting with Kit Lord and walked towards the smokers' wing. She was glad Eric Kennington was not there to see the uprooting of his garden caused by the actions of the fire brigade the night before. She gently touched the shoulder of the fireman who had been posted outside the room and who had fallen asleep on one of the garden benches. He jumped to attention.

Identifying herself, Elspeth requested that she be allowed access to the room.

"It's against orders, ma'am."

"I'm here as a member of the Kennington Organisation security staff, and therefore my concern goes well beyond curiosity. I need to have some idea how much damage was done to the room last night and need to advise our headquarters in London."

"But, ma'am, . . . "

Elspeth used her age and position shamelessly. "I, of course, have an access key card and will leave you to guard the room from others." Without waiting for another protest from the young man, she went to Room 17's door and found that it could no longer accept her card. She shoved open what remained of the door and involuntarily drew in her breath both at the sight and the smell of the room. The destruction was total. The skeletons of the few pieces of furniture than had escaped complete annihilation stabbed at the air in thin, useless spikes. The mattress was heavily burnt and had become a sodden mass of charred stuffing; the coverings had mostly been consumed by the fire and had disintegrated into ash among the charred bedsprings. The central portion of the mattress had been damaged less thoroughly because that was where the body had lain. She coughed from the sharp fumes that hovered somewhere between taste and smell. The window on the far side of the room had been shattered, and glass lay strewn under the warped window frame. The remnants of the curtain rods hung askew across the window opening, the curtains having been one of the first victims of the flames. Elspeth looked up towards what remained of the ceiling. The plaster was cracked and a piece of it had fallen to the floor. The fire sprinkler pipes had been exposed and hung securely by wires from the singed roof trusses above. Fortunately, the structure of the building had held, and the fire had not spread to the adjacent rooms.

Little was left of Martin Hagen's possessions. Elspeth kicked at what looked like the remains of a suitcase, and it disintegrated under her foot. She looked around the room for anything that had survived intact but saw nothing retrievable.

She went into the bathroom. The room was less damaged, although anything flammable had been destroyed by the flames from the adjoining room.

Nothing remained of the towels that had hung on the now-twisted towel bars. The glass door to the shower hung at an odd angle from its hinges. The silver backing on the mirrors that lined the walls was discoloured in paisley-like black patterns. The marble sink top was intact, but the glass bowl that once was the sink had cracked from the heat and the gold taps were warped beyond use. On the counter top were the remains of the metal frame of Martin Hagen's shaving kit, its leather sides crumbled to nothing and its contents melted together in blobs of malformed plastic. His electric razor and toothbrush were little more than husks.

Then Elspeth saw a key, partially hidden under the wreckage of a razor. She knew it was no ordinary key. Rummaging in her pocket, she drew out a tissue she had used to apply the last touches of her makeup that morning, and carefully drew the key from the residue of Martin Hagen's shaving kit. The small key, stamped 'KB' for the Kennington Bermuda, was one given to guests when they put their valuables in one of the hotel's safety deposit boxes. Elspeth looked at the number engraved on the key and made a mental note of it. Her training earlier in her life at Scotland Yard told her to replace the key where she had found it for the crime scene investigators, but this led her to a moral dilemma. She suspected that the contents of the safety deposit box held items that Martin Hagen was using to demand money from his victims, and she wanted to know what it contained. Undoubtedly a search would be made at the scene of the fire, and Martin Hagen's remaining possessions would be gathered together and sent to the police, and, after examination, on to his next of kin. What sort of next of kin would a person like Martin Hagen have? A wife, children, ageing parents? One's mind boggled at his being related to people who shared his life and loved him. Perhaps they did not know his true calling. Elspeth made a quick decision, one she knew she might later regret. She wrapped the key in her tissue and put it in her pocket.

She was several moments late for her meeting with Kit Lord, but he did not know her well enough to know if this was uncharacteristic. He looked up as she entered his office and looked worried. "You have been to the room, I see," he said.

Realising that she must have brushed against some of the items she had examined in Room 17, she nodded.

"Kit, the destruction is quite thorough, but, fortunately, it was restricted to the bedroom and bathroom and didn't spread beyond there. We must, I think, give credit to the Kennington Organisation for being so careful with its fire prevention methods."

Kit was not put off. "The fire sprinklers didn't go off."

Elspeth shook her head. "No, they didn't."

"They should have."

"I know."

"What are we to tell London about that?"

Elspeth considered this carefully. "I know the fire department will have the same question. Do you know the fire chief?"

"We've met. He sometimes comes here with his team for his regular inspections. They're supposed to be monthly, although sometimes the schedule slips."

"How long has it been since the last time?"

Kit went to his file cabinet, opened one of the drawers and drew out a notebook. "Six weeks," he admitted.

"What do they do to test the fire sprinkler system?"

"Mainly they check the connection between the water supply and the hook up to the sprinklers."

"Has the connection ever been faulty?'

"Not to my knowledge."

"But could it have been last night?"

"I suppose so, but the whole system is new. It was installed when Lord Kennington renovated the buildings two years ago. One would hardly expect it to fail."

"Quite," Elspeth said, hoping her voice implied no criticism on the hotel's part, but she wished the inspection had been made on schedule. "Kit, we must report the details to London immediately. They will want to send someone out to assess the destruction caused by the fire. In the meanwhile, I think it will be our job to do damage control with the guests and speak directly to the fire department."

They talked further about their approach to London and finally agreed that the manager of the hotel should call the regional office overseeing Bermuda, Kit should call the central security office, and Elspeth should call Lord Kennington, a task she did not relish. She decided to make the call from her room. Leaving Kit's office, she put her hand in her pocket and touched the offending key. Why did its presence bode so ill?

15

When Elspeth returned to her room, Richard was busily at work on his laptop, muttering to himself. He was robed in a light cotton dressing gown, which she had bought for him when she was passing through Japan. He had not shaved, which was so rare that Elspeth went to him, kissed him on the forehead and asked if he was adopting the current hirsute fashion of Hollywood stars.

"I can't make the data come together," he said more to the air than to Elspeth. "Sorry, my dearest, but they want something conclusive in my report, and all I can find is conflicting information. I don't know which evidence is true and which is not, or if there lies some irreconcilable paradox in the task I've been given."

"Dickie, be a love. I need to call Eric about last night, and the phone call won't be an easy one. Can you spend the next fifteen minutes showering while I ring him? Then I promise I'll be more attentive, although I can't offer an answer to your problem." Nor can I for mine, she thought, fingering the key in her pocket.

He grinned at her. "Now you know what depths I sink into when you're not about. I need your good influence to change my bad habits. When left alone, I tend to be a bit lazy."

She laughed and gently shoved him from the sitting room.

The call to London was less awkward than Elspeth had imagined. Earlier she had purposely not told Lord Kennington about the princess being blackmailed, and she wavered as to whether to do so now or not. In the end she decided to protect the princess, at least for the moment. Eric would be more concerned with the fire than the stolen brooch. Therefore, Elspeth related in great detail the efforts of the fire department in controlling the blaze, the ability of the design of the building to withstand spread of the flames beyond the bedroom and bathroom, and the efficiency of the staff in assuring the guests that there would be no further danger. He grumbled, as she knew he would, but then conceded that Elspeth and the hotel staff had handled the emergency exactly as they had been instructed to do. He said he would send a team out from London to handle the damage, thus allowing Elspeth to get back to her main task. Elspeth mentioned nothing about the key.

She had not been in contact with the people in the bungalow since the fire. She had vague recollections of seeing Francis Tilden among the onlookers the night before, and she hoped he had reported the localised nature of the blaze to the members of the royal party. She heard Richard's movements in the bathroom and assumed that at any moment he would emerge dressed and clean-shaven. She quickly dialled Greta von Fricken's number and asked if she could come across the garden to tell them more fully about what had happened the night before. Greta said she would ring back shortly but also said that the activity in the hotel the previous evening had disrupted all their sleep. Elspeth was making conciliatory noises when Richard came back into the sitting room. He brushed his silky cheek to hers invitingly. She obliged him but only briefly because her call with Greta delayed any further tenderness. He looked disappointed.

"Dickie, I must go over to the bungalow. I'll need to leave you to your conundrum and can't promise I'll be back for lunch.

She went into the bathroom and drew out her makeup kit. She dropped the safety deposit box key from her handkerchief into the plastic bag where she kept her cotton buds and then breathed a sigh which was somewhere between guilt and relief. She would decide what to do with the key once she could talk to the princess alone.

The smell of the fire still clung to the air as she crossed the garden, although none of the exterior hotel structure beyond Room 17 had been marred by the flames. Elspeth noticed that several of the younger male guests stood by the tape barrier put up by the firefighters and were talking among themselves. She could not see the fire officer who had barred her way earlier and hoped he had retired to the fire station without mentioning her entry into the burnt-out room. She let herself through the bungalow gate and looked to see if anyone was about. Mary Tilden appeared round one of the corners of the building and greeted Elspeth with a broad grin.

"They're all waiting for you inside. I was told to come out and find you."

"To scold me about my absence from the hotel last night?" Elspeth asked.

"No, for once I think they're all glad you're here and hope you can explain what happened."

The entire royal party was gathered in the large sitting room. Klaus von Fricken was supervising the coffee, and Greta was carrying a silver tray of croissants, brioche, and sweet rolls around to those present. The social hierarchy of the group was apparent. The prince was served first and declined Greta's offerings, and the princess took a sweet roll with the tongs offered, placing it on a small plate. Both Hope Tilden and her husband took a croissant. Harald Wade sat quietly to one side and declined both coffee and confection. Mary made her way to the coffee bar and poured herself a large mug, adding cream, and shook her head at Greta.

"Ms Duff," the prince said. "Perhaps you can

tell us what occurred last night. Francis assures us that we have no cause for worry. I understand you were on duty all night."

"Most of it, but Francis is correct. I did stay until we knew the fire was completely out, and the danger of it spreading was past. As of early this morning everything has been contained, and we are now trying to establish the possibility that the fire was the result of a guest falling asleep with a cigarette. That's one of the most common causes of hotel fires. Lord Kennington takes special care to make sure the smokers' wing is designed to prevent any great damage from such occurrences."

She did not mention the malfunction of fire sprinklers or the fact someone had died in the fire. The prince seemed satisfied, but Elspeth caught Francis Tilden's eyes on her. He cocked one eyebrow on his handsome face as if to say 'we'll talk later'. Francis was no fool. Elspeth glanced over to the princess, who averted her eyes. Elspeth urgently wanted to speak to her alone, to tell her about the key, and to ask her if she had crossed the garden to see Martin Hagen the night before, but she knew she would have to wait for an opportune moment to take the princess aside for a private tête-à-tête.

Having answered several more questions about the fire, Elspeth cleared her throat. "Now that you are all here together," she said, "may I ask what seems to be a more pressing question? What of Princess Christiana?"

Silence descended upon the room. Harald Wade shifted in his chair. Hope Tilden rolled her eyes towards Prince Michael and then back at her husband. Mary Tilden coughed over her coffee, and Greta and Klaus von Fricken busied themselves with tidying up. Elspeth, however, watched the one person whom she cared about most, Princess Honorée. The princess folded her hands in her lap and looked down at the Persian rug on the tiled floor.

"Your Highness," Elspeth said to the prince, "I consulted a map yesterday and if your yacht makes good time, it should be arriving tomorrow. The weather at the moment seems mercifully calm for this time of year, and I assume your yacht has powerful engines." Elspeth did not lower her eyes from his and hoped her serious expression would provoke an explanation, but he did not respond.

"Have you heard from them?" Elspeth asked, not letting him avoid answering. "If I'm to help you, as you requested, it might be prudent for you to tell me."

He looked down his nose, as if to claim royal prerogative, but she did not flinch.

She continued. "I'm here to assist you, as you know, and cannot do so if you don't tell me when the princess is due to arrive. If the press decides to pursue the story of the fire last night, my job will become doubly difficult, and your chance of privacy here compromised radically." Then she softened her tone. "I'm sure you are aware of this."

Elspeth wondered how many people spoke to him as frankly, but her words had their effect.

He cleared his throat before answering. "I expect the yacht early tomorrow morning. I've instructed the captain to put down anchor well outside the hotel's marina before sunrise."

"And, how will the Princess be brought to the hotel? I assume it may not be willingly."

"It will be willingly, Ms Duff. I've spoken to my daughter, and she has agreed to come calmly and speak to us."

"Will you tell me why the change in her attitude?" Elspeth knew she was stepping beyond the boundaries of her needing to know, but if she did not ask, she would be hampered by only half knowing. From his expression, she knew he was well aware of this.

"We trust you," he said. "Honorée had spoken very highly of your conversations with her, and Hope and Francis have attested to your personal background. Ms Duff, you have not been totally candid about who you are."

Elspeth smiled at the remembrance of the dinner with the Tildens the evening before. "I try to keep my personal life separate from my professional one. They seldom cross, although in this case they have."

He nodded acknowledgement and continued. "Christiana has agreed to speak to us on one condition."

"Which is?"

"That Harald Wade be present."

Elspeth looked around towards the shy, young man in the corner. His pale skin turned scarlet.

She turned back to the prince. "I assume you've agreed."

"I have," he said arrogantly. "There can be little harm in it. Harald knows where we stand."

"Have you made arrangements for transporting the princess to the hotel? Even at that early hour, there could be people about, or, worse, members of the media."

"We have thought of that and are planning accordingly. I have asked Mary to row out to meet the yacht 's launch and bring Christiana back, and have instructed the captain to anchor the yacht far enough away to be out of sight of land. Mary goes out snorkelling each morning and always takes one of the hotel dinghies. She has never seen anyone else about at that hour," the prince said. "She'll go a bit further out tomorrow, so when she meets the launch and Christiana joins her in the dingy, no one should pay attention."

"People do look out from their hotel windows," she said with painful memories of the night Richard arrived. "Mary should take care as she and Christiana approach the shore."

"Both Mary and my daughter are strong swimmers. I'm having them swim the last bit before they arrive at the beach, so that they would seem like hotel guests out for a morning swim."

"What time is this all to take place?" Elspeth asked.

Mary got up from her seat and walked towards the window that looked out to the gate that led down to the beach. She gestured toward the ocean. "We plan to rendezvous at a quarter to six. It should take me no more than twenty minutes to row back close to shore and anchor before swimming to the beach. Uncle Michael and I figured that the whole thing should be done just before dawn. The nights are generally clear here, and I should be able to reach the launch without any problem." Mary seemed eager for the adventure.

Elspeth turned back to the prince. "I'd like to be present when Princess Christiana comes to shore in case there's any difficulty. It's probably a good idea that none of you venture beyond the bungalow walls."

"Is that necessary?" he asked.

"Rather, precautionary, which is the way I prefer to work," Elspeth replied. "Mary and the princess will recognise me because I'll be wearing a floppy hat and multicoloured caftan."

"Doesn't that make you look like any other woman on the beach?" Mary asked.

"It does. Tell Mary and the princess then that I shall be carrying . . ." Elspeth tried to think of something identifying that would be readily available ". . . a red bucket." Elspeth remembered seeing one in the hotel gift shop. Hopefully, no one had yet bought it, as it had an outrageous price tag for a children's toy that could easily be obtained in Hamilton for a third of the price. "And I'll seem to be gathering shells in the first light of day. I'm told good ones are washed up with the morning tides, although I've never been out on the beach that early to see."

The prince smiled at her remarks. "As you wish. If anything changes, we 'll let you know. In the meantime come and join us for drinks this evening," he said. "And bring Sir Richard."

"Now that your secret is out, there is no sense hiding him under a bushel," Princess Honorée said. These were the first words she had uttered since Elspeth had entered the room. "Oh, and Ms Duff—or do you prefer Lady Munro?"

Elspeth smiled. "I use my own name, even when I'm with Richard, except at very stuffy diplomatic functions."

The princess smiled. "Do you remember my telling you about my grandmother's earrings when we were walking on the beach? Come along into my bedroom and let me show them to you."

Thank you, Princess, for making my task easier, Elspeth thought. The princess had never mentioned the existence of these earrings, so Elspeth assumed she wanted to talk about the brooch and Martin Hagen, but did she know he was dead?

Elspeth's eyes crossed the princess's, who gave no indication that she had just lied. "I should be delighted," Elspeth said. "They sound quite remarkable."

The bungalow's simple name on the map of the hotel in the lobby gave no indication of the luxury of its fittings. Elspeth had later learned it had been built for the brother of the original estate owner, his family of six children and their personal servants. The 'bungalow' had twelve rooms, varying in size, but most of them were significantly larger than most modern-day hotel rooms and were easily converted into spacious bedrooms. The common rooms needed little alteration, although they had been brought up to Kennington hotel standards under the direction of Lord Kennington himself. The garden enclosure was originally made for the brother's widow, who would not go beyond the walls after her husband died, and it became a place where she would pass her time among the luxuriant foliage until her death thirty years later. On her husband's demise she had called in the best landscape architects of the era to lay out the space. Lord Kennington had not changed the plan but had supplemented the plantings. Flowers bloomed in a riot of colour, attracting local birds, who frequented several birdbaths which the gardeners or rainfall replenished every day.

Honorée led Elspeth across the garden to the master bedroom wing. The original owners of the plantation had been early Victorians who had accumulated vast wealth during the slave trade era and adhered to the custom of a husband and wife having separate rooms. These were grand in scale and positioned to catch the winds off the ocean in the days when cooling could only be achieved by natural methods. Honorée led Elspeth into her bedroom suite, its interior refreshed by the outside air.

"It's delightful here," the princess said. "It reminds me of the hot summers in Alberta, where Hope and I slept on a sleeping porch. My grandfather never installed air conditioning. I think that's why I enjoy places that don't have artificial cooling. Michael disagrees with me, but here we can have our rooms at temperatures we each like."

Elspeth had seen many of the finer suites in Kennington hotels all over the world, but here Eric Kennington had outdone himself. On her frequent visits to the London headquarters of the Kennington Organisation, she had heard both from Pamela Crumm and from him directly that they felt they were taking a large risk branching out from their traditional hotels housed in historic buildings in urban districts to develop exclusive hotels in resort areas. Would people actually pay the outrageous prices he charged for a stay in his resort hotels? The Kennington Bermuda was the first such hotel, and Lord Kennington had spent an inordinate amount of time to make sure it was significant architecturally both on the inside and outside. He generally did not advertise his hotels, but he made sure that several of the more serious British and American architectural and interior design magazines covered his efforts in Bermuda. He had chosen the palest of apricot for the exterior stucco walls of the bungalow and then let his gardeners grow vines with small fragrant white flowers up the walls and along the trellises. Wooden shutters were hinged above the windows and kept the rooms cool from the sun.

Honorée led Elspeth through French doors, which were ajar. Inside was a dream world, all in white, with touches of beige and cream colours. Lord Kennington could never leave an area in his hotels devoid of fresh flowers, and the room was filled with vases of lilies, jasmine and fragrant white roses.

Honorée's face beamed as she entered the room. "You've no idea how welcoming this is after the royal palace, which was built to withstand cruel winters and the dark enemies of Michael's forbearers. Please never let him know that I said that. He would find me ungrateful, but I do love the cheerfulness of this space."

Elspeth could see why. No wonder the widow of the original occupants had no reason to venture beyond the walls of her garden, particularly in times that were hostile to unattached women.

Honorée's expression of delight at her room faded as she led Elspeth to a sitting area near the French doors. Elspeth seated herself, and Honorée went to the doors and closed them. An overhead fan with white onyx blades turned slowly overhead.

Sitting on one of the wicker chairs, whose cushions had two-toned white stripes, Honorée clenched her jaw and looked directly at Elspeth. "It was Martin Hagen's room, wasn't it?"

Elspeth nodded.

"Was he there when the fire started?"

Elspeth wanted to break the news gently, but there seemed no way.

"They found a body in the room. It was burnt beyond recognition. In all probability it was Martin Hagen's."

"So he's dead," the princess said slowly, her eyes hardening.

"We can only assume so. He was to leave the hotel this morning at my insistence, but no one has seen him since last night in the dining room. They're doing an autopsy, which will determine the cause of death, although it probably was due to smoke inhalation. The identity of the body will have to be established, but there can be little doubt it was Martin Hagen."

"I'm not sorry," the princess said. "He was an evil man."

Elspeth had met many scoundrels in the course of her work, but blackmailers were among the worst of them because they preyed on people's shortcomings for their own gain. By her own reports Martin Hagen had shadowed Princess Honorée over a period of time. In a foolish effort to protect her daughter, she had become trapped in the quicksand he provided. No wonder she found him evil. Was she now trapped by his death? Elspeth knew she needed to be cautious in order to keep Honorée's confidence, but Honorée might have information that could shed light on what happened in Room 17 the night before.

"Did you go to his room last night, Princess? Before the fire?"

Honorée looked away and raised her head to

examine the ceiling. "I have to trust you, Ms Duff. I did go there—by appointment. I couldn't pay what he asked, and I needed to plea for time. I thought that once Christiana was here, we could go to Michael and tell him the truth. l need her to admit to him what she had done. Michael is a proud father. Hearing what we had to tell him would hurt him deeply." Honorée twisted one of her rings round and round as she spoke.

"Was Michael Hagen in his room last night? Did you speak to him?" Elspeth asked.

"Yes and no. Before I could knock on the door, I heard voices inside, raised voices. I recognised his voice but not the other one."

"Was it a man or a woman?"

"I'm not sure. His voice was obvious; the other voice was low. It might have been a man or maybe a woman with a deep voice. I couldn't hear what they were saying. He seemed to be threatening her, but I only heard words like 'tomorrow' and 'more next time' and 'your family'. I tiptoed away shortly afterwards."

"Did anyone see you?"

"I don't think so."

"Did you hear anything else?"

Honorée turned her eyes towards a large porcelain vase, white on white, filled with golden rushes at the corner of the room. "I heard a pop," she said.

"A pop?"

"Like a balloon bursting. It startled me."

"Did it come from the room?"

"Possibly or perhaps from the kitchen or even from the beach. The garden walls masks sound direction, so I can't be sure it came from the room, but I was shaken enough that I ran back across the garden and into our compound. The others were having a noisy game of cards and didn't look up when I crossed the outside window and went to my room. I'd earlier pleaded a headache."

This new bit of information puzzled Elspeth. What was the possibility that Martin Hagen was pursing two victims at the hotel, not just one? If there were two victims, why would he invite them both to his room at nearly the same time? Logic would make one think that the other person, if he or she was Martin Hagen's victim, had burst in on him without any pre-arrangement. The Kennington Bermuda had sufficient accommodation for forty guests, and the voice that Honorée heard could have been any one of them, or perhaps someone from the outside. It occurred to Elspeth that the fire could have been deliberately set, but that would mean that the person behind the mysterious voice had somehow overcome the blackmailer and rendered him incapable of escaping the fire. Such an act would suggest that the person was stronger than Martin and therefore more likely to be a man, or perhaps a very strong woman. Elspeth remembered Martin was lightly-built but he did not look weak. But what was the 'pop'? There was always the possibility that the princess was not telling the truth, but Elspeth did not want to consider this. The protection of the royal family was her charge and implicating any one of them in foul play would compound her task.

Elspeth decided to begin another line of questioning in an attempt to understand more about Martin Hagen's relationship to the princess.

"Did he ever show you the brooch?"

"He did. He had it with him. He showed it to me the first time I went to his room."

"Where did he keep it? In a drawer, in his pocket, in a case?"

"He had a case, a thin metal one the size of a small laptop computer only a bit thicker. When I went to his room, he opened it and held out the brooch for me to see."

"Did he allow you to handle it? Are you sure it

was the real thing?"

"It definitely was the brooch. He had wrapped it in tissue paper, which he unfolded, and he laid it out on the table to let me examine it. Several years ago, the clasp had become loose and I had taken to a jeweller who soldered it back on. The solder was almost invisible, not quite, but I don't think it couldn't be disguised, or copied accurately. That's how I knew the brooch belonged to the royal family."

And you left your fingerprints on it, Elspeth thought, but said nothing.

"When he put it back in the case, did he wrap it back in the tissue paper before doing so?"

Honorée scowled. "I believe he did."

"Do you remember if the case had a lock?"

Honorée nodded. "One on each side like the ones on a briefcase, with three numbers on each dial rather than a key."

"Were there other things inside it? Try to remember if you can."

"He opened the case for only a moment, but I saw several envelopes inside, blue ones with stamps on them."

"British stamps?"

"I don't recall. The stamp on top was quite gaudy, but nowadays every country tries to outdo the others for the most colourful philately, don't they? Certainly our country does."

"Did you see anything else in the case?"

"The case itself seemed to be padded with a silvery material."

Fireproofing, Elspeth thought. She remembered the room she had examined that morning. No such case remained in the room, but a safety deposit box key had, and it now was lodging in the cosmetic case in her bathroom hidden among cotton buds. Its current location could hardly be considered secure.

16

Crossing the garden once again, Elspeth was deep in thought when Lilian Balfour interrupted her.

"Why, Lady Elspeth," she said, "isn't it a beautiful day!"

Elspeth winced at the misuse of her title in combination with her given name. This form of address was never used unless one was the daughter of an earl, marquis or duke. Many sophisticated Americans understood the correct use of British titles, but the general's wife was obviously not one of them.

"Mrs Balfour, I trust the general is feeling better this morning."

"You know how much our warriors give to their country these days," she said. "Poor Bill. The army gives him a bit of rest and recreation, and he now spends it in bed. I can't even coax him out to one of those lawn chairs outside our room."

"What a pity," Elspeth said using her normal voice, since she had given up reverting to her American accent in the presence of Mrs Balfour.

"You seem to go over to that bungalow over there a lot. Is someone special staying there?" Lilianne winked.

Elspeth had disliked this woman from their first meeting but had to admit that the heavy mascara on her false eyelashes in no way blinded her perception of what was going on around her. Lilianne may have been compensating for the general's absence by snooping, but Elspeth suspected that Lilianne had acquired her curiosity long before arriving in Bermuda.

"We have friends staying there," Elspeth

replied.

"Oh, that Canadian couple from Canada. He's quite handsome for a black man, and I still say she does look like Princess Honorée, who I saw once in London in a jewellery store and recognised immediately. I was sure it was her when the shop owner called her 'Your Highness' and told her the piece had already been sold."

Despite her early upbringing in the Highlands of Scotland, where in those days one hardly ever saw people of different races, Elspeth had learned from her parents a deep respect for all the varieties people around the world. Besides, as a child, her grandfather had taken her into his library at Tay Farm, opened a great atlas, and told her stories of people in every part of the globe. Elspeth never forgot these special times with her grandfather, who died when she was ten, and through his stories she had grown to admire the similarity among the different peoples around the world. Racial prejudice revolted her and always had. Lilianne's slight of Francis Tilden rankled her, but she clenched her teeth and said nothing. Just because one could afford to pay the rates at a Kennington hotel, there was no guarantee that social enlightenment came with the price tag. Elspeth wanted to be rid of Lilianne's presence as soon as possible and excused herself rather bluntly.

Elspeth skirted the dining room, which was now filling up with lunchtime diners. She did a rapid visual survey of the room but did not see either Ken or Lars and assumed they were at the bungalow. Her mind went back to the previous night. What had the princess said? She had heard a pop and it might have come from the kitchen. Elspeth wanted to ask Ken or Lars if they knew what made the sound. They might have been in the kitchen as late as midnight, where any untoward noise would probably have been noticed there and commented upon.

Hungry and tired, she made her way back to her

rooms where she found Richard gone, but he had left a note saying he thought a walk to the local yacht basin would clear his head. Her husband was a passionate sailor and could not resist the temptation of the sailing boats at the marina.

She rang for a salad, which arrived quickly despite the noontime hour. She ate it hastily, scrawling a note to Richard telling him of their invitation for drinks at the bungalow, and then added a postscript in her large hand. "Wake me at five." She went to their bedroom and fell into a deep sleep.

She fought for consciousness as someone was shaking her by the shoulders. "Elspeth, wake up!" Opening one eye she saw her husband. She opened the other eye, which confirmed what her first eye had seen. Her head felt wrapped in the cotton wool of dreamless sleep, and she did not want to emerge from it, so she closed both eyes once more.

"Elspeth, wake up!" he said again, this time more urgently. She fought off the urge to ignore him and so opened her eyes again.

"What time is it?"

"Half past three," he said.

"Didn't I say five in my note?"

"You did, but Kit Lord just rang. He wants to see you in his office. It's about the body caught in the fire."

She came to full consciousness.

"Did he say anything else?"

"That he needed to see you immediately, before talking to the police"

"Police?"

"He said it was murder."

The comfort of the cotton wool in her head vanished. She jumped from the bed, grabbed a comb which was on the side table and drew it quickly through her hair. She found her sandals by the bed and made for the door.

"I'll be back as soon as I can. If I'm late, please give my excuses to our hosts. Tell them I'm sorry." She brushed a kiss on his forehead and was gone.

Kit was waiting for her in his private office. She found him on his computer and scrolling down a list of names.

"Elspeth, thank god!"

"Tell me, Kit."

He gave the news without preface. "The victim in Room 17 died from a gun shot at the base of his skull. There was no smoke in what remained of his lungs."

"Has he been identified?"

"Not positively, but it must be Martin Hagen. He's the only guest missing." Kit's expression changed, his eyes evading hers. "Did he say anything yesterday when you met him? Anything that might explain why he was murdered?"

Elspeth's thoughts whirled. She had not reported to Kit, to London or even put in her computer notes the threats that Martin Hagen had made to Princess Honorée, but she had believed the princess's story of blackmail from the beginning, and increasingly, her account of the events of the night before. Had Elspeth misplaced her trust in the princess? Elspeth had encountered killers in her career with the Kennington Organisation more times than she liked, but if a murder had indeed been committed and if the princess might be implicated, then Elspeth needed to use all her investigative experience and intelligence to find out the truth. Martin Hagen was a blackmailer; there was no doubt about that. He had intimidated the princess, but he could have lined up other victims at the hotel as well? Who had written the letters enclosed in the envelopes in the case the princess had described? If the princess's observations were correct, it could be any guest in the hotel. If she had lied, she had done so convincingly.

Elspeth took a certain self-satisfied pride in seeing through people's fabrications, but she also was aware that true sociopaths could lie so convincingly that even a polygraph could not detect their duplicity, and their prevarications were undetectable even to a mental health professional. The princess, however, did not strike Elspeth as being a sociopath.

Elspeth thought of the princess and then, by contrast, her twin sister. Hope and Honor. Hope for the future; honour for the past. How strange it was that the twin who had chosen to reclaim her family's reputation in Europe, and to make her life among the musty corridors of minor European royalty, was now the one who had reason to commit a capital crime to protect her marriage and her daughter. Elspeth did not want to think this way, but events had led her to do so. How far was she expected to go to protect the royal party if murder had been committed by one of their members? The affair of Christiana's marriage to Ali Ayan now seemed insignificant.

"What have they told you, Kit?" she asked.

"They assumed that the body had succumbed to smoke inhalation. The room was sealed, and the fire had fully engulfed the room. No one could have survived that, which is why the fire brigade chose to contain the fire rather than enter the room to find the fire's source. I think everyone assumed that the person in the room had fallen asleep and dropped a cigarette, thus causing the fire, since the room was in the smokers' wing."

"I understand that but, Kit, hasn't anyone asked why the fire sprinklers didn't engage? This omission seems puzzling in light of the discovery that the body probably was shot before the start of the fire. Did the murderer want the body to be consumed completely by the fire so that there would be no evidence of the shooting? If so, how did he or she dismantle our fire protection system? In Britain every suspicious death triggers an autopsy. It can't be different in Bermuda since it's a British overseas territory. Didn't the murderer know this? Kit, if this is indeed murder, and it seems it is, we need to alert London and the legal staff."

"But aren't you . . . ?"

"No, my job here is to protect the residents of the bungalow. London needs to send someone to represent the hotel against damages."

"Damages?"

"Legal ones. Because the sprinklers didn't go off, the Kennington Organisation could be accused of negligence."

Kit swallowed hard.

"You told me the inspection was overdue," Elspeth said.

"We are in Bermuda, and sometimes we do not act as promptly as you do in London," he said defensively.

"I understand, but the Kennington Organisation has deep pockets. I've no idea who would want to sue us over Martin Hagen's death, but we cannot dismiss the possibility. Kit, we must take every precaution."

Elspeth did not say these words lightly, because she knew her own assignment at the Kennington Bermuda could be connected to what had happened in Room 17 the night before.

"Now let's find out what we can about Martin Hagen. What address did he give when he checked in?"

Kit scrolled down the computerised guest list and read out an address in Knightsbridge. "Do you know it?" he asked Elspeth.

"I know the area. He must have been doing well recently to live there. Let's Google him and see what else we find."

Kit turned to the computer and tapped on the keys. The Martin Hagens in all the English-speaking world were numerous, so Kit narrowed the field to

'Martin Hagen, Knightsbridge, London, UK'. There were no hits, and various combinations of the name and place produced nothing more.

"He has covered his tracks well. Normally a web search will at least turn up a phone number. Or, he hasn't given his real address, which doesn't surprise me," she said. "Kit, log into the hotel computer network and find out how many times Martin Hagen has checked in and out of Kennington hotels in the last seven years. You probably don't have the authority here to do this but contact London and see if any of his stays overlapped with visits by any of the other guests staying here now. Also, I want to see the security tapes which cover the area outside Room 17 from the time he checked in until the fire was reported. Hopefully they haven't been destroyed yet."

"No, we generally keep them for about a week. He was only here for a few days."

"Good. Have them ready for viewing later this evening, just by the two of us, and have the security technician show you how to rerun them if you don't already know how. Let's keep them from the police until they ask for them, although I fear that won't be long now."

Elspeth's mind raced. Martin Hagen's murder put demands on her assignment that she preferred not to have. Eric Kennington would certainly involve her with the police, if for nothing else than to keep them from interfering with the royal party.

"When are the police due to arrive?" she asked.

"I asked if I could go to the police station instead. I said I would be there at five."

"Do you want me to come as well?" Elspeth hoped she was not infringing upon Kit's authority, but she also knew he was less experienced than many of the security officers at the larger hotels. She always trod lightly when dealing with the younger members of the security staff. Her position as personal assistant to Lord Kennington gave her freedom to act that in-house security officers did not have, but she was always cautious in exerting her power over them. Therefore, she asked Kit rather than assuming her prerogative as the lead security officer when she was in residence at any of the Kennington hotels.

Kit looked relieved. "That would be brilliant! I've met the Chief Superintendent of Police, but I've never been faced with a murder before. Have you?"

"Unfortunately, yes. One is obligated to cooperate with the police, of course, but there's also the need to keep the guests away from any unpleasantness." She did not add that to achieve this one occasionally had to withhold evidence in the early stages of an investigation, particularly if the police did not ask.

"Then please come," Kit said.

The police station was in the centre of Hamilton in a multi--storey modern building at the corner of Victoria and Court Streets. They entered through the double doors at the front, and the woman at the desk said they were expected.

Detective Chief Inspector Lawrence Hart, a tall, dark man in uniform, straightened his tunic as Elspeth and Kit entered the room. His posture was rigid and his face stoic. The main part of his office was orderly, but stacks of files seemed about to spill out from a bookcase beyond his desk, which was empty of everything but a computer monitor, a keyboard, a pen set, and a single file of papers.

"Mr Lord?" he asked, although the policewoman who had led Kit and Elspeth down the corridor to the DCI's office had announced his visitors. "And who is she?"

Elspeth recognised the reaction and froze him with her glare. Having encountered racial prejudice earlier in the day, she now was faced with a police officer who seemed to devalue her because of her gender and, she assumed, because of her stylish attire. Although she had risen quickly from her nap and had not attempted to change from the clothing she had put on earlier for a meeting with the royal party, she resented the DCI's look, which seemed to suggest his disdain for a female who dressed expensively and with obvious elegance.

Elspeth glanced towards Kit, who seemed nervous, but she let him take the lead. He frowned.

"Sir," he said, which immediately put him in the inferior position. Elspeth would have called him by his title, which would have kept their status on a par, but she held her peace. Kit was still learning.

"You wanted to see me, us," Kit continued, his voice cracking. He did not introduce Elspeth or state her position at the hotel, and so she reluctantly intervened.

"Chief Inspector, as your constable said, my name is Elspeth Duff," she said simply. "I work for the security staff of the Kennington Organisation in London." She did not clarify her role vis-à-vis the Kennington Bermuda, but she did add, "I'm here for other reasons, but Mr Lord and I are working together on the fire. It is, of course, of major concern to our corporate office in London."

The DCI looked startled at Elspeth's assertive tone.

"Ms Duff was at the scene of the fire for most of last night," Kit said, "while I was seeing to the safety of our guests. She can tell you more than I can about what happened."

The DCI flared his wide nostrils, as if the presence of a woman at the scene offended his olfactory senses. Elspeth met his gaze, but she damned the stereotypical thinking of some policemen around the world. She coped with their prejudice for the sake of her work but had never become reconciled to its inappropriateness.

Elspeth hated to pull rank, but she did so. "I used to work for Scotland Yard," she said blandly. "The Kennington Organisation has always found that useful as I'm fully aware of police procedures." She did not mention that her service with the Metropolitan Police had been over three decades before, and she had held a lowly position.

The DCI shifted in his chair and straightened his tunic once again.

"I welcome you both," he said in an obvious effort to regain his superiority.

Kit seemed oblivious of the subtle jostling for power that had just occurred between the DCI and Elspeth. Kit reached for his tie and adjusted it for no reason. His nerves were apparent. Elspeth wished it were otherwise.

Elspeth waited for Kit to take back the lead, but he did not, so she filled in for him.

"Will you be more specific as to the cause of the death of the body found in Room 17? Have you been able to identify it? Was he, I assume it was a he, dead before the fire started? I saw the flames in the room and wonder if much of the body is recognisable? I know I'm asking a lot of questions, but is it possible for us to see the pathologist's report?"

The DCI flinched at Elspeth's rapid-fire requests. "Ms Dunn . . ."

"Duff," Elspeth said smiling, but feeling impatient.

"Ms Duff, we work more slowly here in Bermuda than they do in London. I'll have to ask the chief superintendent if you can have the report, but it may be a few days before it is complete. The pathologist's secretary is shared with the rest of us, and she has multiple tasks beyond typing the pathologist's report. We are lucky to have her, as she used to be a medical recorder and knows the terminology, but we do not want to rush her. In any case, I believe the pathologist has not finished his examination."

Elspeth wondered how many cases the pathologist was currently processing and doubted it was more than one, as she suspected Bermuda had a low murder rate.

"Perhaps then you can tell us the essence of the report," Kit said, his tone more patient than Elspeth's.

The DCI rustled through the papers in the file folder and found what from across the table looked like handwritten notes.

"The pathologist, Dr. Kirby, informed me immediately when he found a bullet in the victim's brain. It entered the base of the skull, just above the third vertebra and penetrated the medulla. Dr. Kirby surmised that death was instantaneous as there was no internal bleeding. The body was badly burned but most of the internal organs were still intact. He didn't find any smoke in the lungs, and at least initially he assumes that the victim was dead before the fire began."

Kit glanced over at Elspeth but said nothing.

Elspeth stepped in again. "Then the cause of death was from a gunshot. Did Dr. Kirby indicate what sort of gun?"

"Not specifically," the DCI said, "but he said it was a small calibre pistol, the sort that could be easily hidden and is most often used by ladies."

"Implying that our murderer is a woman," said Elspeth.

"So it would seem. You both must realise that the police will have to question the guests at the hotel, particularly the women guests."

Elspeth drew up in her chair. "Detective Chief Inspector," she said in her haughtiest voice, "the guests at Kennington hotels pay premium prices not to be disturbed. The management of the hotel cannot allow you blanket access to our guests, or even all our women guests. In fact, you will have to provide us good reason to question any of the guests. I suggest that you let me and Mr Lord conduct a preliminary investigation to find the people whom the victim had contact with during his stay at the hotel, assuming of course, that you first identify the victim. At this point we are assuming that the victim is, or rather was, the person booked into Room 17, but that's not yet firmly established." She spoke with the knowledge the police could obtain a search warrant and interview whomever they liked, but she wanted to avoid this.

Kit squirmed in his chair. Obviously he had never thought of standing up to the police. Elspeth had no qualms in doing so; in fact she had done so many times before. Practice makes perfect, she thought wryly.

DCI Hart did not look convinced. "I'll need to talk to the chief superintendent," he said. "The decision will be his."

Elspeth rose from her chair, hoping to imply that she had only the slightest respect for the DCI's position.

"Please do," she said, "and let us know."

Kit Lord looked startled at Elspeth's arrogance.

"Thank you, Chief Inspector. I'm sure we can reach an acceptable way of handling this," Elspeth said.

Kit Lord followed her meekly from the room.

When they were to on the street, he blew out his breath. "Do you always deal with the police that way?"

Elspeth laughed. "No, of course not. Only when I feel they want to put me down. That raises my hackles, but, we do need to keep the police out of the hotel. I suggest that when we get back, you call the DCI and make muttering noises about my abruptness and something about this being what you have to bear when someone, particularly a woman, comes from the Kennington head office. I suspect you'll get his immediate cooperation, which we may need further down the line."

Elspeth saw Kit's lips begin to quiver and eyes sparkle. "I fear, Ms Duff, that you are not an easy person to deal with if you feel an injustice has been done."

17

The bravado that Elspeth displayed at the police station did not last long. As she sat in the cab alongside Kit Lord on their way back the hotel, she was worried. She did not want to let Kit know this, because she felt she had won his admiration since the fire, and she did not want him to think of her as coming up short. She needed his full cooperation but also to distance herself from him and pursue plans forming in her mind. Because of her position, and by inclination, she sometimes deviated from standard hotel procedure, but Kit did not need to know this, at least not yet.

They did not speak on the way back to the hotel, and Elspeth sensed Kit was uncomfortable with her silence. His nervousness spilled out perceptibly. He kept shaking his head and massaging his hands.

Finally he spoke. "I've never been involved with a murder before." His voice broke, and then he cleared his throat.

"It's not a pleasant thing. Martin Hagen, by all accounts, was not an admirable man, but he didn't deserve to die violently. Whoever did this must have had compelling reasons to commit a murder rather than going to the authorities. Kit, we must get to the bottom of this before the police do, and keep them out of the hotel as long as possible. We have several resources at our immediate disposal, and I suggest that as soon as we get back to the hotel, we sequester ourselves in your office and go over our options. I hope you didn't have plans for the evening."

"None that can't be cancelled."

"Good. It may be a long night." Elspeth spoke these words with regret. Richard was due to leave in the morning, and she now had no chance to join the royal party for drinks. She was thankful that Richard had his own connection to the Tilden's and that her company was not central to the success of the gathering at the bungalow.

"Give me a few minutes to freshen. Let's meet at seven o'clock. Order dinner for us, something easy to eat, and an urn of coffee. We might need it. In the meantime, get the security tapes set up."

They parted company in the lobby, and she made her way back to her rooms. Showering quickly and changing into casual clothes, she looked regretfully around the room and knew Richard's things would be gone in the morning. Her condition that she keep her job after their marriage suddenly seemed ill-considered. She was unhappy that when they were together at one of the hotels, she would, by necessity, have to leave him to his own devices while she worked. Their marriage was still recent enough that the pleasure of his company filled her with unbound love and warmth. She tried to write him a note to explain her absence but found her words feeble. Finally she penned:

> *"I'm so sorry, Dickie, but I can't be with you this evening. I'll be with Kit Lord. Get dinner for yourself and stop by the security office to say good night if you can. I promise to make this up to you next time we are together. E."*

They watched the tapes carefully. The security cameras were set up so that they only ran when there was motion. Martin Hagen had arrived four days before, so Elspeth and Kit rewound the tapes from the cameras set in the garden and directed towards the smokers' wing, beginning on the night Martin Hagen had arrived.

People crossed to and from the wing at frequent intervals. At 17:05:27 Martin Hagen arrived at his room carrying something that looked like a small briefcase under his arm; while a porter carried two cases. Elspeth asked Kit to stop the tape and zoom in on the briefcase, which matched the princess's description. She made no comment, however. They continued watching the tape covering the night Martin Hagen checked in and noted that Martin left his room at 19:16:10 and headed in the direction of the dining room. He reappeared at 20:32:13. So far nothing seemed out of the ordinary.

At 22:20:26, however, an unidentifiable female figure in a large hat and long skirt appeared and knocked at the door to his room. The door opened quickly. The woman left fifteen minutes later. The princess, Elspeth thought. The next frames, however, startled her. A woman, without a hat but still unidentifiable, knocked on the door and was admitted. Elspeth asked Kit to zoom in and frowned at the closer image, which, on careful observation, resembled the princess. Kit had had little contact with the princess and did not seem to have identified her. The rest of Martin Hagen's first night was undisturbed.

Activity on the next day was normal. Guests, including Martin Hagen, came and went from their rooms, and during daylight hours he had no visitors.

They had been viewing the tapes for an hour, so Elspeth suggested they break for dinner. Kit had ordered an array of sandwiches and finger food from the bar buffet. They ate quickly and returned to their work.

Day two of Martin Hagen's visit revealed the same two nocturnal visitors, one wearing a hat, the other not. But there was another visitor too, who visited before dinner when it was still light—Lilianne Balfour. She stayed for ten minutes and then fluttered out of the room with a little dance, hardly the actions of a blackmail victim. Elspeth was puzzled by this, but

Lilianne was flighty enough that she could have any reaction to blackmail.

Day three, the day of the fire, was different. The woman in the hat appeared again, but the hat was different. Her stay lasted a bit longer, leaving in a half hour rather than fifteen minutes. Twenty minutes later there were signs of the fire in Room 17, as small flames started licking under the curtains in the window.

Elspeth leaned back in her chair and rested the back of her head in her hands as she stretched out her neck.

"So, what have we discovered, Kit? I'm not sure exactly. Obviously, Martin Hagen's nocturnal visitors were all women, and because of the late hour they were probably hotel guests. Did you recognise them?"

Kit shook his head. "I recognised Mrs Balfour, but I couldn't see the others well enough to make any positive identification."

Elspeth was relieved that the princess did not appear clearly on the tapes, and that her secret was intact.

"Have you heard anything back from London about Martin Hagen's previous visits to our hotels?" she asked.

"Nothing yet. They have someone cross-checking and promised a report by tomorrow."

"Good. I think if there were any overlaps between Mr Hagen's visits and those of any one of our other guests, we could have our first indication of who his visitors were. It bothers me that he could get away with blackmail in our hotels without us being aware of it. Had he not approached me, we might still be in the dark about why he was here. By the way, did he make arrangements to check out this morning?"

Kit brought up a list on the computer and scrolled down it.

"Hmm," he said. "Yes, he did. He paid in cash."

"In cash? What is the amount of his bill?"

"With meals and extras, just over six thousand pounds."

Elspeth blew out her breath. That's a lot of money to pay in cash. Are there limits on how much cash you can bring into Bermuda?"

"I think it's ten thousand dollars, but I can find out for sure."

"Find out about non-UK citizens too. We don't know for sure if the women who visited him were all from the UK. Certainly Mrs Balfour isn't. You know, Kit, something is strange about Mrs Balfour. Have you seen her husband?"

"Her husband?" He seemed at a loss. "She's staying here alone."

Elspeth was confused and then reacted. "Google General William Balfour."

Kit busied himself with the keys of his computer while Elspeth tried to assimilate his last bit of information. On several occasions Lilianne Balfour had said, or at least implied, that her husband was here at the Kennington Bermuda with her. Why had she lied? Was she delusional? Did she need the presence of a man to justify her being at the hotel? Or, was she purposely trying to deceive Elspeth?

Kit said, "Bingo!"

"What did you find?"

"Major General William Balfour was killed in the attack on the US Embassy in Saigon in March 1965. He left behind a wife and two daughters, one named Lilly Anne, who was born in 1954. That would make her the same age, more or less, as our guest with a similar name. What do you make of that?"

"I'm not sure, but Martin Hagen may have been demanding money from her in return for his silence. It smells like a 'fishy fish', as my son said as a child."

Kit laughed for the first time that evening.

It was approaching ten o'clock, and Elspeth's lack of sleep the night before was creeping up on her.

"Can you think of anything more we can do tonight, Kit? I could do with some sleep after last night, and I'm sure you could too. Let's call it a night and get together after breakfast in the morning. Nine o'clock shall we say?"

When Elspeth returned to her rooms, she found Richard dozing in bed with Elspeth's copy of Jane Austen fallen from his hands. He looked up sleepily as she entered.

"Long night, my love," he said sympathetically. "I hope you can get some sleep tonight."

"Mmm," she said as she snuggled down next to him. "Have you been enjoying Jane in my absence?"

"I'd forgotten how witty her books are. I haven't read them for years. I think I tackled several of them when Marjorie had them sent out to Africa, although the machinations of damsels in Bath and Brighton in the early nineteenth century seemed far from the hostile affairs we were dealing with at the time. Francis and Hope were out there too, as you know. We probably shared Jane with them as well. Good books in English always made their rounds."

"How were drinks at the bungalow?"

"Pleasant but stiff. I wished you'd been there. You were asked after, of course, and I made excuses about your being involved with the fire investigation. As I left, Princess Honorée asked if you would call her in the morning and the others sent their regards. You seem to have made quite an impression on them. The prince also said he would contact you in the morning with the updated arrival date, whatever that means."

If staying on schedule, Princess Christiana's arrival would be imminent. Elspeth had almost forgotten in light of the other events at the hotel.

Elspeth drew her thoughts inwards and was

determined not to let them interfere with her last night with her husband. "Let me get ready for bed, Dickie. I'll be just a minute."

She made her way to the bathroom and pulled off her clothes. She fetched her silk pyjamas and caftan from the walk-in cupboard and sat down to remove her makeup. As she pulled a cotton bud from her bag, her fingers touched the safety deposit key. She slipped the key in the pocket of the caftan and decided she must do something about it in the morning, but her mind was too tired to form a definite plan.

When she climbed into bed next to Richard, he drew her to him and said lazily, "Oh, this note came for you." He reached over to his night table and produced a cream coloured envelope with the Kennington crest on the flap.

She took it and put it in his book. "I'll deal with it in the morning. I have other things on my mind tonight."

It was Richard's turn to say 'mmm'.

The wake-up call came as the vaguest hint of dawn filtered through the French windows that led out to their patio. Elspeth turned and drew her one of her pillows over her head. Richard lifted it, kissed her cheek, and said, "I must be off, my dear. Will you come out to the lobby to say goodbye?"

"Nnn," Elspeth mumbled, turned over and put the pillow back over her head. He kissed the back of her neck and rose to prepare for his trip. When he emerged from the bathroom, Elspeth had pulled on her caftan, and was running a comb though her hair, which, because of its skilful cut, fell obediently into place. Her eyes were only half open.

They said their loving goodbyes, and Elspeth, having found her sandals, walked out with him to the lobby. Other guests were waiting for the van to the airport. Two couples, who seemed to be friends, stood by the trolley with their luggage and chatted about their upcoming flight, and Dorothy Ayers was at the desk settling her bill. The latter turned and saw Elspeth and Richard, and navigated in their direction.

"Elspeth, my dear, is this your husband? Sir Richard, Elizabeth told me all about the wedding. It sounded divine!"

Elspeth explained. "Mrs Ayers is the mother of one of Lizzie's friends in East Sussex."

Richard made all the right noises, and Elspeth knew him well enough to suspect that he was hoping his flight would not be the same one as hers.

Elspeth struggled for words to say to Dorothy Ayers. "Dorothy, I didn't expect to see you. Didn't you say you were leaving yesterday?"

"Those were my original plans, but I had to stay another day. It's so beautiful here, and I have nothing scheduled at home, so why not extend my visit? In any case, I didn't sleep well on the night of the fire and thought I'd get another day's rest."

Elspeth wished that Dorothy had not mentioned the fire and looked over at the two couples to see if they were listening. They were absorbed in each other's company and did not seem to have heard.

"Sir Richard, are you flying to Heathrow?"

Elspeth could see almost imperceptible relief cross Richard's face. "No, I'm off to Philadelphia and later to Malta."

"Malta! I've always seen it as such a romantic place. The brave Maltese who overcame every obstacle during the war."

"They are a brave, dignified, and very warm people. You haven't been there, I presume? You must come someday."

"How delightful. I should love to come."

Elspeth wondered if Dorothy assumed that Richard had just issued an invitation, but, before this could be made clear, the van arrived. Elspeth put up her cheek for Richard's final kiss and whispered, "Call me when you get to Philadelphia." As he left her, she had no idea how important these last words would become.

Elspeth was inclined to go back to her room and get a few more hours of sleep, but as she made her way out of the lobby, the receptionist called her over.

"Ms Duff, was that your husband? The staff are all talking about him and how distinguished he is. Is he really a high commissioner? He looks like a historical figure."

Elspeth suspected the receptionist was barely out of her teens, so did not mention that many of the older generation remarked on the uncanny resemblance between Richard and Earl Mountbatten of Burma. To think the young woman would even know how the late earl figured in history was expecting more of modern education than was likely. Instead she said, "Yes, others have said so. He's the British High Commissioner to Malta." She would have left it at that, but she saw an opportunity open.

"You are Cynthia, aren't you?"

The young woman seemed flattered that Elspeth remembered her name and flushed slightly.

"Do you have access to the safety deposit boxes?"

"We have a key here at the front desk," she said, "but it takes two keys to open one box. We give the other one to the guests who request a box. It gives them a sense of control."

"How many people have access to your key?"

"We keep it in a locked drawer, but everyone here at the reception desk can open it. It isn't like a bank, where you have to sign in and out. We want guests to feel that we can't open their boxes without them being there, so we give them a separate key, but it still takes two keys to open a box."

Elspeth's mind was working quickly. Could she open Martin Hagen's box since she had his key? She could ask Kit, but that would be admitting that she had taken the key from the fire scene. Although she hated to take advantage of her position in the Kennington Organisation, she did so shamelessly, drawing herself up to her full height.

"You know that I'm here as a member of security staff, don't you?" Elspeth said to Cynthia.

"We all do."

"I need to get into one of the boxes. Oh, don't worry, the guest entrusted me with her key." This wasn't exactly true, but Cynthia did not need to know.

"No problem," Cynthia said. Elspeth smiled in thanks. Cynthia unlocked the drawer and handed a key similar to the one from Martin Hagen's room. She then led Elspeth round the corner from the reception desk and unlocked the door to the safety deposit box area.

"I would appreciate it, for the guest's sake, that you not mention this to anyone."

Cynthia grinned and said, "I won't, for sure. I'd love to have a job like yours someday."

Elspeth smiled her broadest smile. She was well-aware of its effect on others; it usually charmed them. "It's not as easy as it seems," she said earnestly, but her statement was lost on Cynthia.

Once alone in the secure area, Elspeth drew out Martin Hagen's key from her pocket and checked the number on it. Unimaginatively it was 17. She inserted Cynthia's key in the drawer and then, taking precautions, wiped Martin Hagen's key with her handkerchief and, after wrapping it carefully, inserted it into its slot. The door opened noiselessly, and she drew out the metal box inside. Elspeth wished she had thought to bring gloves, but instead she carefully wrapped her fingers in her handkerchief and withdrew the slim briefcase that Princess Honorée had described so exactly. Elspeth feared the security dials on the front of the case might be engaged, but the locks opened without effort. She held her breath as she looked inside. She found two clasped envelopes, one large, one small. Taking precautions not to leave her fingerprints on anything, she opened the larger envelope. Inside were newspaper clippings dated thirty years before. A young woman was shielding her face and the headlines screamed 'Baby Killer released from hospital,' and the subtext read "Declared sane three years after smothering her baby'. The woman was unrecognizable. On top of the newspaper was a handwritten note that read, *"Tell me how much you want. I will meet you by the stature of the bear in Paddington Station at three on Tuesday and will bring the money to you."*

Elspeth carefully put these papers back in their envelope. Next, she opened the smaller packet. A brooch of gold with emeralds set in the art deco style fell from its tissue paper wrapping. Elspeth did not need to be told what it was, but it posed a dilemma for her. The evidence in the first envelope was traceable. Princess Honorée's brooch was not, unless one was intimately acquainted with the royal family. Elspeth stared at the brooch, and then slowly slipped it into her pocket.

Now what should she do with the key from Room 17? Her first thought was to slip it on to the key rack inside the door of the secure room. Looking at the assortment on the rack, Elspeth assumed that they were the keys to the boxes not being used by guests. She was about to hang up Room 17's key when she noticed that the key in her hand had been blackened in the fire and so would therefore stand out among its neighbours, which were clean and bright. She thought of going back to Room 17 and replacing the key where she had found it, but she had no idea if the police had secured the scene. More than likely they had. Finding no quick solution to her problem, she slipped the key back in her pocket.

When Elspeth returned to the lobby, Cynthia was helping a guest check out. Elspeth walked behind her, held up the key Cynthia had given her and placed it on the counter, and she mouthed 'thank you'. Cynthia turned and gave an idolising smile.

Nine o'clock was approaching and Elspeth became acutely aware she had not rung the princess, nor had she dressed for the day. She hastened back to her rooms, made quick phone contact with Princess Honorée, and begged for a half an hour to dress. At nine-thirty, fully prepared for her day with the guests in the bungalow, Elspeth presented herself at their gates, the brooch tucked safely away in her room safe. Only after the gates were open to her did she remember that she had not called the prince about Princess Christiana's scheduled arrival time.

18

Princess Honorée met Elspeth at the gate, which was unexpected.

"Please come to my rooms," she said, "before the others know you're here." The princess was swathed in a gold brocade dressing gown that seemed too heavy for Bermuda's climate, but which accentuated her royal status. Her hair was faultlessly arranged, and her makeup applied with skill. She wore high-heeled sandals with pointed toes, which were fashionable at the moment but made Elspeth's feet hurt just looking at them.

Elspeth followed her into the silvery haven of her bedroom suite and took the seat she was offered on a white rattan chair. Little had changed in the room since Elspeth had last been there, but the flowers were fresh and there was an urn of coffee and some rolls and fresh fruit on the sideboard. Elspeth accepted a cup of coffee from the princess, who seemed agitated and kept tugging at the tasselled belt of her dressing gown. "What have you heard about the fire? Was it Martin Hagen? Am I finally rid of him?"

Elspeth shook her head. "As yet the body has not been identified, but all the circumstantial evidence points to it being him. The police will have to get dental records or a DNA report from the UK for positive proof because the body was burned beyond recognition. But, Princess, I don't think you need to worry any longer. I've found the brooch, and I'll see that you get it back soon. What you chose to do with it after that will be your own decision."

The princess pressed her lips together and looked up at Elspeth. "May I ask how you discovered where it was??"

"I'd prefer not to tell you," Elspeth said. "Let's just say that it belongs to you and not to the person who had it." Then she took a long swallow of coffee.

The princess's face flooded with relief. "Is there any way I can thank you?"

"By simply never mentioning what I have just told you. The brooch has already caused far too much harm. I suggest when I give it to you that you hide it away for a long time to come."

"But where?"

"In plain sight, in your jewellery box until you return home. Or perhaps give it to Hope. I assume she doesn't know its history. Find some excuse."

"Ms Duff, are you always so . . . devious?"

"Devious? I want to protect you. As long as the brooch was in someone else's possession . . ." She did not finish.

"Will you get in any trouble?" the princess asked.

Elspeth raised an eyebrow and suppressed a grin. "I hope not, but I consider it a risk worth taking. As far as I know, only we two know who had the brooch, and that person is no longer here to protest his loss."

Princess Honorée closed her eyes and tears slid down her cheeks and into the corners of her mouth. She wiped them with the back of her beautifully manicured hand. "Elspeth," she said and then paused, "You have taken a great burden off my mind, and you have saved me and my daughter from more pain. I would like to repay you in any way I can."

"Perhaps it seems a small thing, Princess, but listen to your daughter's heart and not her words when she arrives."

The princess cocked her head and frowned.

"Your daughter is young and has obviously been foolish," Elspeth continued. "You could tell her that you now have access to the brooch, although I beg you not to tell her the circumstances. Just the thought that the brooch will soon be returned to its rightful owner may change her feelings towards her earlier rashness and your attempt to help her. From what I have heard of your daughter, she seems to be a bit impulsive. I can understand because I've been accused of the same thing."

The princess smiled, and Elspeth flushed, wondering if she had said too much. "Now I must see the prince about her arrival time. Do you know if he's up yet?" Elspeth asked.

"I believe he's having breakfast with Mary."

Elspeth laid down her cup, thanked the Princess for the coffee and left the room silently. She did not look back. She had no idea if she had helped the cause of Princess Christiana or not.

She found the prince, Mary, and Hope in the dining room. The prince was serving himself from the breakfast buffet, Hope was taking up her napkin from one of the places set at the table, and Mary was sipping a cup of tea. An uncomfortable silence lay over them.

Hope looked up. "Elspeth, we missed you last evening. I congratulate you, however, in the change you have brought about in Richard. I've never seen him so relaxed and happy."

Elspeth did not want the conversation to focus on Richard, or on herself, so she simply smiled and said, "Yes. It has been quite wonderful for both of us. I was sorry not to have joined you last evening, but with the fire . . ." She let them form their own conclusions.

The prince took his place at the table and started spreading butter and jam on a piece of toast. He seemed to be ignoring Elspeth and Hope's conversation. Hope motioned for Elspeth to take whatever she wished from the sideboard, but Elspeth settled for another cup of coffee. How many breakfasts could she eat?

She decided to address the issue of Princess Christiana's arrival. "Your Highness, is the princess still scheduled to be here tomorrow morning?" she asked without preface.

He put down his toast. "I've not heard otherwise," he said, and resumed his breakfast.

"Are your plans still intact?"

He nodded, and then turned to his eggs and bacon. Elspeth took a long sip of her coffee and then cleared her throat before voicing her concerns.

"Are you all comfortable with your various roles?"

Hope looked up and appeared to be puzzled.

The prince frowned. "Hope and Francis have nothing to do with our plans for my daughter. Will you excuse us, Hope?" His tone was imperious. She left the breakfast room with her plate only half finished. Elspeth was not quite sure what the dynamics among the three people in the room were, but she felt Hope was annoyed with her brother-in-law and was put out by her dismissal. Hope looked at her daughter, but Mary was suddenly completely absorbed in her cup of tea. After Hope's departure, Mary rose and selected an orange from the fruit bowl. She returned to the table and slowly began to peel the fruit, dividing its flesh into sections. She glanced over at her uncle, as if expecting something from him. He did not seem to notice.

Elspeth watched the two of them and tried to assess what their feelings were towards each other. She guessed that Mary was not overawed by the prince, but also suspected the he did not have the least inkling of this. He attacked a rasher with relish before addressing Elspeth's concerns.

"Nothing has changed. Do you still plan to be on the beach? It's not necessary," he said.

Mary took up a section of her orange. "I think it's a good idea, Uncle Michael. You shouldn't go outside the compound, and, if anything goes wrong, Ms Duff can phone for help."

"What possibly could go wrong?" he said, looking at Mary as if she were a child. "We've thought of every eventuality."

Elspeth judiciously studied her coffee. Always have a Plan B, she thought to herself, but obviously the prince was so used to getting his way that he felt that fall-back arrangements were not necessary. He took up the newspaper that was lying at his place and opened it in front of them. Their conversation was obviously over. Elspeth's eye caught a stop press at the corner of the front page. "Tropical Storm growing in the western Atlantic." There was a small map that Elspeth could not see clearly without her reading glasses, which were back in her suite. She made a mental note to find a copy of the paper when she left the bungalow. She looked up and caught Mary staring in her direction.

"Mary, let's go out to the beach together," she said.

The prince grunted and went back to his paper. Mary raised an eyebrow and glanced at him. Soon afterwards the two women left the dining room and the prince to his meal.

Elspeth walked beside Mary as they crossed the beach to the water's edge. The tide was flowing out. Mary leaned over and picked up a sea snail, which promptly withdrew into its shell.

"Smart creature," she said. "He has a built-in fortress he can retreat into at will. It's a shame we humans don't have similar defences."

"Perhaps we do, Mary. Some cultures, like the Chinese, find their own privacy while surrounded by the masses of humanity around them. Unfortunately our culture, particularly among the youth in the twenty-first century, glories in full disclosure. Bare it all!"

Mary, who was scantily clad, smiled. "Do we? I suppose all our exposed flesh is another way of hiding, you know. People look at your body, but they do not see your mind or your heart. I think the way we dress is more a diversion from our true feelings and thoughts than an exposé of them. Look at the photos of Christie. Is she flaunting that she loves Harald? She does, you know, love him. Desperately. That's why she's demanding he be present at the family contretemps."

"Does he know?"

"Quite frankly he's clueless about her real feelings toward him, which is one reason Christie loves him. He stumbles about, loving her, feeling unworthy, bending to the family opposition and yet never wavering in how he feels towards her. I'm making him sound like rather a wimp, but he's not. He is brilliant in his field and as an academic has a magnificent chance of becoming a don or even the head of a college at Oxford or Cambridge. Among normal mortals, he would be any parents' dream of a match for their daughter. But instead he has fallen hopelessly in love with a princess, even if she is one from a minor kingdom."

"And the princess?"

"Christie's hopes are as convoluted as his. If she were not a Princess, the nuptials would have taken place long ago, and they would now be settled in academic bliss. Ms Duff, this whole thing with Ali Ayan is Christie's way of pleading with her parents to let her marry Harald."

"You implied that earlier," Elspeth said. "Affairs of the heart, no matter at what age, are never simple." She did not elaborate. Instead she asked, "Mary, have you talked to your cousin since she boarded the yacht?"

"Yes, several times."

"What is her mood?"

"I'm not sure. I would say defiant, and then

again, hopeful."

"Do you think the princess could be happy with Harald at Oxford or Cambridge, tending to the needs of undergraduates at one of the colleges? You know, that's one of the tasks of the wife of a don or head of college."

Mary walked along beside Elspeth for a long way before replying. "I think she would like nothing better in life."

"Will you support her in this?"

"Yes, Ms Duff, with all my heart."

"Then I wish the princess good fortune tomorrow. I'll see you on the beach before six."

"You bet," Mary said and turned back towards the bungalow

19

When Elspeth reached her suite, her room phone was ringing. She faltered before picking the handset up. Her close contacts all had her mobile phone number and would have rung her using it. She reluctantly gave in to the phone's demand.

"Elspeth Duff here," she said shortly.

"Ms Duff?" a man's voice said at the other end of the line. People seldom listened when one answered the phone. "DCI Hart."

Elspeth was tempted to say, "Is that Chief Inspector Hart?" but she restrained herself from the temptation of impertinence. She knew she must not give in to her earlier feelings of annoyance at the policeman.

"Yes, Chief Inspector," she said instead.

"You have asked that we not come to the hotel, but things have come to light that make it necessary for me to speak to you. Therefore, I'm going to ask you to come here."

"I would prefer that. Do you have any new information on the post mortem?"

"On the victim, yes, but also your activities."

"Shall we say in an hour?" Elspeth said, attempting to establish superiority, but caught off guard by his last comment.

"No, Ms Duff. We are only ten minutes' drive from your hotel. I will see you in half an hour."

This gave Elspeth little time to prepare for her visit. She picked up her mobile and pressed the stored number for Kit Lord.

"Are you in your office?" she asked when he answered. "I need to talk to you as soon as possible."

"No, but I can be there in two minutes."

"I'll meet you there."

Kit was waiting for Elspeth as she came into the security building. He held the door to his office open and followed her in.

"Why do the police want to see me?"

He turned his eyes away from hers. "I've just returned from the police station," he said. "They're asking questions about the night of the fire, but also about your activities yesterday morning. Apparently the fireman on duty reported that you had gone into Room 17 alone the morning after the fire."

"Did you confirm that?"

"I couldn't lie."

"What else did the Inspector ask you?"

"What your relationship was with Michael Hagen."

"What did you tell him?"

Kit was obviously uncomfortable. "They asked me if you had any 'negative experiences', I think those were his words, with Mr Hagen."

"What did you say?"

"I felt I had to tell him the truth."

"What truth?"

"That he had threatened you."

"I see. Did you tell him the reason for the threat?"

"No. Since I wasn't present when Mr Hagen met you, I couldn't give him any details."

"Did you mention why I was in Bermuda?"

"I didn't think that was relevant to Michael Hagen or the fire."

"Thank you for that," Elspeth said, hoping her voice did not sound sarcastic. Kit Lord, if he were to rise in the Kennington Organisation Security Department, would have to develop more tactical ways of dealing with police enquiries. Bleating out the truth was one thing; answering discreetly another.

"What else did he ask you?"

To his credit, Kit now looked disconcerted. "He asked if you had tried to tamper with any evidence."

"And what did you answer?"

"I felt I had to tell him about your going into the safety deposit boxes. Cynthia told me you had."

Elspeth winced. Kit's naïveté was perhaps a quality he might be able to overcome in time but at the moment it presented huge problems for her. He, of course, had no idea why she had gone into Room 17's safety deposit box or that she had removed the brooch. Elspeth knew when the chief inspector questioned her, she would be hard pressed not to tell the truth, but she had to think of ways to skirt the issue. She looked at her watch. She had twelve minutes before her interview with DCI Hart, and she wanted to be on time. There was no reason to aggravate him this early in his investigation.

Elspeth left Kit's office with a brief nod and said, "I'll let you know how it goes when I talk to the chief inspector. I'm due at the police station in a few minutes."

As she walked in the police station, her mind swirled. She knew she would have to answer the DCI with as much truth as his questions demanded, but also with as much evasion as necessary to protect the guests of the hotel and particularly the royal party. Her training in the law and later experiences as a private detective had equipped her with the ability to state honesty what had transpired but to leave out pieces of the truth that were not directly requested. She knew that she might have an advantage over DCI Hart, and she meant to use it. Richard had many times accused her of being devious. The princess had said so as well. In this case that quality might serve her well, although she did not intend to lie outright. Sophisticated twists when reporting on reality could serve her well if only she stayed focused on the chief inspector's questions and did not tell him more than he asked for directly. She knew this was a technique used by lawyers, and certainly a useful one.

The DCI kept her waiting for twenty minutes. Elspeth sat back on the hard chair she had been offered in the corridor and tried hard not to feel provoked, but she was thoroughly irritated when she was at last shown into his office. Only her good breeding and need to maintain her position of calmness kept her from showing her indignation, as she was certain the inspector had purposely kept her waiting. She made her mouth smile although she did not feel any pleasure inside.

"Ah, Ms Duff," he said, as if she had dropped by casually. "I'm a busy man and hope I didn't keep you waiting long. But, after my discussion this morning with Mr Lord from your hotel, I felt it necessary to ask you a few questions. You know, of course, that the body found in Room 17 was killed by a gunshot that entered the back of his skull, and therefore we are dealing with murder. We don't have many murders here in Bermuda, particularly of foreigners, and consequently, we take those that happen very seriously. You've asked that we stay out of your hotel, but I fear if I don't get straight answers from you, I will have to obtain a search warrant. I'm sure you'll give us your full cooperation." His implication made Elspeth cautious.

"What would you like to know, Chief Inspector?" She hoped she sounded cooperative although he was carefully watching her.

"I understand that you were at the scene of the fire two nights ago."

Elspeth nodded. "Yes, I was there most of the

night."

"When did you first become aware of the fire?"

"When the alarms went off," she said.

"And where were you when that happened?"

"I had retired for the evening and was asleep in bed in my suite."

"Were you alone?"

She flushed. "I beg your pardon, Chief Inspector. What possible bearing does that have on the fire?"

"Were you?"

"No, I wasn't." She did not elaborate.

"I understand you had spent the evening with a man and another couple at the Waterloo Restaurant and had a large meal and several bottles of wine."

"We dined at the restaurant, as you already know. It wasn't a raucous affair, but rather a party with old friends."

"Were these old friends staying at the Kennington Bermuda?"

"My companion was." Elspeth knew this was a partial evasion of the truth since she did not mention the Tildens.

"Was it he who you were sharing a bed with when the alarms went off?"

Elspeth's annoyance grew. "Yes, Chief Inspector, it was. He's my husband." She wanted to add a caustic remark but held back.

"Does Mr Duff always accompany you when you are working, Ms Duff?"

She did not correct his misuse of Richard's name. "My husband had a break in his work schedule and decided to come to Bermuda for a few days."

"So on hearing the alarm, you left him in bed and went out to see about the fire."

"That's correct."

"What did you do when you left the room?"

"All members of the hotel security staff are trained on a regular basis as to what to do if there's a fire. Our major concern is the safety of the guests. Mr Lord and the night manager were seeing that the guests were evacuated to the beach, so Mr Lord asked me to investigate the location of the fire. I was concerned that the fire be contained as quickly as possible."

"Did you know that there was someone in the room where the fire started?"

"I had no idea, but it was always a possibility. Room 17 was in the smokers' wing of the hotel. Smokers do fall asleep sometimes before extinguishing their cigarettes. I thought this was the most likely explanation."

"You did?" The inspector sounded suspicious.

"Yes," she said defiantly.

"You didn't go to Room 17 before that, did you?"

Elspeth was caught off guard at his question.

"No, inspector. Why would you assume I had?"

"I understand you and the guest staying in Room 17 had words earlier." He looked smug.

"If you mean Mr Hagen, yes, we did."

"Tell me what passed between you."

Damn Kit, Elspeth thought. He didn't need to tell the Chief Inspector about her confrontation with Martin Hagen.

"Chief Inspector, my job with the Kennington Organisation is to see that all our guests enjoy their stay without any interference from other guests. As you can imagine, because our guests pay a great deal to stay at a Kennington hotel, most of them are well-heeled, and as such are sometimes targeted by people who wish to defraud them. The security staff is constantly vigilant to see that such things don't happen. Mr Hagen seemed to be one of the predators. I'd crossed him once before at another of our hotels and had put him on what we call our 'watch list'."

"Did he know this?"

"I have no idea."

"When was this?"

"About six or seven years ago, as I remember. When I got to the Kennington Bermuda on this trip, Mr Lord mentioned this to me, although I had little or no memory of Mr Hagen, or the reason I'd tagged his name earlier."

"I expect he recognised you. You're not a person to be overlooked when you come into a room."

Elspeth wasn't certain if this was compliment or not.

The chief inspector continued, "So Mr Hagen approached you. What did he want?"

Elspeth knew that the policeman could go on whittling information from her bit by bit, so she decided to give a brief version of what happened on the night that Richard came to Bermuda.

"He had seen my husband arrive. It was quite late, probably sometime after eleven. I hadn't expected him, my husband, I mean, so I asked to have my rooms readied for him. As we waited, we wandered out on the beach and . . ." she groped for an appropriate word, ". . . and greeted each other, eh, rather lovingly, shall we say. We have only been married a short time and were perhaps a bit . . . incautious. Mr Hagen must have seen us, because the next day he accused me of bringing a man into my room for immoral reasons. Mr Hagen threatened to go to Lord Kennington with this information if I didn't arrange for his hotel bill to be either cancelled or accommodated."

"Did you tell him the truth about who the man was?"

"No. It shouldn't have been his business who came to or went from my rooms. I simply asked him to leave the hotel the following morning, after he had paid his bill in full. I have that authority."

"What you are telling me is that he tried to blackmail you."

"That's exactly what I am telling you, Chief Inspector. Mr Hagen tried to blackmail me, although he had no basis on which to do so. I knew I had to do everything possible to have him removed from the hotel in case he decided to approach any of the guests in the same manner. We are very protective of our guests, as I have just explained."

"Did you have any concrete evidence that he was blackmailing others in the hotel?"

Elspeth knew she needed to treat lightly around this subject. "Not at the time."

The chief inspector saw through her evasion. "And afterwards?"

"Mr Lord has probably already told you this, but we reviewed the security tapes for the night of the fire, particularly those located near the smokers' wing where Mr Hagen's room was located. On the night of the fire a woman visited his room. I suspect, Chief Inspector, that if we could identify this woman, we would know who shot the occupant of Room 17 and set the fire. Unfortunately, when Mr Lord and I reviewed the tapes, we weren't able to see anything but the top of her hat."

"Could it have been a man?"

"I think not. The posture was wrong."

"I sense you're a keen observer, Ms Duff, and must use this talent when protecting the guests in your hotels. Nevertheless I'll be issuing a warrant for those tapes."

Elspeth's mind rushed back to the tapes and their graininess. She was almost certain that the princess could not be identified, but there was the complication of Lilianne Balfour having said she had seen the princess. Had her suspicion been sufficiently allayed by

Elspeth introducing Hope Tilden at dinner the night of the fire? Lilianne Balfour was not easily distracted, and Elspeth wondered how much her deception had worked. A woman of Lilianne's background would probably have noticed that the woman who furtively crossed the lawn on succeeding nights had a different hairstyle from her twin even though they were identical in many other ways.

"I'll see if Mr Lord can resurrect the tape of the night of the fire. Kennington guidelines recommends we delete the tapes after forty-eight hours," Elspeth said. She did not mention that the Kennington Bermuda had been lax, and the tapes of earlier nights still were intact and showed more than one woman going to Martin Hagen's room.

Elspeth rose as if she now had fully imparted what she had come to say, but was brought short by the chief inspector. "I am not finished," he said slowly.

She made her mouth smile and focused her eyes on the wall beyond him.

"Really, Chief Inspector? I don't know what else I can add," she said with feigned innocence.

"Why did you go into the safety deposit box room on the morning after the fire?"

Elspeth considered her position. How far could she twist the truth in order to deny her having taken the key from the fire scene and her need to protect the princess? She eventually would have to admit to the former, but she had no intention of revealing the presence of the brooch in Martin Hagen's box. Making a hasty decision to tell only half the truth, she said, "I found a safety deposit key in Room 17 when I went there after the fire was extinguished. As you know, the fire was still considered an accident and the death of the occupant an unfortunate result of it. None of us knew a crime had been committed."

"But you already suspected Mr Hagen was a

blackmailer."

"He had tried to threaten me, but I suspect he had negative feelings towards me because of the last time we had met at a Kennington hotel. His so-called 'blackmail' could easily have been retribution for my earlier actions against him."

"Weren't you curious to see if he had anything in the safety deposit box that might incriminate you or one of your guests?"

"I think I've already told you that there was nothing he could substantiate that would force me to wipe off his hotel expenses, or pay them."

"How much did he owe?"

"About six thousand pounds," Elspeth said. The amount seemed reasonable to her, but she could see the DCI's eyes widen.

"Six thousand pounds. That's a large sum of money."

"He had been at the hotel for four days," she said as if to justify the bill. From the DCI's expression, she knew that the rates at a Kennington hotel were probably well beyond anything he could have imagined. "I think you might now understand how necessary it is for us to protect our guests. They pay a great deal of money to stay at the hotel and be cosseted," she said.

"Indeed," the DCI said, clearing his throat.

Elspeth had hoped she had satisfied the inspector's curiosity about the safety deposit box, but she was wrong.

"What did you find in the box?" he asked directly.

"Not a great deal," she said. "A few newspaper clippings and some letters. None of these papers meant anything to me." She did not mention the brooch.

"And did you leave these papers where you found them?"

"Of course. They weren't mine to take."

The DCI leaned over his desk. "Did you remove anything that incriminated you, Ms Duff?"

"Absolutely not," she said indignantly. "Martin Hagen may have wished to blackmail me, but he had no grounds to do so."

"You are sure?"

"Inspector, you may examine the box yourself. I already know you will, but rest assured, I removed none of the papers from the box." This was literally true.

"Are you planning to leave Bermuda soon?"

This placed Elspeth in a dilemma. Her assignment would be finished when the royal party had concluded their business at the hotel. If Princess Christiana arrived on schedule the following morning and if the family confrontation took place shortly after that, they well might leave the day after tomorrow. When her job was over, she would return to London as soon as possible, but she did not want to admit this to the policeman.

"I've an open ticket and can leave at any time," she said.

"I suggest that you stay until we find Martin Hagen's murderer. At this point, I can't force you to do so. I only recommend that you take seriously what happened at the hotel two nights ago. You may return there now, Ms Duff, but I will stay in touch."s

Elspeth emerged into the sunlight with her head held high and a look of slight disdain on her face, but her heart was beating more quickly than usual. The DCI was more skilled than he let on. His questioning was sharp, and his manner lay somewhere between straightforwardness and latent hostility. Elspeth couldn't judge the success of her attempts to conceal information, but she knew she would have to teach Kit Lord the technique of not giving information to the police which they had not requested. She especially needed to warn him about releasing the security tapes for the nights before the fire. She had planted the idea in the DCI's mind that security tapes were destroyed after forty-eight hours, although they had not been, and she hoped he would take her word that this was routine and had been done on the nights previous to Martin Hagen's murder, although she had not directly said so. She did not feel she could justify erasing the tapes now, but their existence did not need to be dangled in front of the police.

When Elspeth entered the lobby, she asked for Kit Lord, but was told it was his half-day off. Perhaps because when Elspeth was on a job she did not have any time off and had to catch moments of relaxation when she could, or perhaps because she was irritated because of the DCI's treatment of her, she was unjustifiably annoyed. How often did a Kennington hotel have a murder on its premises? Infrequently, although Elspeth had been involved in several over the course of her career with the Kennington Organisation. Each case was carefully handled, and the hotel's involvement kept from the press whenever possible. Elspeth asked for Kit's assistant, who proved to be an eager young man who admitted he was a trainee and who seemed overawed by Elspeth's presence. She directed him to secure the tapes and make a copy of the one outside Room 17 on the night of the fire and asked him to have them kept for her. Exhausted after her morning at the police station, she went to her room, ordered a late lunch and lay down on her sofa to take stock of what had just happened and to decide what to do next. As she waited for her lunch, she tried to formulate what to say in her report to Eric Kennington. He already knew of the pathologist's report because Elspeth had conveyed this information by secure e-mail to him earlier, but she had not received any direction from him on how to proceed.

She could hear his words, so often spoken, 'Elspeth, that is why I pay you such an outrageous salary. I leave the details in your capable hands'. Elspeth's predicament, of course, was that she had not told Eric about the brooch and Martin Hagen's blackmailing the princess. She did not regret this omission, but it would make any interaction with him strained. She expected that at any moment she would get a call from him that transferred the responsibility for the murder investigation from Kit Lord to her. Eric would expect her to handle both her commitment to the royal party and the investigation as well. She made an instant decision. Picking up her mobile, she dialled Kit's private phone number and did not ask him but rather ordered him back to the hotel. She did not know if she had the authority to do so, but on the phone, she made it sound as if she did.

20

Kit Lord phoned Elspeth an hour later, breaking into her nap. She sat up abruptly at the sound of her mobile ringing.

"Elspeth, I need your help," he said, his tone diffident. "Can you come to the security office?"

"Give me ten minutes." She rose, put on her sandals, combed her hair, repaired her makeup and arrived at Kit's office at the time promised. His face was ashen even through his tan. Surely Elspeth's demand was too mild to cause this change in him.

"What is it, Kit?"

"The room service staff just went into Lilianne Balfour's room. They discovered her body lying on the floor by her bed. She's been shot."

"How?" said Elspeth without expression.

"How?"

"Yes, how? Where was she shot? In the head, neck, heart? Is she dead or merely wounded?"

"Will you come with me to her room?" Kit sounded as if he were asking Elspeth to do something that she would refuse to do. "The room attendant who found her thought she was dead. There had been a 'Do Not Disturb' sign on the door since early last night."

"I see. Have you been there?"

"No. I called you when I heard. I thought we should go together."

Elspeth's eyes rested on Kit's face, which froze under her gaze. He noticeably gulped. "I'm not accustomed to crime scenes," he said. "I thought you could help me." His plea fell somewhere between pathos and desperation.

Elspeth softened her position. "Death is never easy, Kit. It's something you'll have to deal with at times. People do die in hotels, although usually from some pre-existing condition or sudden illness. I'm sure you have seen the policy papers on this. Murder, however, is different. It happens so seldom that we have to deal with it on a case-by-case basis. We don't know yet whether Mrs Balfour died by her own hand or by foul play. I think we need go to her room and find out."

Elspeth had no more desire to go to Lilianne's room than she suspected Kit did, but she had had more experience in such matters than he had. If indeed Lilianne had died violently, Elspeth knew she would have to keep a stiff upper lip and not show what she was really feeling. She rose and put her hand on his shoulder. "Safety in numbers," she said, without believing it.

Lilianne Balfour's room was on the first floor at the end of the main wing of the hotel and looked out to the beach and ocean beyond. Elspeth and Kit climbed the open staircase and crossed the first-floor open gallery, finally reaching Lilianne's room, the last from the end. The 'Do Not Disturb' sign still hung on the door handle. Kit inserted his master key card and swallowing, opened the door for Elspeth.

Lilianne Balfour's body was sprawled on the floor beside the queen-sized bed. Her position was awkward. Her right hand was flung out above her head, and just beyond it lay a small, pearl handled pistol. Her dressing gown had come open, and she was wearing a satin nightgown which Elspeth guessed came from an expensive boutique. Her lacquered hair was slightly off kilter but had stayed intact. She was fully made up, lipstick and mascara still in place. Her face was frozen in repose, revealing nothing of her last moments, and her eyelids were drawn down over her eyes. The only defect in her appearance was a small hole in her right temple ringed with a crust of dried blood.

Kit leaned against the wall and looked sick. Elspeth wondered if he had ever seen a dead body this close up before. No one, and she counted herself among them, encountered dead bodies that had met with a violent end without feeling revulsion. Repeated experience did not help, if Elspeth's numerous conversations with pathologists were true. She felt the contents of her own stomach rise as she approached Lilianne's body. Kit looked green, leaned against the wall and made a hasty retreat into the bathroom. Elspeth could hear him retching, as she had done the first time she had seen a murder victim when she worked at Scotland Yard many years before. He reappeared several minutes later and apologised.

"Kit, we all have had similar responses, and you probably will again, if there is a next time. The first time is the worst. I think it would be best if you went down to your office and called DCI Hart. Ask him to bring the pathologist and a member of the crime scene investigative squad. Make sure he meets you at the back entry to the kitchen. He won't like that but be insistent. If you come up the service stairs, no one will notice, I hope. Keep as low a profile as possible. It's the middle of the afternoon and few people should be milling around."

After Kit left, Elspeth took a throw from the back of the small sofa and used it to cover Lilianne Balfour's body. The blanket was not quite long enough and Lilianne's sandal-shod feet extended beyond it. Elspeth then turned from the body and rummaged in her pocket for her mobile. Contending with the police would be difficult but telling Lord Kennington of the second murder in one of his newest hotels, particularly one that was launching his new resort program, would be devastating. Elspeth racked her brain for the right words before she touched the speed dial for Eric Kennington's secure number. Normally Pamela Crumm was her buffer in difficult situations, but Eric had explicitly kept Pamela from knowing the details of Elspeth's current assignment. Elspeth's next hope was that he would be occupied and would not answer her call, but she was disappointed.

"Elspeth," he said, "what now?" His mood was obviously sour.

She swallowed. "There had been another complication here," she said.

"Which is?" he said, annoyance filling his voice.

"Another guest has died."

"Died? How?" Eric was not a man of many words when confronted with a problem at one of his hotels.

"She died from a bullet wound in her temple."

"Suicide?"

"I don't know, but I doubt it."

"Why?"

"There's no powder residue. Eric, I'm not a pathologist, but even an amateur reader of whodunits knows that shots close up produce powder burns."

"Are the police there?"

"Not yet, but I've instructed Kit Lord to get them."

"Elspeth, I find it untenable that the minute I send you to Bermuda on what would seem to be a benign assignment, suddenly there are two suspicious deaths at the hotel." His tone was accusatory.

"Eric, I . . ." she floundered.

"Take care of it! Call me when you have finished doing so, and don't involve the parties in your initial assignment in any way whatsoever. They are to remain completely isolated and are not to be told about this new death." His words were an order. He rang off before she could protest. This was not the first time she wondered if the high salary given to her by the Kennington Organisation was worth the effort that it took to earn it.

She looked down at Lilianne's body, now partially covered by the throw. Who had she been? She had masqueraded as General William 'Bill' Balfour's wife, even intimating he was with her at the hotel, but evidence suggested she was his daughter and that he had died forty years before when she must have been a child. Why did she need to falsify her background? Elspeth needed to deal with the police first, but then she wanted to check if Lilianne was on the frequent guest list at the Kennington hotels, and if she had used the same ruse before? If so, why?

Elspeth knew she had only a few minutes to search the room before the police arrived. She needed to disguise her prying as much as possible, but she did not have a handkerchief in her pocket. With this in mind, she went into the bathroom and found a small towel. Encasing her hand in this she systematically began to go through Lilianne's suitcases, which lay open on the luggage rack and on the second bed. Most of the clothes were tropical weight, but there was a woollen trouser suit and a cashmere jumper, which indicated that Lilianne had come to Bermuda from a colder climate or was returning to one. In the dressing room Elspeth eyed a woollen coat with gloves stuffed into the pockets, further indication of Lilianne's previous location or future destination. On the dressing table in the bathroom, Elspeth found a large vanity case holding numerous cosmetics of varying hues and several bottles of medications. She recognised two of them, one being a sleep pill and another a common prescription painkiller. She returned to the bedroom and found a telephone pad and pen, which she used to take down the names of the other medications. She shoved the pad and pencil in the pocket of her jacket and proceeded on with her search. So far nothing she had found seemed to incriminate

Lilianne of any nefarious activity. Elspeth emptied the contents of Lilianne's large Prada bag on the undisturbed bed. She saw the usual contents of a woman's handbag, cosmetics, a French purse with over eighty dollars in American and Bermudian banknotes, a packet of tissues, a pen, a credit card case, several receipts from local shops, an address book, a set of keys, and her passport. This last item revealed that her name was Lilly Anne Cissy Balfour, her nationality American, and it only had a few immigration stamps, the document being issued only three months before. It was a rarity that modern day guests did not have a mobile phone, but Elspeth did not find one in the room or handbag. She made a mental note to have a log made of the telephone calls Lilianne had placed on the hotel phone since arriving at the hotel.

Next Elspeth made an inventory of the dressing room. Lilianne seemed to have anticipated a variety of activities in Bermuda, and her wardrobe reflected this. Clothing included sports outfits, fluffy afternoon dresses, and formal wear. She had several sun hats and a variety of shoes ranging from trainers to sandals to smart high heels. All the clothes were expensive but probably ready to wear. Elspeth examined the labels, which showed that Lilianne had shopped primarily in New York, London, and Paris.

Elspeth returned to the main room and quickly placed the contents of Lilianne's handbag back into the Prada bag. She did stop long enough to take note of the address on Lilianne's driving license, listed as Fredericksburg, Virginia. She hurriedly finished reloading Lilianne's handbag because she heard footsteps coming up the staircase from the kitchen. The police were arriving and none too silently. Elspeth quickly returned the hand towel to the bathroom, straightened her hair in the mirror and went to the door.

As they entered the room DCI Hart did not look pleased, and Kit Lord appeared as if he would prefer to disappear into thin air. The pathologist, an older man with crinkled grey hair and deep wrinkles, seemed interested only in the form under the throw. A willowy young man behind the others was carrying a large case, which he put on the floor beside the body and drew out a video camera. Elspeth doubted he had ever been at a murder scene before because he paled under his dark skin when the pathologist drew back the covering from Lilianne's body, but she gave him marks because he came forward with the camera and followed the pathologist's instructions with great precision.

DCI Hart drew Elspeth and Kit aside.

"I can't stay out of your hotel now. One death by foul play is bad enough, but two leaves us no option but to start our own investigation of your guests. Ms Duff and Mr Lord, I expect your full cooperation," he said, turning from one of them to the other.

Elspeth stepped forward, pre-empting any assistance Kit might offer.

"Chief Inspector, I've been in contact with our head offices in London and have been put in charge of the investigation here, thus freeing Mr Lord for his other duties. Again, I must insist that our guests not be disturbed unless you have direct evidence that they were involved in the deaths of Mrs Balfour and Mr Hagen, since by now there can be no doubt who the victim in the fire was. Kit, please find us a corner in the security office where the Chief Inspector and I may work, preferably somewhere where others can't hear us."

Elspeth could not be certain how Kit Lord felt about being taken out of the investigation. On her own part, she now felt in control, but could she direct the DCI's attention away from the guests in the bungalow? She was well aware that if the DCI were given free rein, he soon would come upon the presence of the royal guests, particularly if he further investigated the identities of the women on the security tapes. Elspeth had not yet reviewed the tapes recorded the night before outside of Lilianne's room and began devising ways to see them before the police demanded them.

Elspeth smiled her most professional smile. "Chief Inspector, I'm sure we can find a way not to disturb the guests, and together we can gather all the information you need in another way. Let me know what you require, and then give me time to assemble what you need."

DCI Hart raised his eyebrows, as if questioning the extent of Elspeth's cooperation. "I'll need to see a list of all your guests at the hotel."

"I can provide that," Elspeth said with a steady voice. Inwardly she was grateful that the royal party did not appear in the hotel register. "And?"

"I'll want to see the videos from the camera in the upper hall outside of Mrs Balfour's room. I saw one when we came up the stairs."

"I'll see that you get a copy."

"I also want to find out what the relationship between Mr Hagen and Mrs Balfour was."

'So do I,' thought Elspeth, 'but I want to find out before you, Chief Inspector', but instead she said, "We all do."

"I also want to find out which of the guests had connections to one or both of the victims."

"That may prove more difficult. I'll see what I can discover and let you know."

"No. Ms Duff. This is something we will discover together."

Elspeth's mind raced as she tried to find some way to divert his attention before she had a chance to review the tapes.

"Relationships between guests in hotels are

usually casual, and we have no way of confirming them." Elspeth knew she was stonewalling the DCI and suspected he knew it too.

He stared at Elspeth, but she did not flinch.

"I expect your full cooperation, or I'll get a search warrant. I'm sure you would prefer to avoid this," he said.

"I would," she responded. "Chief Inspector, I'll let you continue your work here." She checked her watch, seeing it was three o'clock. "Meet me at the front desk at four and we can go back to the security office. I'm grateful that you're wearing plain clothes today, and ask that when you come to the hotel in the future you continue to do so."

"I want to finish here first. Let's set our appointment for four-thirty," he said.

"All right," she replied, grateful that she had an extra half hour.

When Elspeth left the room, she felt her exchanges with the DCI equally balanced the power play between them. She also felt he was as aware of this as she was. DCI Hart was no fool, and Elspeth knew she had to remember this in dealing with him.

Elspeth descended the stairs slowly, feeling tremendously conflicted. She had been neglecting the guests in the bungalow, but by doing so, she had been trying to protect them. She was torn between walking over to the bungalow and explaining her absence or going directly to the security office where she could review last night's CCTV images before DCI Hart arrived. The tapes seemed more important, so she took her mobile from her pocket and dialled the number for the bungalow. Francis Tilden answered. Elspeth tried to recall how much the occupants of the bungalow might have learned about the murders. The princess, of course, was aware that Martin Hagen was dead, but were the others?

Elspeth took a risk. "Francis, I want you to make sure that no one from the bungalow goes out into the hotel grounds. Your presence here had become even more sensitive than it already is, and, as you know, I've been charged by Lord Kennington to keep you out of the public and the police's eyes. May I ask your help in doing this?"

"What do you want me to do?"

"Just stay put."

"What about tomorrow morning? I know things are afoot"

"Tell the prince I'll be there. Mary can proceed as planned. When I'm on the beach, I can deflect any unwanted onlookers if necessary." Elspeth knew her words were optimistic.

"It sounds both you and Michael have a plan," Francis replied, "but you can rely on us as well."

Elspeth made her way to the security office and found a technician at the CCTV monitors. She smiled as Elspeth came in the room and then reached over for an envelope with Elspeth's name written out in capital letters. "It came in from London," the technician said. "I printed it out for you because I thought it would be easier to read."

Elspeth undid the clasp and pulled out the computer-generated sheets. She saw a list of the times Martin Hagen had visited Kennington hotels, eight visits in ten years. The computer had collated the guest lists at the times of his visits, looking for matches between any of the guests currently at the Bermuda hotel and Martin's other visits. Only one overlapped. Lilianne Balfour had been a guest at the Kennington hotels three out of the eight times that Martin Hagen had been at one, all of her visits being during the last two years. Here at last was the beginning of a possible the link between them. But what did it mean? Was Martin blackmailing Lilianne, and had he pursued her in each case? Her masquerading as the general's wife rather than his daughter might be the basis of blackmail, but Elspeth was still uncertain why Lilianne had perpetuated this deception.

"Can you get me access to London's security office?" she asked.

"Of course, Ms Duff. Here, use my workstation. I'll log you in."

Elspeth tapped in two questions to the central security office and sent it with the highest priority tag. Then she turned back to the technician. "I need to see last night's tapes from the cameras in the upper hallway of the main building."

The technician left the monitors and took Elspeth over to the central control console. "What time shall we start?"

"Start at five yesterday evening and fast forward so we can see when there was activity outside Room 121. The technician's skilled hands typed in a series of commands and the tape began to roll.

Between 17:00 and 20:30 guests went up and down the corridor to the gallery's staircase and disappeared quickly from view, obviously on their way to their rooms or to the gardens below. The tapes went blank until 21:15, when there suddenly was a flurry of activity. Lilianne Balfour came up the exterior staircase and tripped over the last step. She looked well into her cups, and drunkenly staggered towards the door to her room. She fumbled with her handbag, the same one Elspeth had examined, brought out her key card and tried to insert it in the slot. It took several attempts before she was successful. She entered her room and the camera went silent.

Shortly afterwards a woman in a hat entered the corridor and knocked on Lilianne's door.

"Zoom in on that woman," Elspeth said. The technician did as she was bidden.

"What do you see?" Elspeth asked.

"Just the hat, a floppy cloth one."

"No, pan down. What else do you see?"

Elspeth and the technician surveyed the video, frame-by-frame, zooming in on details, but there were few clues as to the mysterious woman's identity. She was dressed in a loose-fitting garment, much like a Hawaiian muumuu or loose-fitting caftan. Her garment covered her feet. Elspeth examined closely the hand that rapped on the door, but it was devoid of rings. The woman was not wearing any other jewellery, but she carried a small burgeoning handbag in her left hand.

"There might be something here," Elspeth murmured, more to herself than the technician. "Zoom in on the hands again."

The black and white images at this enlargement were fuzzy. All they could see were carefully manicured hands with grey toned nail lacquer. Pink or light red, thought Elspeth, looking at her own nails. She preferred the latter colour.

The tape did not record any further activity until twenty minutes later. The lady in the hat slipped from the door and made her way down the stairs from the gallery to the landing below. The handbag was draped over her arm but appeared to be slimmer than when she had entered the room. *Cherchez la femme.* But the tapes gave no indication other than a fine manicure as to who the woman was. Her identity remained shrouded under her hat.

Elspeth checked her watch and saw it was close to half-past four. DCI Hart would be arriving in the security office at any minute, if he were on time. She could not be sure of this, as Kit Lord had told her that an urgent need for punctuality in Bermuda did not match Lord Kennington's. She sat down in the chair in front of the central security monitor and tried to pull her thoughts together. The DCI would want copies of last night's tapes, and she instructed the technician to put them on to a memory stick, along with the ones from the night of the fire. Elspeth debated whether to tell the chief inspector the information about the overlap in Martin Hagen and Lilianne Balfour's visits at several of the Kennington hotels, but decided that she would not disclose this information until she was asked for it. She did not consider this an actual obstruction of justice, rather as a test of the DCI's acuity.

What else would the DCI ask to see? Her mind raced among the possibilities and landed abruptly on the safety deposit box. She had admitted to opening it and looking at its contents, but she had skirted the truth when describing everything in it. She had carefully and with forethought taken the brooch and saved it for Princess Honorée. Suddenly it dawned on her that the princess, like most women in the hotel, had worn a floppy hat to protect her from the sun and had done so when she and Elspeth had walked out on the beach together. Elspeth had not paid particular attention to the style of the princess's hat but remembered it was a generic broad-brimmed sunhat similar to her own. The princess was well-manicured and easily could have stripped her hands of any identifying rings. The loose-fitting clothing seemed incongruous, but what better disguise? Elspeth knew she had but a few minutes before the DCI arrived and so directed the technician back to the tapes of the night of the fire. Frame by frame they reviewed the activity of the woman entering Room 17. She wore the same hat and the same loose-fitting garment, and she was carrying the same bag.

Could the woman be the princess? She had said she had seen another woman enter Martin Hagen's room, but was she lying? Elspeth usually did not pray, but she did now. Please let it not be the princess.

21

DCI Hart kept Elspeth waiting for twenty minutes. This seemed to be his modus operandi, and therefore Elspeth was as annoyed as she had been when he had done the same thing at the police station. The delay, however, gave her more time to strategise. She would need to tell the truth to the chief inspector, but she did not need to pour out every detail. Her husband would accuse her of deviousness as he had done frequently in the past, but she preferred to call it prowess. She imagined him shifting his hazel-green eyes in her direction and looking down his long nose in incredulity. She grinned at the thought. Dearest Dickie! How she tried his sense of propriety. Elspeth also considered the delicate situation in which her employer had placed her. Damnable Eric! Protect the royal party at all costs, find the murderer and keep his, or perhaps her, identity from the media. Suddenly she was amused at the contrast of her feelings towards the two; Richard and Eric Kennington were the closest men to her in her everyday life.

The tea Elspeth had ordered for the police was now cold in its pot, although Elspeth had poured herself a cup earlier and eaten two watercress sandwiches and one with smoked salmon. She avoided the sweet cakes. DCI Hart strutted into the security office with his crime scene investigator in tow. The latter was dressed in a light blue shirt and navy trousers. Elspeth was glad he was out of uniform, but then speculated that the man might not be a member of the police force, but a civilian hired to do his job. For this she was thankful, as his presence would not alert guests, unlike the presence of the uniformed police. Elspeth knew well enough that she would have the advantage if she manipulated the direction of the conversation.

"Chief Inspector, I've asked our technician make copies of the security tapes both on the night of the fire and last night, but I thought you might like to review the originals to confirm that we had not doctored what we are giving you. As you will see, our camera only starts to record when there is motion in the area. We frequently see the flights of doves that fly through our outdoor areas," she said with a chuckle, "but normally what we record is the comings and goings of guests to and from their respective rooms. It isn't our intention to catch people in compromising liaisons, although we do on occasion, but rather to monitor any intruders or suspicious activities in the public spaces. As I have already explained, the tapes are constantly monitored for the security of the guests and are normally destroyed after forty-eight hours because we intend their use to assure the protection of our guests, not as a judgement on their morality. To do the latter would be disaster to any hotelier, as you can appreciate. Kit Lord reviewed these tapes with me earlier and will attest to their being complete, but you may watch them if you wish."

DCI Hart's hooded eyes did not give his thoughts away. "I would appreciate viewing the original tapes. Thank your technician for making copies for us. Before I begin, Ms Duff, please show me where the safety deposit boxes are kept. I understand the occupant of Room 17 had one, but I also would like to verify if the occupant of Room 121 did as well."

Elspeth hoped this would not happen, although she should have suspected it would.

Trying to hide her consternation at her oversight, she said, purposely haughtily, "Of course. I'll have to ask Mr Lord if he has the keys to the box 121 for

Room 121. I assume you didn't find one in Mrs Balfour's room."

"We did not, but you were in her room before we arrived, so you'd know better than we do. Didn't you take the key from Room 17?"

Ouch! She could not deny this; in fact, she had virtually admitted this to the DCI when she had described the contents of Martin Hagen's box.

"Let me call the front desk," she said. "They control the safety deposit boxes." She raised the handset on the house phone and put it on speakerphone.

"Front desk," a voice unfamiliar to Elspeth said.

"Elspeth Duff here at the security office," she said. "Has anyone from Room 121 used the safety deposit box recently?" Elspeth knew that the telephone at the reception desk would confirm the origin of her call.

There was a pause. "You may access the records personally if you wish, but I don't see that anyone has used that box since early last month," the receptionist said. Elspeth breathed a sigh of relief. It seemed Lilianne Balfour had not trusted hotel security.

"Thank you," Elspeth said over the speakerphone, and at the same moment she watched the face of DCI Hart. He nodded but looked irritated.

Then he said, "Now, Ms Duff, I wish to see the contents of the box associated with Room 17 and have them photographed."

As they left the security office, the crime scene investigator eyed the teacakes left uneaten on the tea trolley.

"Have one," Elspeth said, motioning toward them. "I'm sorry the tea is no longer hot, or I would offer you a cup. Chief Inspector, do have something to eat as well. The Kennington hotels are quite famous for their teas."

DCI Hart brushed away the offer and frowned

at the investigator, who had taken a large slice of sugar-frosted almond torte and was smiling contentedly after biting into it.

The lobby was crowded as they entered it. The hotel van was disgorging a well-heeled group of guests, who were burdened down with cameras, sun hats, and bags of purchases. Fortunately they seemed oblivious to Elspeth and the police. Elspeth sighed with relief. The receptionist gave her the master key to the boxes. She had found the key for Box 17 in her pocket and knew the moment called for a bit of bravado.

"I've brought the key along so we can open Box 17," she said. "It's the one I found in Room 17 and used to open the box this morning." She brought the key from her pocket and made sure she left her fingerprints on it, since she had admitted to opening the box, but she had wiped her prints clean after doing so. DCI Hart instructed the crime scene investigator to put on latex gloves and take the key from Elspeth. He opened the box after struggling a bit with the key Elspeth had handed him. It had been warped slightly by the fire and was difficult to insert, as Elspeth had learned earlier. The drawer finally came open and the investigator drew out the inner box.

"Before we examine the papers, Jones, I want you to dust them for fingerprints. Ms Duff, I also want to take your fingerprints."

"There's no need," Elspeth said. "They're on file at Scotland Yard, as I used to work there."

The DCI raised his eyebrows. "Then I assume you understand police procedure," he commented.

"I do."

"Including tampering with evidence?"

"That's a fairly basic tenet of the law."

"And doing so carries penalties," he said steadily.

Elspeth nodded coldly, but her heart was

pounding. She knew she was skirting the law. She turned to watch Jones dust the contents of the drawer. He went about it slowly but methodically. Finally, he looked up.

"They're clean of prints," he said.

DCI Hart bent over the drawer and then looked back at Elspeth.

"I thought you said you had examined these this morning."

Elspeth held his eye steadily. "I said I had opened the box and seen the papers. I didn't go through them."

"Why did you open the box, Ms Duff? What were you looking for?"

"I wasn't sure."

"Then why look at all?"

Elspeth was intelligent enough to know this question was coming and was prepared. "I suspected that Martin Hagen was not here on holiday but on business, and as his business seemed to be blackmail, I wondered what pieces of incriminating evidence he might have, and which guest or guests it might involve. Chief Inspector, at that point there was no evidence that Martin Hagen was murdered."

"Had Mr Hagen died as a result of an accidental fire, what would you have done with the contents of this drawer?"

She evaded the question. "I didn't recognise anything in the drawer, so I simply shut it."

"Are you sure, Ms Duff?"

Elspeth began to feel perturbed that the DCI kept using her name, as it smacked of an official interrogation. She wasn't under oath, so she countered in kind.

"Chief Inspector, my curiosity was piqued, but I know well enough not to disturb something that might later be related to a crime, particularly blackmail. I was unsure what to do and so doing nothing seemed to be the best policy."

"Are you sure you didn't take anything out of the box?"

"All the papers you see there are the ones that I found this morning. There weren't any others. I didn't look through them, other than to see that there were both newspaper clippings and a handwritten note." It took all Elspeth's training at her mother's knee to keep an innocent face. Her mother had been the drama teacher at Blair School for Girls where Elspeth had received her education before entering Girton College and where her mother had first cast her in numerous roles from the time she was twelve years old.

When she had opened the safety deposit box, Elspeth's concern had been the brooch and not the papers. Her cursory examination of the papers at the time had seemed unimportant, but now she wished she had taken a closer look.

Jones carefully laid out the envelope on a table near the boxes. Slowly he extracted each sheet. Three pages from the tabloid press, dated September 1975, showed a woman shielding her face from the cameras and the screaming headlines to the effect that the woman who had been convicted of murdering her baby son had been released after five years in a prison mental hospital after being declared fit to re-join society. None of the blurry newspaper photographs proved useful in identifying the woman. Her name was given as Catherine Justine Dorothy Clemmons, originally of Portsmouth. The only other paper in the box was the one Elspeth had seen earlier. The note was scrawled across a piece of plain paper and acceded to the blackmailer's demands. The paper was written on good stationery, but it bore no watermark or distinct marks.

Jones finished his work and then pulled a large

plastic envelope from his bag and inserted the papers into it. The DCI seemed satisfied and asked that they return to the security office.

Once they arrived, Elspeth again tried to take the upper hand. "I'll order coffee, Chief Inspector. It sounds as if we'll be settling into a long evening's work viewing the tapes."

The DCI regarded her suspiciously, but finally gave in. "That would be acceptable," he said, "considering how late it's getting. Jones, you are past the end of your shift. Return to the station and give the sergeant on duty the memory stick and the contents of the safety deposit box. Have him put them on my desk. I'll see you in the morning."

After Jones left, DCI Hart addressed Elspeth directly. "Ms Duff, I don't trust you completely."

Elspeth stared at him directly and did not move a muscle. "Why, Chief Inspector?" she asked innocently.

"Because you serve two masters, the truth and your employer's dictates. I wonder which one is more important to you."

She considered her answer carefully. "Perhaps they are not incompatible."

He cocked an eyebrow at her. "But the difficulty comes when each of us decides what we want to do with the truth, to bring a criminal to justice or to protect high paying guests."

Once again Elspeth realised that she was dealing with a seasoned officer of the law and that she would have to tread lightly. His assumption had hit the mark.

"Do you first want to review the tapes from the night of the fire or those from last night? It may take several hours."

"Then let's get started," he said. "I think we should review them in order."

The technician was inserting the first tape when the coffee arrived. Elspeth had made sure large sandwiches were included on the tray, as she suspected the DCI would not allow them a break for dinner.

They went through the tapes, almost frame by frame, particularly when the woman in the hat entered Room 17. The DCI had the technician zoom in closer, but little could be seen of the woman beyond the hat and a loose-fitting garment. She had a small handbag, but the black and white recording only showed that the hat was grey, the long skirt was dark with a pattern at the hem, and the bag was black and seemingly innocuous. The taped stopped until the fire became visible in the window of the room. The DCI was quick to remark that the woman who had entered Room 17 had spent a long time before leaving. To Elspeth's relief the princess had not come close enough to the camera to be recorded. After a long pause the camera swung around and focused on the next visitor, the person clearly being Elspeth herself. The DCI sat up and took notice.

"That's you, isn't it, Ms Duff? Where did you come from?"

"From my room, as I told you earlier. I was awakened by the fire alarms and came directly to the scene of the fire. Her explanation sounded feeble as she repeated it, as she had no proof. In such an emergency, she doubted that Kit Lord or the night manager would remember her presence other than on the periphery.

The DCI requested that they roll through the tapes one more time, and he began taking notes in his police notebook. He then asked to see the video taken outside Lilianne Balfour's room. While waiting the chief inspector absently took a sandwich.

"This is excellent," he said. "I don't think I have tasted one like it before."

Elspeth smiled. "The Kennington kitchens are noted for their unique food," she said in explanation, hoping the sandwich would mollify him.

He went through the new film frame by frame.

The woman with the hat and long skirt appeared at 21:20. He had the tape stopped.

"Do you see anything about the hat or skirt to distinguish it from the person we saw on the night of the fire?" he asked. "You women tend to know more about these things than I do."

"No, the hat is quite ordinary. Ones like it are sold in our gift shop here in the hotel. In fact, I bought one myself because I'd forgotten to bring a hat from London."

The DCI looked sideways at her and said, "Indeed," with so little inflection that Elspeth could not decide what he meant. The woman in the hat knocked on Lilianne Balfour's door and then put her ear to it, as if trying to see if anyone was stirring inside. The door opened a crack and was blocked by the security chain. The woman outside spoke into the void created by the gap. The door closed and then was opened just wide enough to let the woman in the room. The tape stopped again. Twenty minutes and thirteen seconds registered on the timer on the tape before the woman in the hat let herself out of Room 121 and disappeared from the view of the camera.

"Do you have a camera in the internal staircase as well?" the DCI asked.

Elspeth nodded to the technician, who scrolled down her computer. "Yes, Ms Duff. Shall I play it?"

"Yes, start at 21:00. That should show if the arrival of the woman who visited Lilianne Balfour came up the exterior stairs to the gallery that leads to Room 121."

The technician wound the tape back.

"It seems," the DCI said, "that the woman who entered Lilianne Balfour's room didn't come up the outside steps, but rather from the inside of the hotel." He asked that the tape in the corridor be rerun. Indeed, the woman's figure was first spotted coming from the direction of the other upstairs rooms. "Which," he concluded, "leads one to suspect that the murderer was a resident of the hotel."

Elspeth was puzzled for a moment at the word 'resident', but dismissed it as meaning 'a registered guest'.

It was now well past seven o'clock. Elspeth dismissed the technician, who cast her a grateful glance.

"Is there anything else I can do for you, Chief Inspector?" she asked

"Yes, I want you to come with me to police headquarters, but first I want you to collect your passport."

"It's in my suite."

"I assumed it might be. I'll follow you there. Also," he said, "I need to caution you." He recited the words from memory.

"Are you detaining me, Chief Inspector?"

"Yes, Ms Duff, under suspicion of committing the murders of both Martin Hagen and Lilianne Balfour."

22

Elspeth had been in police interrogation rooms before, first at Scotland Yard and then once as a potential suspect in Cyprus, but she never had been directly accused before of committing not one but two murders. She was escorted to a police car at the hotel's delivery entrance, but thankfully she had not been handcuffed. When they arrived at the police station, she was taken into a bare room with a table, four steel chairs, a video recorder and the smell of tobacco smoke, alcohol and fear. The absurdity of her arrest flooded over Elspeth, but she knew the DCI was serious and her incredulity would do her no good.

She was left alone with a woman police constable, who Elspeth judged was in her late fifties and intractable. Elspeth made no effort to engage this woman in conversation but took the time she had to assess her position before the DCI returned. She was bothered that he had confiscated her passport on their entrance to the police station, as without it she had no recourse either to the British authorities in Hamilton or had any chance of leaving Bermuda until she had cleared herself of any suspicion of wrongdoing. She was unclear on the exact diplomatic relationship between Hamilton and London, Bermuda being a British overseas territory, and she did not know if because of her British citizenship she had the same rights that she would have had in the UK. The constable, a plain and severe woman, glared at Elspeth. Elspeth averted her eyes from the hostile stare. There was no outside window, so Elspeth glanced at her wristwatch to see the time, seeing that it was now well past eight o'clock. The DCI kept her waiting another half hour. He entered with a police sergeant in uniform.

After motioning to the sergeant to turn on the video camera, the DCI took the lead. "You are aware, are you not, that we are recording this interrogation?"

"I am," Elspeth said.

"State your name in full.'

"Elspeth Fiona Duff."

"And your residence?"

Elspeth gave the address of her flat in Kensington.

"Where were you born?"

"In Perthshire, Scotland."

"State the name of your employer."

"I work directly for Lord Kennington of the Kennington hotel chain."

"And your position there?"

"I'm a special security advisor, like a trouble shooter, and I travel to various Kennington hotels if he thinks I can resolve any difficult situations there."

"Tell me why are you currently at the Kennington Bermuda?"

Elspeth had prepared herself for this question as she had waited for the DCI.

"The Kennington Bermuda is one of the newest hotels in the Kennington Organisation chain. Lord Kennington sent me out to see if the guests were sufficiently shielded from the eyes of the sensational press. You may appreciate that this is a constant concern, and he had no idea how much the local Bermudian press might be interested in our guests. He assigned me to find out." She spoke this half-truth without blanching. "Lord Kennington is always concerned about the possibility of predatory guests. Martin Hagen certainly fit that description."

"For the record will you explain that?"

"After Martin Hagen threatened me because I'd previously reported him as a suspicious guest, I had assumed he fell into the category of 'predatory guest'."

"Did you report this to Lord Kennington?"

"Not yet because I haven't had time." This was not exactly true.

"Did you confront Martin Hagen?"

"I did and I told him he was to leave the hotel."

"Ms Duff, our last interview was not taped. This one is. Please repeat what you told me earlier."

Elspeth recalled how equivocal she had been earlier in the DCI's office when she was describing Martin Hagen's approach to her. She cleared her throat.

"Recently I was married, and my husband was able to come to Bermuda to visit me. While waiting for his luggage to be delivered to my suite, we went out on to the beach. Because we thought we were alone, we embraced, and afterwards went to our shared suite. Obviously, we were seen, and the next morning Martin Hagen approached me and accused me of initiating an illicit relationship with a guest in the hotel and inviting him to my room for the night. He threatened to inform Lord Kennington of this fact. The accusations were without foundation, as Lord Kennington was not only a member of our wedding party, but he has also sanctioned Richard's visiting me when I'm on assignment. Had our relationship been otherwise, there might have been a reason for Martin Hagen to try to blackmail me. Apparently, Martin Hagen did not know of Richard's relationship to me."

"Did you enlighten him?"

"No, there was no need to do so. I simply ordered him to remove himself from the hotel. I have the power to do so."

"Did he object to this?"

"I expect so. He had asked me to forgive his hotel bill of six thousand pounds, about nine thousand

Bermudian dollars, but I'd refused to do so, instead asking he leave the hotel after his bill was settled in full."

"Did he pay it?"

"I understand he did—in cash."

"In cash?" The DCI's eyebrows rose. The police sergeant let out a snort of disbelief. When was this?"

"I can check with the hotel's accounting department."

"Martin Hagen must have resented you making him pay."

"Undoubtedly."

"What did he say when you asked him to leave?"

"He threatened to call Lord Kennington. I doubt he could have penetrated the many layers of staff Lord Kennington has placed between himself and public complaints. Only a few of us have direct access to his office line."

"Do you feel he had a reason to contact Lord Kennington, one you would have wished would go away?"

Elspeth frowned. Where was the DCI going with this?

"No, Chief Inspector. Eric Kennington and I work on close terms."

"Did you find any papers in Room 17's safety deposit box you wished to hide from him?"

"No. There were no papers in the box other than those you took earlier this evening."

"Will you swear to that?"

"Yes, Chief Inspector."

"I don't believe you."

"Why?" she ventured.

"Because you admitted to having opened the drawer, but you left no fingerprints. If you had wanted to see what was in the safety deposit box, your fingerprints would be on some of the items in the box. We did get a copy of your prints from Scotland Yard. You obviously didn't want us to know you had investigated what was in the drawer."

Elspeth cursed herself for only focusing on the brooch when she had initially opened Room 17's box. Indeed, she had admitted to opening the drawer earlier, but that did not account for the fact that she had done so with a handkerchief in her hand. She thought quickly.

"I didn't want my prints on the papers for the simple reason that they might obliterate the ones underneath them."

"Then you were assuming that the papers were direct evidence that Martin Hagen was a blackmailer."

"I assumed so, yes."

"But you did not report this to us."

"Chief Inspector, I did not have any direct evidence," she protested. "And I didn't yet know Martin Hagen had been shot. I assumed he died as a result of the fire."

"Tell me, Ms Duff, where you were earlier in the evening on the night of the fire."

"My husband and I dined with old friends of his at the Waterloo Restaurant, and then returned to the hotel, probably getting there about half past nine or a little after that. Then we retired to bed."

"What were the names of your husband's friends?"

"Tilden," Elspeth said cautiously. "Richard had worked with Francis Tilden many years ago, and they met by accident here in Bermuda."

Elspeth waited for the DCI to ask where the Tildens were staying, but thankfully he did not and changed the topic instead.

"You said you were awakened by the sound of the fire alarms."

"Yes, I was."

"Can anyone confirm where you were between the time you returned to the hotel and your being awakened?"

"My husband could, but he left Bermuda this morning."

"Has he returned to London?"

"No, he works in Malta and was taking a flight from Philadelphia to Rome this evening and then on to Valletta on a late morning flight. I don't know his exact itinerary."

"I see. So, he's unavailable."

"He may still be in Philadelphia."

"What was your connection to Lilianne Balfour?" the DCI asked, changing the direction of his questioning again.

"She came up to me several times in the hotel. I was anxious not to pursue any further relationship with her and put her off several times. Because of my position in the Kennington Organisation I was trying to be discreet as possible, so I was polite but distant when Mrs Balfour approached me."

"How and when did she approach you?"

Elspeth had not considered the numerous times Lilianne had spoken to her as having any bearing on her assignment at the Kennington Bermuda and therefore did not remember the times exactly.

"The first time, I think, was when she saw me in the lobby and complimented me on my clothes. In the moment I thought it was probably a ploy to strike up an acquaintanceship. She actually invited me to dinner with her as her husband was indisposed, which, in retrospect, is rather strange, since she was travelling alone. Of course, I didn't know it at the time. I demurred, as I didn't want to have anything to do with her."

"And the next time?"

Elspeth put two fingers on her forehead and thought. "It was the morning after my husband arrived.

I had left him sleeping and had gone out for a cup of coffee and a bite of food in the breakfast room. Mrs Balfour came in shortly after I did and invited herself to my table. She began this strange charade of winking at me and suggesting that women 'our age' had not necessarily lost our attraction to men. She said she had seen me and a man embracing on the beach the night before. Like Martin Hagen, she seemed to have made assumptions about my actions."

"But she did not try to blackmail you."

"No," Elspeth said, trying to suppress a grin. "She congratulated me."

Neither the DCI nor the police sergeant seemed amused. In fact, DCI Hart frowned threateningly.

"Did it occur to you that shortly after Mrs Balfour congratulated you on your sexual prowess that Martin Hagen tried to blackmail you for the same thing. Then within the space of two days they both were murdered."

This caught Elspeth short, and the grin died off her face. "I don't believe there's a connection."

"I do, and you seem to be in the middle of it. They both were killed by the same person. Do you know how to handle a gun?"

"Yes, although I don't like them."

"What sort of gun?"

"My grandfather was a great hunter in Scotland, where I grew up, and taught me how to shoot a hunting rifle when I was about eleven years old, and while at Scotland Yard I was trained to shoot a pistol."

"Do you own a gun?"

"Absolutely not. I lived in the Los Angeles area for a very long time and saw the havoc the gun culture has caused there."

"Your presence at the murder scene, your skill with a pistol, and the fact that the woman entering both Martin Hagen and Lilianne Balfour's room wore a floppy cloth hat leads me to an irrefutable conclusion. The woman with the hat was seen leaving the room, and you appeared on the tape shortly afterwards but you were now hatless. Both the ballistics and the security tapes you showed me confirm this. The murderer is a woman of approximately your size, wearing a hat similar to the one you admitted owning, and competent enough with a pistol to kill two people. I have no choice but to remand you into custody. The police constable will take you to the jail, where you will be charged with the murders of Lilianne Balfour and Martin Hagen. You're allowed one phone call." He turned away from her, rose from his chair, and appeared ready to leave.

Elspeth could feel the blood rush from her head. "I'd like to phone my husband but will need to use my satellite phone. Is that allowable?" she said, suddenly afraid. "I usually carry it in my pocket, but they took it away from me when I came in."

DCI Hart motioned to the police constable to retrieve Elspeth's mobile.

Oh, please let Dickie still be in Philadelphia, she prayed. Once she retrieved her phone, she touched in the speed dial key for Richard's mobile. It rang four times. Her heart pounded. Had he already left? How long was the flight to Rome? It would be well into tomorrow morning before she could reach him if he did not answer now. The phone rang a fifth time and then his familiar baritone came on the line.

"Elspeth, my love, to what pleasure do I owe this call?" His voice was jocular.

Relief spread through her. "Oh, Dickie, I'm so glad I reached you. I've been arrested for the murder of Martin Hagen and Lilianne Balfour. Yes, I realise you don't know that she was murdered as well, but the police think I killed both of them. I need you to help me! I'm not sure what you can do from Philadelphia, but please let Eric know and have him get me a solicitor as quickly as possible."

"Dearest one, please slow down and start from the beginning." Floods of memories going back over forty years washed over Elspeth. When she and her cousin, Johnnie Tay, got into mischief when 'Dickie' Munro had visited Johnnie, his university pal, during the summers between their years at Oxford, Richard was always the one to find a way to appease whoever needed to be placated for the disruption caused by their pranks. But, although the current circumstances brought these memories to her mind, their exuberant antics all those years ago had never involved anything as serious as an accusation of double murder. Elspeth swallowed hard, despairing at her present need.

"Dickie, I seem to be in a frightful mess, but none of it is true, except that the murders *did* happen." She knew her voice sounded lame.

"I've been blessed by the incompetence of modern air travel," he said. "For goodness knows what reason, we have a two-hour delay before we take off. I'll see what I can do. And, dear one, you are magnificent. Don't forget that."

She blinked hard to keep her tears away. Half of her hated her current dependence on her husband; the other half was filled with thankfulness for his care, commitment, and love.

The constable took Elspeth's phone from her and indicated that it was time to leave the interrogation room. The chief inspector noted that the interview was at an end, clicked off the videotape and indicated that Elspeth should follow him out of the room. DCI Hart whispered orders to the constable.

The sergeant at the charge desk was a large, jocular man, whom seemed more fit to admit people to a county fair than to a jail. He asked Elspeth to surrender her jewellery including her rings, her watch, her belt, and her sandals, and would have taken her handbag, but she had none.

"Don't worry, love, if they let you out you will get them all back. If not, they will be sent to whoever you designate."

She signed a chit for them.

A constable led her into the core of the police station, where the holding cells were located. The constable took the key the sergeant had given her and unlocked the sliding gate to the cell block.

"In here," she said, indicating a cell halfway down a corridor. As she stepped in, Elspeth looked about her. The walls of the cell were unadorned concrete, as was a shelf that served as a bed, bench, and the only resting place in the three-metre square space. A dirty pillow, coarse blanket and well-used sheet sat on it. One of the walls had a steel water closet with no tip-up seat and a hose bibb above it. At the top one of the walls was a small barred window that during the day let in light and during the night a breath of fresh air. The only light was a single bulb fixture imbedding in the concrete wall beyond human reach and protected by a metal grille.

"The lights go off at ten-thirty," the constable said as if Elspeth had a watch.

Elspeth spread the mat provided on the concrete bench and took note of her surroundings. The space reeked of carbolic that only vaguely disguised the smell of urine, vomit, and the unique smell of unwashed humanity. A few obscene words had been scratched into the concrete wall and attempts to eradicate them had been only partially successful, whether by design or lack of interest. She put her pillow at the head of the bench, spread the sheet and blanket over the mat and turned down the edges as homage to the Kennington hotel room staff, who would have added two chocolates wrapped in the distinctive celadon-coloured foil marked with the name of a famous Parisian chocolatier. She shook her head at the absurdity of the contrast.

Putting fantasy aside, Elspeth sat down on her newly made bed and contemplated what had just happened to her. Even with Richard's intervention or the appearance of a solicitor hired by Eric Kennington, she had no chance of being released until morning. Under normal circumstances this would be uncomfortable but not drastic, but at six in the morning she had promised the prince that she would be on the beach to watch Mary take her dinghy out to meet Princess Christiana and prevent interference from any other people on the beach. Elspeth looked around her cell to see if there was any means of escape, but found none. She could yell a protest to anyone within earshot, but she felt doing so could only be fruitless. So she settled down on her bed and drew her knees to her chin.

The only way out was to discover the real murderer—and quickly. She began to review all the facts that she had on hand, sorting them one by one. Normally she would have done this on paper or on her computer, but, having neither at hand, she mentally laid out every detail she could remember and tried to sort them into a logical order.

She first went over everything the princess had told her about Martin Hagen's approach to her and their subsequent meetings. According to the princess, he had met her when she was presenting a plaque and stalked her from there, always in public places. But how had he known about the brooch? Elspeth's mind jumped to the statement she had just given to the DCI, that Lilianne Balfour had approached her the morning after Richard had arrived and several hours later Martin Hagen had tried to blackmail her. The DCI had put these two events together, but Elspeth had not. She could suddenly hear Lilianne saying that she had seen the princess in a jewellery shop in London when she was trying to buy back the brooch Christiana had left there.

Of course! Martin Hagen and Lilianne Balfour were in league. She scouted out information that could be used for blackmail, and he approached the victim. They had been at the Kennington hotels together several times before. Why hadn't Elspeth made the connection earlier? But this led her no further in discovering who had murdered them both. Undoubtedly it was one of their prey, but who? Elspeth set her jaw, concentrating hard. The princess was the obvious choice as she had both motive and opportunity. The only pieces of evidence Elspeth had found in the safety deposit box were the brooch, the newspaper articles and a handwritten note. This gave her some options. She could continue to dispute the police evidence against her, stalling until the royal party had left Bermuda and Princess Honorée was out of police sight, but in doing so she would be countermanding Eric Kennington's directive for her to protect the royal party. By six in the morning she would already be derelict in her duty. Or, she could assume the princess's innocence and dig more deeply to identify the woman in the hat who had gone to both Martin Hagen's and Lilianne Balfour's rooms. Elspeth had few clues as to her identity, but, there was evidence, the other papers in the safety deposit box. If Martin Hagen and Lilianne Balfour had been at the Kennington Bermuda to intimidate the princess, they also must have been there to confront the woman in the newspaper stories. Elspeth now wished she had looked more closely at them.

Her thoughts were broken by a terrible cacophony of women's voices coming through the slot in the steel door of her cell. Elspeth rose and peered out of the door's small window, which had been left open.

"Blimey, get yer bleedin' 'ands orf o' me," a voice from the East End of London said. Through the narrow slot in her cell door, Elspeth saw the woman uttering these words and laughed at the outlandishness of her scant wardrobe, makeup and hairstyle. She wore leather shorts that did not even attempt to hide the bottom of her buttocks, a bright mauve halter-top with red stripes that, with a breath, could have exposed far too much of her enhanced breasts, six-inch high platform sandals, and nothing else. Her hair was unnaturally black with raspberry spikes that projected from her skull, and her body was pierced so frequently that it hurt Elspeth to look at it although all the accessories had been removed, probably at the behest of the charge sergeant. Her exaggerated makeup disguised any features she might have been granted at birth. With her was a woman with a quieter voice, who had enhanced her eyes with lines of kohl, thick red lips, and dreadlocks interlaced with gold and silver beads that were losing their shiny veneer. She wore a very short and tight sleeveless cheongsam made of an iridescent satin material that was wrinkled over her large belly. Her voice was soft and flowing in the West Indian style.

"Hush, Cat," she said.

"Mush, 'ush yerself, Maze," Cat said.

The constable showed the two drunken ladies into a barred cell across from Elspeth, who was glad for a moment's diversion. The two women companions accepted surroundings with the casualness of habitual guests, which it seemed they were. They threw the bedding on the mattresses on the concrete benches opposite each other and sat down gracelessly. Cat blew out her breath and looked curiously towards the door to Elspeth's cell.

"I'm Cat," she said, as if Elspeth had been deaf to the previous conversation. "Wach yer in fer?"

Elspeth smiled, "Do you mean what I'm charged with?"

"Blimey, Maze, it's a toff." Maze seemed unimpressed and began to unfold her mattress.

"Murder," Elspeth said. "Not one but two."

"Yer jokin', ain't yer?"

"No."

"Y'guilty?"

"Is anyone who comes in here guilty? Aren't we all innocent?"

"Naw. We're just a bit tipsy. But murder!" Cat seemed to find Elspeth's accused crime an anathema, had she known the word, and turned away as if shielding herself from an untouchable human being.

All right, thought Elspeth, so I am a piranha, more dangerous than the men they solicit on the streets. How important the hierarchy of crime is to criminals. But, perhaps, drunken streetwalkers were always afraid of murderers in their line of work.

Feeling strangely shunned, Elspeth returned to her bench and drew her knees back up to her chin. She was no closer to finding out who had murdered Martin and Lilianne than she had been before she had been brought to the police station. Her thoughts took her away from the low murmurs between the two women across the way until the lights were shut down and only the dimmest of bulbs in the hallway kept the new inmates visible. Elspeth did not move for a long time and finally put her face in her hands. She could think of no escape. Soon she heard the night-time breathing of the two drunken women and wondered with a grin if they were relieved to have the night off.

She must have dozed, as the sound of the door to the cells sliding open awakened her. The desk sergeant approached her cell. Looking embarrassed he said, "Lady Munro, we didn't know who you were."

Elspeth looked around to see whom they were addressing and then realised that she had been called by the title she seldom used. She wondered what pressure Richard had brought to bear, for it must have been of his doing.

"Blimey, lye-dee so an' so, yer cudda guessed

233

from 'er accent," a voice said from across the way. "Maze, we've been in the presence o' royalty."

Elspeth laughed. "Not so, ladies. I'm just an ordinary citizen like you."

"'Ardly, but good luck to yer. An' don't go committin' no more murders."

"I'll try not to," she said in parting, "unless forced to."

"Lady Munro, the Chief Superintendent of Police is in his office and wants to speak to you," the sergeant said, ignoring Elspeth's words to Cat and Maze. "Let me return your things before you see him."

23

The Chief Superintendent of Police was waiting for Elspeth in DCI Hart's office and obviously had just come from a formal gathering. He was dressed in black Bermuda shorts with a taffeta stripe down each side, silk knee-high socks, evening slippers, a bright red cummerbund wrapped round a pleaded white shirt, and a white dinner jacket. His first words explained his dress.

"I've just come from a reception at the governor's mansion under orders from His Excellency to free you. The governor was explicit in saying you were to be returned to the Kennington Bermuda under your own recognisance. Lady Munro, you must have influence in high places because I've never been asked to do anything like this before, particularly in the middle of the night. The governor said he knew your husband, Sir Richard, as they were at Oxford together. He also mentioned your cousin, Lord Tay, whom he knew at Oxford as well."

Inwardly Elspeth ground her teeth. She worked with the rich and privileged on a daily basis, but one thing about her job that always rankled her was the presumption that titled people expected to be granted favours that mere citizens were not. Her husband knew her feelings, but he must have chosen to overlook them in order to get her out of jail. One of the conditions of their marriage had been that she keep her own name, but right now, with her need to be on the beach at six in the morning, being 'Lady Munro', as much as she hated the title, served its purpose, and she did not refuse the chief superintendent's offer. She would speak to Richard later, delicately of course, as he obviously had gone to great trouble to contact the governor from the Philadelphia airport. Richard had a facility at doing these things. Elspeth had no way of knowing whom Richard had called to make direct contact with the governor, but she bowed to his success. Richard so frequently surprised her with his many contacts and how quickly he could call in favours.

"But, Lady Munro, we will have to keep your passport. I cannot convince DCI Hart that you had no involvement in the murders. I'm also curious why you haven't changed your name on your passport. I understand you have been married to Sir Richard for a number of months."

"Almost five," Elspeth said, but gave no reason for the name on her passport.

"I hope you will cooperate fully with Chief Inspector Hart. He's one of the most competent men on my force."

"So I have realised," she said. "Where did he train?"

"At Scotland Yard and later with the Los Angeles Police Department. It seems you have much in common."

Elspeth was troubled by this remark. She had told DCI Hart about Scotland Yard, and having lived in the Los Angeles area for many years. Perhaps the chief superintendent had been told of her past. Elspeth thought she might use the Los Angeles connection later on if needed. She tried to remember the names of officers in the LAPD whom she had worked with in the past and that she could use now. None came immediately to mind, but she knew they would eventually.

"Thank you, Chief Superintendent, and please thank the governor as well. I'm certain I'll be much more comfortable at the hotel." Her face broke into a smile as she said this.

He caught the humour in her voice and drew his lips in a thin smile. "I'm sure you will as well. I'll keep in touch with the chief inspector on the progress of the case. In the meantime, I've asked one of the sergeants on duty to drive you back to the hotel—in one of their unmarked cars."

Since nibbling at the sandwiches in the security office while viewing the tapes, Elspeth had eaten nothing, but she wasn't hungry. She took some yoghurt from the mini-bar in her suite, found a packet of cheese and biscuits and made a makeshift meal that was filling but not satisfying. After ordering a wakeup call at five, she took a hot bath to wash away the smells of the jail and changed into her silk pyjamas. How odd it seemed that only last night she had done the same thing in anticipation of slipping into the bed with Richard. Tonight, it felt terribly empty without him, but she only had a few hours left of sleep. She dared not take a sleeping pill, which on occasion she did, for fear of not waking on time. Pulling the fine Egyptian cotton sheets around her shoulders and fluffing up the feather pillows, she had visions of the rough blanket, sheet and spongy pillow in the jail and wondered if Cat and Maze were so accustomed to them that they were able to sleep without noticing their coarseness.

Elspeth wanted to sleep. After the last few nights she should have fallen quickly into deep sleep, but sleep defied her. She dozed fitfully, tossing and turning, missing Richard, and ruminating on her relationship with him. Why did she so often turn to him in moments of distress? This had been true since the day he had come to fetch her at Girton College when she had learned that her fiancé Malcolm had been murdered. Richard had led her gently from her college room, taken her by train from Cambridge to King's Cross Station in

London and then across to Euston Station for the sleeper train to Perthshire, where he had arranged for her father to meet her. Richard had sat with her throughout the journey, holding her hand when she had broken into tears and letting her rest her head on his shoulder when she had dozed off. He had delivered her to her family and then returned to London. Elspeth felt she had never properly thanked him for this.

She remembered the time when her marriage to Alistair Craig was falling apart and Richard and Lady Marjorie had visited them in California. Marjorie had briefly left the room with Alistair, and Richard had come over to her. She had turned towards him, and he held her eyes.

"Are you happy, Elspeth?" he had asked, concern and love in his eyes.

She could hear her voice. "Happy? Not really but I've learned to live with my choices." She had touched his arm briefly, as gesture of thanks for his caring, just before Marjorie came back into the room. After that Elspeth had not seen Richard for eight years, but that long look of his hazel-green eyes had sustained her for a long time. She had not loved him then, not the way she did now, but his constancy was one of the deep cores of her being. Then recently he had literally saved her life twice, in Singapore and again in Nicosia. Now, just hours ago, she had called him and once again he had not failed her. Dickie, she thought, what have I ever given back to you that could repay all you have done for me? Falling in love with him two and a half years ago and their eventual marriage was one thing, but his stalwartness for the past four decades was quite another because it had so often been one-sided. She despaired her own impulsiveness, which she knew sometimes annoyed him, and her tremendous need for his friendship and support over the years.

Her strong self-reliant side said that she could

certainly survive independently, but could she really? How often she had called him to rescue her. Damn, she thought, I've needed him all these years, and, sighing, she turned over restlessly. Finally sleep came, her last conscious moment seeing 2:47 on the clock at her bedside. It blared back at her at 4:59, just a minute before her wakeup call.

Her first thought through the fog that swirled in her head was the realisation that she had not bought the red pail that was to identify her on the beach; in fact, she had not even looked to see if the hotel shop had one, and she had just under an hour to be out on the beach. First, she rang room service for coffee and a light breakfast, at the same time wondering what her meal might have been in jail. Next, she called the front desk and asked if the night manager would ring her right back. She stressed the urgency of contacting him. He called five minutes later and was courteous when he heard her request, although she could tell he had doubts about why she was asking this.

"I'm not sure, Ms. Duff, that they sell beach pails in the gift shop."

"Then where can I get one before six o'clock this morning?"

"I believe my three-year-old daughter has one, but my wife and children won't be up as yet."

"Do you live close-by?"

"I do."

"Could you go home and fetch the pail for me? It's vitally important for my mission here." As she spoke Elspeth knew that what she was asking seemed absurd, and she wished that she had thought of something more adult to identify herself on the beach.

He sounded confused, but as she outranked him in the Kennington Organisation and because he probably knew she was acting under the direct orders of Lord Kennington, he conceded to her demand.

"I'll be back in about fifteen minutes and will bring the pail to you," he said.

Her breakfast was delivered shortly afterwards. Had she been more awake when she had called room service, and had she known she could find the red pail, she might have asked for something more substantial than what was on the tray, but even the lightest of Kennington hotel breakfasts was filling and the coffee in the urn was hot and strong. She poured herself a cup and chose an almond croissant. She knew it would be cool in the wind on the beach and dressed accordingly, in light woollen trousers, a cotton polo-necked jersey, and a fleece she had tailored to meet her preference for longer over-jackets. She found the hat that resembled the ones on the tapes. She chose her shoes carefully and for practical purposes, in this case a pair of trainers. She loathed them generally, thinking they didn't flatter a woman's foot, but she always carried a pair to be used either when she wanted to hide her identity or knew she might be involved in strenuous physical activity. Both cases might apply this morning.

The night manager knocked discreetly on her door soon after she had finished dressing. He produced a red plastic pail that he said was much loved by his daughter. Vestiges of sand both inside and out and a white plastic handle attached only on one end showed it had been recently used. But despite its disrepair, it was red, which was all Elspeth needed. He had added a white plastic shovel. Elspeth wondered what he thought she would be doing with the pail. She thanked him without any explanation of its importance.

She glanced at her wristwatch, and, if she ate hurriedly, saw she had time for another cup of coffee and a succulent Anjou pear. She took one of the colourful cloth napkins and wrapped a croissant in it, thrusting it into the pocket of her fleece for later consumption. She put her mobile in the other pocket.

The beach was colder than she expected, and a strong wind was coming off the ocean. She wished she had brought her windcheater, but she did not want to return to the hotel. The temperature would warm up soon, she hoped. At the bungalow the day before she vaguely remembered seeing mention of an approaching storm, but in light of all the other events, she had not had time to check the local forecast or find a local morning newspaper. She hoped the wind was not a precursor to a tropical storm. Because the gusts dislodged her broad brimmed hat, she took it off and drew out the chinstrap, which she secured tightly. The brim still blew about.

Dawn was just beginning to break, and a thin orange streak of light appeared through the clouds on the horizon. She feigned gathering shells but focused her attention on the pier where an unoccupied dinghy, probably Mary's, bobbed up and down. Had something gone wrong? Elspeth checked her watch again.

Just past six o'clock however, two figures appeared from the back gate of the bungalow. Mary's tall and lithe figure was unmistakable, but Elspeth had to strain to identify the other person. Both figures were wearing wet suits, had swimming masks with snorkels hanging round their necks and gripped swimming fins in their hands. She took out the binoculars that she had thrust in her pocket at the last minute. She focused them and saw that the second person was Harald Wade. Surely, this was not in the prince's plan. Harald carried a large webbed sack that bulged formidably. Elspeth slowly made out its contents, another wetsuit, mask, snorkel and fins. She speculated that the members of the younger generation were taking the prince's plan and turning it to their own advantage, but she was unclear what that entailed. Mary and Harald saw Elspeth, or perhaps her red pail, and waved. They lowered themselves into the dinghy, and Mary turned the lever to start the engine, which sprang into action. The dinghy made its way out into the ocean over the waves made choppy by the increasing force of the winds.

Elspeth ended her pretence at gathering shells. She was curious about the two occupants of the dinghy and their bag. How much danger were they courting? The threat of bad weather was increasing, and Elspeth had an uneasy feeling about the contents of the bag they were carrying. What was the intent of the wet suit? Would it fit Princess Christiana? What did Mary and Harald have in mind? And, how far were they willing to go to defy the prince?

She set down her ridiculous red pail and ran down the beach towards the dinghy, waving frantically. Harald saw her and waved back, giving the V sign for victory. She had no idea what he meant. Before she reached the pier, the dinghy had disappeared into the rising fog. Elspeth stopped and watched them go. What did all this mean?

Had she not been so deprived of sleep, she might have gone over to the pier to find a boat to chase the two young people, but she knew nothing about boating and was prone to seasickness. In any case, if she took any vessel moored at the pier, she expected she would be committing piracy or some similar crime. The wind was now increasing in velocity. Elspeth knew her waiting at the pier would prove fruitless, even if Mary had planned to bring the dinghy back to the hotel beach, but Elspeth now instinctively felt that Mary and Harald had another scheme in mind.

She turned back towards the hotel and went to fetch her red pail, but the tide had come in, swirling around the place where she had left it, and it was gone. Was this a metaphor for what had just happened? Let that not be so.

Her mobile suddenly rang out, and she growled

at the jaunty tune she had chosen for her ringtone. Its cheerfulness did not reflect her current mood.

"Elspeth Duff here," she yelled into it.

"My dearest, you need not shout, although you do sound as if you are in a wind tunnel. You must have escaped from jail."

Elspeth laughed at her husband's voice. "Dickie, what tales to tell. You never let on you knew the governor."

He chuckled. "There are certain advantages of an Oxford or a Cambridge education, as you must have learned."

"I've never used my connections so shamelessly," she said with a huff.

"I don't find springing my beloved wife from jail by using any connection at hand shameless," he said. "I'm no longer out of sight than . . . " She did not let him finish.

"Dickie, things here are very serious. As I told you, someone killed Martin Hagen and Lilianne Balfour, and I've no proof that it wasn't one of the party I was sent to protect. Where are you, Dickie?"

"In Rome. I should be in Malta by late afternoon. I'm expected at dinner with the prime minister and his wife. Shall I give them your regrets?"

"Regards, but not regrets. They know where I stand, and you can't lie to them."

"They seem quite taken with you, Elspeth."

"Tell them I hope to see them the next time I'm in Valletta. Could we ask them round for dinner at your new digs?"

"Our digs."

"Our digs," she said repeated awkwardly. Before their marriage, Richard had moved out of Lady Marjorie's cousin's house on Triq Il Torre in Sliema to a house he had found in Valletta. Elspeth had visited many times but always felt a guest, as she had imposed nothing of her own on the residence other than leaving clothes in the walk-in cupboard she shared with Richard. He was well looked after by his housekeeper, a Maltese widow of indeterminate age but exacting manner. Elspeth always felt the housekeeper viewed her as a curious adjunct to the high commissioner's life rather than as his wife. "But I haven't thanked you for getting me out of jail, even if you shamelessly gave the governor my title."

"I had no time to explain," he said. "Best to let him reach his own conclusions. I didn't mean to disregard your request to use your own name, my dear, but only to find a quick way to get you out of jail. I assumed it worked."

She smiled. Richard was a diplomat to the core, even with her, and for that among many other things she loved him.

"In time to return to the hotel for a few hours' sleep," she said. "I missed your being there."

"Elspeth, your phone has a hollow sound to it. Can you adjust the volume?"

"No, it isn't the volume. I'm outside on the beach, and the weather is kicking up."

"What time is it there?"

"Almost half past six."

"Why are you on the beach?"

"May I tell you later? It's too complex right now."

"Of course. They're calling my flight. I love you above all things and promise to give you my full attention when you get to Malta. Will you be there for the weekend?"

"I can't really say. The police still have my passport. I love you too," she said, but was not sure if he heard her. The line began crackling and he did not reply.

Elspeth had little choice but to return to her

rooms. The wind was now quite strong, and she was battered by its intensity. The sun still had not risen but the horizon continued to lighten. She climbed the stairs up from the beach, let herself in through the door to her patio and pulled the French doors closed. Her whole body longed to go back to bed and sleep, but she knew she would need to be back at the pier in less than half an hour to see if Harald and Mary had returned there with Princess Christiana in tow. She had grave doubts. In her mind she sensed she had failed. Eric Kennington might not have factored in the complexity of his request, but she could not ignore it. She knew there was a good chance that Princess Honorée could be guilty of the murders. As a royal, did she have diplomatic immunity? Elspeth thought she must ask Richard about this the next time they spoke.

The coffee in the urn was still hot, and she emptied the last of its contents into the coffee cup she had left behind earlier. As the plate of rolls had been removed, she reached in her pocket to get the croissant she had put there, and, despite its flattened condition, she munched away at it, hardly taking in its buttery flavour.

What was her best move now? The wind hit the French doors and they rattled. She went to secure them and through the iron pickets of the gate to the beach, she could see large whitecaps forming. How seaworthy was Mary's dinghy? With the increasing swell, could Princess Christiana be lowered into the dinghy from the yacht's launch without disaster? Was that the reason for the wetsuit? In the event they were tossed into the ocean, could they swim for land? Elspeth suspected that Mary and Harald had not taken the weather into account when they were making preparations, and that the ocean gear might be meant for another purpose. Elspeth had no choice but to go back to the beach. She abandoned her hat and was grateful for a pair of gloves she found in the pockets of her windcheater. A sudden downpour sent her scurrying for the gazebo, which offered only slight protection from the rain and wind. She took out her binoculars again and began scouring the edge of the fog bank. The birds had abandoned their search for breakfast, and the only visible life was several crabs that scuttled across the beach. Nothing emerged through the mist. The roar of the waves and the howling of the wind were deafening, and she wished nothing more than to beat a retreat into her room, pull her blankets over her head and be rid of any responsibility for Mary Tilden, Harald Wade, and Princess Christiana, but her sense of duty was stronger than her need for sleep. In the moment the life of a diplomatic wife seemed a rosy alternative, but the thought was fleeting. Elspeth set her jaw and continued to search the ocean. Then she saw it. Mary's dinghy rode the crest of a terrifying wave and was catapulted onto the shore. It had been smashed to smithereens, but no bodies were in it. Elspeth's best hope was that Mary and Harald, aware of the growing ferocity of the ocean, had crawled aboard the launch carrying the princess and been transported out to the prince's yacht, which surely was large enough to withstand the storm, but there was no way she could verify this.

Elspeth made her way down the beach to where the dinghy's remnants lay. Only the staves of the hull and pieces of fibreglass remained.

24

Elspeth circled the wreckage of the dinghy, which had been torn apart. The boat's engine was missing, the bow ripped away, and only the aft section had been cast ashore. Elspeth could not determine if the sea had destroyed the boat or if its impact with the beach had, the missing pieces of the dinghy having been washed back out to sea, like the red pail she had brought with her. Satisfied that the shards of the boat had nothing more to tell about the whereabouts of Mary, Harald, or Princess Christiana, Elspeth turned wearily back to the hotel. She felt an enormous surge of defeat. She had no alternative but to go to the bungalow and tell the prince and princess what she had just seen, but how could she tell them tactfully?

Elspeth's original task had been to deflect the curiosity of the press and keep the royal party safe from outsiders. She had not been a part of the plan to get Princess Christiana to shore nor had she been able at the last minute to make Mary and Harald return to the pier. They were intent on their mission and had waved cavalierly at Elspeth as they had plunged the dinghy into the waves. Elspeth had had no recourse to stop them, but she somehow felt responsible.

She checked her watch and saw that the hour was fast approaching seven. She now faced the unpleasant task of returning to her suite and ringing the royal party. Twenty minutes would make no difference in her doing so, and therefore she indulged herself in a hot shower and rapidly changed her clothes into something she felt was more suitable for her visit to the prince and princess. Clean and respectable but not refreshed, Elspeth picked up her house phone and was put through to the bungalow. Hope Tilden answered the call.

Elspeth arrived at the gate just moments later, and Hope let her in.

"Have they returned?" Hope asked. The question answered Elspeth's unfounded hopes that the three young people had survived the crash of the dinghy and been in touch with the royals.

Elspeth cleared her throat and considered what to say. Hope Tilden, the consummate diplomatic wife, would have known how to phrase the truth to make it sound as positive as possible, but Elspeth knew no way to convey what she had seen other than stating the obvious. She drew in her breath and was glad she was alone with Hope. Hope's daughter might now be a victim of the ocean, but Hope appeared to have a level head and, Elspeth suspected, could take the news she was about to impart calmly.

"Hope," Elspeth hedged, "do you know why Harald Wade went out with Mary this morning?"

"Harald? I'd no idea he had. I heard the prince plotting with Mary and knew something was afoot."

"He was with Mary in the dinghy when they set off. Both were in wetsuits and were carrying what appeared to be another one. Do you have any idea why?"

"No, none. Harald has always been a late riser. None of us noticed his absence. You saw him with Mary?"

Elspeth nodded. "Does Prince Michael know about this?" she asked.

"Know about what?" the prince said as he entered the sitting room.

Elspeth was startled. How much had the prince heard? She did not want to blurt out that the dinghy had crashed into the shore without any of its occupants aboard and that there was the distinct possibility that they could have drowned. Elspeth searched for alternative ways to tell the prince what had happened.

"Your Highness, when I went out on the beach this morning, Mary and someone else were boarding the dinghy. Both were in wet suits. They also had a rubber webbed bag with another wetsuit in it. Was this in your plan?"

"Absolutely not," he said.

"Have you heard from either Mary or the launch?" Elspeth asked.

He shook his head. "We're trying to stay close until my daughter arrives. Tell me, Ms Duff, what did you see on the beach this morning?"

Elspeth no longer had an excuse to evade the inevitable.

"I was on the beach at six, and shortly afterwards I saw Mary and another figure come out of the bungalow and get into the dinghy. Because they were carrying a wetsuit, I assumed this gear was for Princess Christiana. At first, I couldn't identify the person who was with Mary, but after looking through my binoculars, I recognised Harald Wade. Did you know he was going with Mary?"

"I had no idea. It wasn't part of our planning."

"I assume that Mary, given her academic interest in marine biology, is a proficient swimmer."

Hope nodded. "She's also a certified scuba diver and a trained instructor as well."

"Harald Wade is a strong swimmer as well," the prince said. "He swims for exercise every day in the palace pool."

"And Princess Christiana?"

"Mary and she both swam frequently at the beach when Christie was staying with us in Los Angeles. She could keep up with Mary," Hope answered.

"Could the three of them have plotted not to return to the hotel but instead abandon the dinghy and swim to another part of the archipelago?" Elspeth asked. She was looking for a way to explain the empty dinghy without assuming that the occupants had come to a tragic end.

The prince seemed leery, and Elspeth suspected he still did not trust her completely. "Why do you ask?" he said.

Elspeth raised her head, as she habitually did when imparting unpleasant truths. "The dinghy was washed ashore about half an hour ago without anyone on board." She did not mention the derelict quality of the boat. "I'm not satisfied that the occupants of the dinghy were accidentally washed overboard."

Elspeth watched Hope glance towards her brother-in-law and was not sure if she did so as a caution or a plea. Neither of them spoke.

"Why did Princess Christiana insist that Harald Wade be present when she arrived here? I think this may have some connection to his going with Mary this morning."

"My daughter has the misconception that she and Harald are in love and that their happiness depends on them being married. Nothing could be more unsuitable."

"Except perhaps your daughter marrying Ali Ayan?"

"Christiana was goading us. She never would have married him. In fact, the detectives who approached her reported that she was relieved when they asked her to come with them."

Elspeth had not been an eyewitness to this scene, but she wondered just how accurate the prince's description of the event was.

"Do you think that Harald and the princess are trying to find a way to, how shall I put it, run away together? And that Mary might be colluding with them?" Elspeth said.

"Impossible." the prince said.

"I'm not certain. Michael, surely Elspeth has made a good point," Hope said.

"I find it unconscionable."

"Well, I don't," Hope said, vehemence in her voice. "Christiana is no longer a child."

"Hope, you would do well to adopt some of your sister's humility."

Hope countered, "Honor may give into you, Michael, but she's stubborn in her own way, and I know your daughter is too. It would be like Mary and Christiana to hatch a plot to let her meet Harald before confronting us all. After all, Christiana is of age and can make her own decisions."

"Are your suggesting that I should allow the third in line to our throne to throw herself at a mere doctoral student who doesn't have the family background suitable for the position of her consort?"

"I think he has no intention of being her consort. Probably he just wants her to be his wife," Hope said.

"That sounds like a naïve concept that only a North American could conceive."

"You must acknowledge that love can be stronger than tradition," Hope said.

"Not for a member of the royal family. Look at the Duke of Windsor," he countered.

"Harald is not a twice-divorced American like Wallis Simpson. His roots are established in Oxford academia, and he's certainly respectable. You wouldn't have taken him on as your secretary if he were otherwise."

"I took him on as my secretary, not as my future son-in-law. Had I known he had ambitions in that direction, I would certainly have found someone else."

"That's not the point," said Hope. "Right now

we must find out what happened to the three of them. Elspeth, do you have any ideas of how we might locate them?"

Elspeth's mind flew through the possibilities. She decided to ask questions rather than answering Hope.

"Does Mary have a credit card in her own name?"

"Don't all young people these days? Mary manages her own financial affairs and supports herself through grants and part-time jobs, usually in her chosen field. Francis and I often slip her a few dollars, but she always claims she doesn't need them. Mary knows she must stay out of debt because of my husband's diplomatic position."

"Will you check her room to see if she has taken her credit card and her passport with her?"

"It's a strong possibility," Hope said before hurrying from the room.

Elspeth turned to the prince. "Your Highness, can you break your silence and call your yacht. We should know if the launch took Princess Christiana out to the dinghy."

"I gave them orders to do so," the prince said, as if his commands were unquestionably obeyed.

"We need to know what happened when the launch and the dinghy met. Was the exchange made quickly? Beyond the beach the ocean's cold, and Mary and Harald could easily have convinced the launch's crew to allow the Princess to put on the wetsuit before she went over to the dinghy. The other possibility is that Mary and Harald boarded the launch and let the dinghy go. I think we need to know."

The prince looked shaken. "Have you considered that they might have been washed overboard from the dinghy after my daughter got on board?"

"Perhaps, but I want to think differently. Were it

not for the wetsuits, I'd be more worried that they have been lost, as the ocean is rough this morning, but I trust Mary knows the sea well and wouldn't allow anything to happen to Princess Christiana or to Harald." Elspeth trusted that her voice sounded confident, although she was partly bluffing.

The prince glared at her. She could not read his thoughts from his expression.

Finally he said, "I know now why Lord Kennington employs you, for your clear mind and cool manner. My family says I should remain positive so I'm putting my trust in your judgement. I want you to find all three of them. Do so as quickly as possible, as I do not want to worry my wife."

No sooner had he charged Elspeth than Hope returned to the room. "Both Mary's passport and French purse, where she keeps her credit cards, are missing. I checked Harald's room as well. His wallet was there but I didn't find his passport."

"Your Highness, ask your yacht's crew if your daughter's passport is gone as well. I'm assuming that because she's not the monarch of your country she travels with an ordinary passport."

The prince's nod confirmed this.

"So, we have three young people who are free to travel. The only complication may be that Princess Christiana, assuming she's here, didn't enter Bermuda through proper channels. This may create a problem. It also suggests that the three of them may still be in Bermuda," Elspeth said. "This should make finding them easier."

Not really easy at all. Since Mary was not a celebrity and was unknown to the press, she might have slipped out of the bungalow to explore the islands and to set up a place where she, Harald, and her cousin could retreat. This left Elspeth in an awkward position. She had no doubt that the police would track her movements once she left the hotel. Although the governor knew both Richard and her cousin, Johnnie Tay, Elspeth had not been cleared of the murder charge brought against her the night before. If she suddenly were seen to be crossing the islands in pursuit of the wayward threesome, the police could very well take umbrage and intervene. Inwardly Elspeth's confidence faded, but she nodded to both Hope and the prince.

"If I'm to get on with it, today's the best time. Call my room number, Your Highness, when you hear from your yacht."

After Elspeth left the room, she was conflicted. She wished to speak to Princess Honorée about the murders, but at the same time did not want to burden her with the disappearance of her daughter.

When she returned to her rooms, Elspeth silenced the ringer on her mobile and called the front desk, asking them not to disturb her until one that afternoon unless one of the guests in the bungalow called. She crawled into her bed, and fell into a dreamless sleep, which was shattered by her wakeup call, four hours later. She lifted the telephone to stop the buzzing and turned back over. Although her body ached from her lack to sleep over the last three days, her mind was instantly awake and aware of the two problems she needed to solve. Which was more important, discovering who had murdered Martin Hagen and Lilianne Balfour or finding Mary, Harald and Christiana? She rolled over again.

Because of her arrest, she was uncomfortable going out beyond the confines of the hotel in search of the wayward young people. Still, where could they have gone, assuming they had not been washed away by the forces of the ocean? Elspeth suspected that Mary had been the leading force behind hiding her cousin from her aunt and uncle. If this were indeed so, where would Mary have taken them? Elspeth rose, although her body protested, and went to her laptop. She connected to the internet and typed in 'Marine Biology in Bermuda'. The response was immediate, leading her to the Bermuda Biological Station for Research. Mary could have visited there, and she also probably knew a number of the scientists who worked there. Surely this was the logical place for her to take Harald and Christiana. Elspeth did not want to mention her theory to the prince as yet. She preferred to find Mary, Harald, and Christiana and talk to them before taking them back to the bungalow.

Next, Elspeth turned on her mobile and saw she had two voice mail messages, the first from Richard and the second from an unknown caller. She decided to listen to the second. The prince did not identify himself, merely asking that Elspeth meet him as soon as possible. The voice mail had been left three hours before. She remembered having asked him to use the hotel phone, not ring her mobile.

Without listening to Richard's message, Elspeth rang through to the prince on the house phone. Greta von Fricken answered and seconds later the prince came on the line.

"Where have you been?" he asked. She could tell he was annoyed, but she did not rise to the bait.

"I'll come right over," she said with dignity.

The prince was waiting at the gate and let her in. They went to the dining room, where the vestiges of the lunch buffet had not yet been cleared. Elspeth was aware she was ravenous, having eaten little lately. At the prince's behest, she poured herself a cup of tea and discreetly sipped it, all the while wishing for more.

"What have you discovered?" he demanded.

Elspeth, unperturbed by his irritation, said, "Please, Your Highness, tell me what you learned from the yacht."

"The launch met the dinghy this morning," he said. "Mary came on board, leaving Harald in the dinghy, and she assisted my daughter into her wetsuit because she said the water was cold and the princess might need it if the waves got any worse and splashed over the sides of the dinghy. The yacht's first mate warned Mary against the vagaries of the tides when the wind was so high. She merely laughed and told him that she was accustomed to the moods of the ocean and had no fear that if the princess were sufficiently suited, she wouldn't suffer any ill effects from her swim to the shore. The two of them boarded the dinghy and were shortly lost in the fog."

Elspeth listened to him respectfully and said, "I don't think that Mary expected the waves or the fog, but she had every intention of taking your daughter and Harald somewhere other than here. She may not have planned to let go of the dinghy, but the weather may have forced her to do so. Your Highness, I think I know where to find them, but you must trust me to do this without your intervening. If they have chosen to defy your wishes, they'll need to be persuaded that returning to the hotel is in their best interests. Please let me try."

He looked at her. She could see he was conflicted, and once again she wished she could read his thoughts. "You seem to have great confidence in your abilities, Ms Duff," he said.

"I'm not a clairvoyant, but I do think if you and Princess Honorée intervene at this point, they will find ways to rebel against you, no matter how good your intentions. I'm a neutral party and may be able to talk sense into them."

"Tell me. How do you propose to do that?"

Elspeth smiled her most persuasive smile, one she had used over the years with difficult guests. "I'm not completely sure. I have to find them first."

He sniffed. "Do so, then, and be quick about it!"

Elspeth did not want to leave the bungalow without accomplishing her second task, and she decided to deal with it directly.

"Before I leave," she asked, "may I see Princess Honorée?" Then, bending the truth, she said, "I think she may be able to help me when I approach your daughter."

"I don't want my wife involved."

"Surely she must be?"

"She's extremely worried about Christiana's whereabouts, fearing she has been lost in the ocean."

"I can well understand that, but please let me talk to her." Elspeth knew her voice was pleading.

"All right," he said, "but spare her the details."

Elspeth was not sure which details he meant but did not ask. "Please let her know. I can meet her in her rooms if that would be easier."

Princess Honorée greeted Elspeth as she came into the suite. She was dressed in an elaborate dressing gown, but from the darkness under her eyes, Elspeth assumed she had been up since before dawn and had slept little the night before.

"Has Michael been trying to protect me?" she asked after greeting Elspeth and leading her to a chair. Elspeth noticed that a fresh tray had been brought with a coffee urn.

Elspeth nodded sympathetically as she accepted a cup of coffee from the princess. "He has. I'll try to explain what's happening, but I also need to talk to you about the unfortunate affair with Martin Hagen."

"I thought you might," the Princess said. "Christiana is one problem, but his murder is quite another. Michael has downplayed Christiana's disappearance from the dinghy sufficiently to make me think that the three of them have found a place of refuge. But, Elspeth, I'm really concerned about what you have found out about the blackmailer."

"Let me assure you first, Princess, that I'm convinced your daughter, niece and Harald Wade are safe somewhere here in Bermuda. I've a strong suspicion where they might be, and plan to pursue this lead once we've finished speaking."

"You sound confident."

"Somewhat. I'll feel better once I've contacted them. When I do, I'll let you know, but in the meantime, we do need to talk about the murders."

The princess looked up, startled. "Did you say murders, plural?"

"They haven't told you?" said Elspeth, surprised,

"About Martin Hagen's death, yes. But another murder?"

"Unfortunately, there has been another, and I believe the second victim was Martin Hagen's accomplice. Her name was Lilianne Balfour, and she was posing as the wife of a general serving in Iraq, saying they were here to celebrate their wedding anniversary. She hadn't accounted for the fact that most people are traceable on the internet and that the general she boasted about was her father who had died during the war in Vietnam. She was alone but seemed to need a reason to justify her being here. I put a trace on her in the hotel records and found that she and Martin Hagen had visited other the Kennington hotels at the same time on several occasions. That points to their being in league with one another. I think the way they operated was simple. She was the front person, looking for wealthy people who had something to hide. Once she had found them, he would approach them and demand payment for silence."

"I have no recollection of meeting this woman."

"If you think back, she may have seen you at a critical moment, the moment you were trying to buy back the brooch from the jeweller. Lilianne told me this in a completely different context. She said she recognised you here because she had seen you at a jeweller in London where the proprietor had addressed you by your title. You mentioned this when you first told me about the blackmail. Do you remember anyone else in the shop when you were there?"

"I was quite upset when the jeweller told me the brooch was gone, but thinking back, I do recall brushing by a woman as I dashed out to the street."

"Do you have any recollection of what she looked like?"

"No, none."

"Did you see this woman when you went to Martin Hagen's rooms?"

"I saw no one. I was being extremely careful, but I think I would have noticed."

"Mrs Balfour recognised you. I tried to convince her that it was Hope she had seen, but, if she was working with Martin Hagen, she probably didn't believe me. The police have made the connection between the two victims, and they are convinced the two murders are the act of a single killer."

The princess looked distressed. "That would absolve me, wouldn't it?"

Elspeth looked directly at the princess, who diverted her eyes. "Unfortunately not, Your Highness. Our hotels use CCTV cameras that are placed around the whole exterior premises for security reasons. The police are in possession of the tapes on the nights of both murders. On both of these tapes there is a woman in a broad brimmed hat who entered the rooms of both Mr Hagen and Mrs Balfour. Later the two of them were found dead. The hat was similar to the one you wore when we went out on the beach."

"But . . ." The princess hesitated. "Have you seen the tapes?'

"I have and I saw a woman in the hat both times she approached Martin Hagen's room. She was not really in focus. The woman who went to Lilianne

Balfour's room was even less recognizable. It could have been any woman staying at the hotel, or a man disguised as a woman, although I doubt that. The figure's way of walking was definitely that of a woman."

Up until this point, Elspeth had purposely concealed that the police had taken her into custody the night before. "Princess, can you tell me where you were on both nights? Did you go to Martin Hagen's room before the fire and then circle back to give yourself an excuse in case you were caught on the CCTV camera? And, where were you two nights ago, the night when Lilianne Balfour was killed?"

The Princess drew back, her eyes wide and her lips pressed together in anger. "Are you accusing me of murder? I thought I could trust you!"

Elspeth reached over and put her hand gently on the princess's arm to calm her. "I'm afraid the police are going to insist on making inquiries into the movements of the women guests on both nights. We've given them the guest list for the hotel but have excluded the occupants of the bungalow. I don't know how long it will take the police to discover the omission. I've told several half-truths to cover for you, but I can't hold the police off forever."

"Half-truths?"

"I've told them I found 'no other papers' in Martin Hagen's safety deposit box. I skirted the fact that I did find the brooch and have put it away for you. I don't know how much longer I can avoid telling the truth."

"Why would they doubt you?"

Elspeth took a sip of her coffee, which by now was lukewarm. She tried to think of a way to sugar-coat what had happened the night before but could think of none. She took in a deep breath.

"I was arrested last night for the murders and put in jail. The police used the flimsiest of circumstantial evidence to justify my incarceration. The experience was extremely unpleasant, I can assure you. I'm a bit shamefaced to admit I used my husband's connections to the governor to secure my release early this morning, as I knew I was expected on the beach. The police still suspect me and have retained my passport, and I'm fully aware that they could be watching my every move. In any case, Martin Hagen had tried to blackmail me although he had no basis in fact, but he did have real material to use against you—the brooch. As you know, I took it from the safety deposit box and plan to return it to you shortly because by right it's yours, not his. I hope I can continue to deny its existence, but, if pressed, I will have to tell the truth. This admission could implicate me for tampering with evidence, which is a serious crime, and possibly you for murder, which is worse."

"You are very frank, Ms Duff," the princess said stiffly.

"I've no choice but to be. I don't want you to be accused of murder. Believe me, it's an unpleasant prospect, but you must be prepared for it if the police do discover that I found the brooch in Martin Hagen's safety deposit box." Gravity filled Elspeth's voice, and the princess winced. "Now, Princess, I must go and find your daughter."

The princess did not rise as Elspeth left her. Instead she put her face in her hands. Elspeth let herself out of the gate.

25

When phoning the Bermuda Biological Station for Research, Elspeth used an old technique that she frequently found brought her success. She called the station's main number, which was given on the internet site. A cheerful woman answered and asked how she might direct Elspeth's call.

"This is Dr Duff from *mumble mumble* University. I'm looking for Mary Tilden," Elspeth said in her American accent, which she lowered, hoping it would become androgynous. "Has she come in yet today?"

There was a pause, and Elspeth suspected the person behind the cheerful voice had covered the receiver. Then she returned saying, "I haven't seen her but one of the researchers here said she was here earlier. "Do you want to leave a message?"

Success, thought Elspeth. "Will you find out when I can reach her directly?" Elspeth said again in her American tones.

The voice went off the line again. It was almost a minute before she returned. "She said she would be back by three. Shall I have her ring you?"

"No, thanks. I'll call her back then since I'm calling long distance."

"Will you give me your name again, please. I didn't write it down."

Elspeth quickly rang off before answering.

She looked at her watch. It was half-past two. She drew out a map of Bermuda and saw that the biological station was farther away than she could walk in half an hour, so she decided to take a taxi. Rather than going into the lobby and having the doorman get one for her, she went out her back gate and skirted around the edge of the beach to the main road. She soon found a taxi queue away from the hotel and directed the driver to take her to the station. She asked that he drop her off at the end of the long, tree-lined road that led to the main building. If Mary was coming back there, Elspeth hoped to waylay her before she entered the building. Elspeth found a bench under the shadow of a palm tree but not in direct view of the entrance. She waited ten minutes before she spotted Mary, who no longer was in a wetsuit but was dressed casually in a tracksuit and wearing trainers and a baseball cap. She seemed immersed in her own thoughts and did not see Elspeth. Elspeth rose slowly and came up behind her. Instinctively Mary turned.

"How did you find me?" she asked.

"Using long investigative experience," Elspeth said, grinning.

"I suppose you want to know about the others?"

"Un huh," said Elspeth said nodding.

"Will you tell my aunt and uncle?"

"At the very least I need to tell them you're safe. They're worried that you had been lost at sea."

Mary considered this. "All right," she said begrudgingly, "but I beg you, don't tell them where we are."

"That won't prove difficult," Elspeth said, "as I have no idea where that is. But, Mary, at least let me know what this is all about. We can discuss later what you want me to tell the prince and princess."

"Ms Duff, Christie and Harald love each other, and they want to get married. If they return to the bungalow, every kind of pressure will be put on Christie to assume her royal duties and forget Harald, who undoubtedly will be fired."

"Is that why you and Harald arranged this morning's events?"

"The idea was mine, not his. Have you ever loved someone so much that you would give up everything in your life for him?"

Elspeth answered honestly. "I'm the wrong person to ask. Twice I made the mistake of thinking I was in love with someone without fully considering the consequences. Each time it ended badly, so asking me about my experience isn't a good way to judge what has happened between Princess Christiana and Harald Wade. What my own experience has taught me, however, is that lovers need to think long and hard about the far-reaching consequences of their liaison. If they can find a way that truly works for them both, without either one having to sacrifice their individuality, then they may find happiness together, but if either one had to give up too much, I fear they'll eventually hate having sacrificed something important to them. But, Mary, I speak as a middle-aged person, not someone young."

"Will you see Christie and Harald without involving her parents or mine? Perhaps you can talk to them. You must know I'm on their side, but I sense you may have some pearls of wisdom you could give them."

"I often think wisdom comes from paying attention after one has made a number of mistakes. If I'm wise at all, which I cannot guarantee, it's because I've fallen so many times that I now look where I am going. I don't know what I can tell Harald and the princess, but I'm willing to see them. Only tell me where and when."

"Do you have a mobile phone?"

"I do."

"Give me the number and I'll call you."

"I'll be available at any time they're willing to see me."

"Thank you, Ms Duff. And please tell my aunt and uncle that you have spoken to me, that you know we are safe, but you do not know where we are."

"And if they pressure me?"

"You can't tell them anything but the truth. You really don't know where we are, do you?"

Elspeth returned to the hotel by taxi and asked to be left at the bottom of the hotel's drive. She did not see any sign of the police, but she hoped her exit from the hotel had not been noticed since they had warned her not to leave. No matter what happened, her first concern was to let the members of the royal party know that their children were safe and still in Bermuda.

She returned to her suite, and rather than using the house phone, she picked up her mobile. There was one message, the one from Richard that she had not listened to earlier. Guilt spread though her. At what point did her duty to her job supersede her relationship with her husband? She had no answer. So much for the wisdom she had touted with Mary. It would now be evening in Malta, and Elspeth remembered that her husband was dining with the prime minister. She would not be able to reach Richard directly, but she could leave a message. She would have to tell him the truth, that she had put her job first, even when replying to his earlier call would probably only have taken a few minutes. She would have to ask his forgiveness once again, for her own sake, for he was always chastising her for her lack of faith in the depth of their love and their marriage vows exchanged just over five months earlier.

She called him at his new house in Valletta, or rather 'their' new house, as she must learn to call it. She sighed and asked him to ring her when he got home from the prime minister's party. She noted the time and vowed to herself that she would make herself available when he returned the call.

She had no sooner disconnected her call than

her mobile rang again; this time it was Mary, who sounded breathless. "She'll see you, but she wants you to be alone." Elspeth assumed that the 'she' was Princess Christiana, "Do you know the ice cream shop on the way to the station. She'll bicycle there and wait for you."

"I'll be there as soon as I can, if I can get a taxi right away. Have her wait, if necessary. How will I know her?"

"She'll know you."

Elspeth grabbed her windcheater, which, in an uncharacteristic moment of messiness, she had not hung up after her morning excursion back to the beach and hurried from her sitting room. Because of her call to Richard, she had not contacted Christiana's parents, and she did not want to do so whilst riding in the taxi. The good news, or was it, would have to wait until she had talked to the wayward princess.

Elspeth should not have been surprised by the princess, but she was. She had seen press photographs and the tabloid pictures of Christiana on Ali Ayan's yacht and expected her to be someone who was sophisticated at one moment and defiant at another. Therefore Elspeth was taken aback when approached by a young woman in a tracksuit, trainers, and a baseball hat that were identical to Mary's, and who, except for her colouring, was more like her Canadian cousin than the camera had suggested. She was tall, close to six feet, trim but not thin, and radiated fitness and health rather than world-weariness or boredom with life. The princess's intense pale blue eyes, like her father's, were intelligent and alert. Her fair hair was pulled back in a ponytail which she had thrust through the back of her baseball cap. Her Royal Highness, the Princess Christiana looked like a fresh Californian university student, not someone born and raised in the royal courts of a small and staid European kingdom.

She came up to Elspeth as she was paying the

taxi driver and spoke in a deep, cultured British voice. "Thank you for coming, Ms Duff," she said. Her tone gave away only the slightest hint of her royal standing.

"Your Highness," Elspeth said instinctively once the taxi had driven away.

"Please call me Christie. I think under our current circumstances that would be best. Would you like an ice cream? You'll have to pay as I don't have any money with me."

The princess seemed amused at saying this. Elspeth was not sure if this was because Christiana, like Queen Elizabeth, did not carry money on her person.

The wind was still blowing, now in gusts, and so they took their paper cups of ice cream and found a table in the lee of a wind by a wall outside the shop. No one else had ventured out so they could speak privately.

Christiana began. "I asked Mary to arrange for me to see you alone because I felt you could act as an intermediary between me and my parents. I'm afraid that Mary and I have been totally underhanded. I never had any intention of coming to Bermuda to be browbeaten by them into returning to court. When Mary came to see me the last time on Ali's yacht, we cooked up our plot, that I would agree to be 'kidnapped', if you will, and brought here. Ali and I never did plan to be married. In fact, he is a good enough friend and has enough mischief in him to play along, knowing what my real intention was. I'm afraid there was no way I could hide my parents' prejudices against him."

"What was your intention?"

"To elope with Harald. We have been planning it ever since my father said no to us a year ago. Are you shocked?" Christiana took a spoonful of ice cream, her eyes challenging Elspeth.

Elspeth did not reply at once. "No," she eventually said.

"Will this put you in a difficult spot? Mary said

she thought it might."

"It might, but would you consider talking to them first?"

"For what purpose? I already know where they stand. My mother is almost worse than my father on this issue, although the ultimatum was his."

Elspeth considered her assignment, to protect the royal party, but not to be a counsellor to any of them. Yet this case had become extremely personal for her, and Christiana's plan for elopement brought back memories in Elspeth's life that, in retrospect, always brought sorrow. Instinctively she wanted to spare Christiana the pain caused by her impetuous elopement with Alistair Craig and their later estrangement and divorce.

"Unfortunately, when dealing with your family, I can't get rid of personal feelings from an earlier time," she said ruefully. "Normally my past life doesn't come with me when I'm on assignment, but I keep finding parallels between my situation then and yours now, which might make me unfit to be an intermediary. Because of my own life experiences, I can see both sides to your situation and, therefore, may not be an impartial party."

Christiana looked askance at Elspeth. "Are you taking their side?" she asked. "Mary said you wouldn't."

"I'll be honest with them, Princess. I also won't take your side. I made the mistake you may be about to make when I was about your age, and I have regretted it for most of the rest of my life because I could have handled the whole thing better, for myself and for the others involved. Your circumstances are far different, but the consequences may be the same. I'd like to talk to you about this, not here, but in a place when we can be more private—and be out of the wind." Elspeth was aware she was shivering. "Also, I would like to continue to speak to you alone, without Mary or Harald being present. I don't know if I can offer any great insight, but

I can tell you about the mistakes I have made in the past and hope I can offer some guidance to you. Would you be willing to come with me to my rooms at the hotel where we could talk over something warmer than ice cream? I promise we can go in the back way without being noticed, and no one will know you are there. I also promise I won't let your parents or your aunt and uncle know you are with me."

Elspeth was not sure if Christiana would consent. The young woman rose, threw her half-finished cup in the dustbin and looked at Elspeth. "Mary said I should trust you," she said.

"You can. My only wish is for a happy resolution to this situation. If you are willing to learn from my mistakes, then I'll tell you all about them."

"No time like the present," the princess said with an insouciant look. She pulled her baseball cap more firmly on her head and followed Elspeth as she hailed a taxi.

During the taxi journey back to the hotel, Elspeth tried to find a way to tell the story of her own elopement in a way that would be meaningful to the princess without seeming condescending. Tactfulness was required if Elspeth were to be effective.

As Christiana freshened up after their return to the hotel, Elspeth boiled water in the electric kettle for tea and found an assortment of biscuits especially made for the Kennington hotels by Fortnum and Mason. When Christiana reappeared, she had shed the baseball cap and let out her hair, which was stylishly cut, long, and wavy. She looked regal now, despite the tracksuit and trainers.

"Tell me about Harald Wade," Elspeth said, handing a mug to the princess.

"About Harald?"

"Please. I've only briefly met him and have no idea of he who is, not his position but inside."

"I love him," Christiana said.

Elspeth smiled. "Of course, or we wouldn't be here, but I need to have a sense of him, and why you love him."

"He's very handsome in his shy way, and intelligent. He can say the sweetest and then the most brilliant things. When I'm with him, I just want to hear him speak, even if he is just discussing the weather or my father's upcoming appointments. When he is about to leave the room, I feel I never want him to go. I think about him all the time."

"What would it be like if you were together all the time?"

"Blissful!" Christiana's infatuation was plain, but Elspeth wondered how this might translate into a life-time commitment.

"After you elope, where will you live?" she asked.

"We'll find a dear little cottage near Oxford. I'll tend the garden, and he'll bicycle into college every day to do his research and see his students. We'll have three children, two boys and a girl, and they'll be handsome and brilliant like their father and follow him to Oxford."

"And you? Other than tending the garden, what do you see yourself as doing? Please forgive me for asking, but you see I eloped for my first marriage without asking that question. Later I was sorry I didn't ask. The man I married had all the mystique of romance in his life, his manner, and his way of living. I met him in London, after the tragic end of my engagement when I was at Cambridge. He held an important position in Hollywood and, after several dreary years of mourning my fiancé's death, he offered the escape I thought I needed, to the land where dreams are made. Alistair, my husband, promised to take me away from all that had hurt me in the past. He did, but I never considered where I was going other than away to a dream filled with happiness. I left the UK without a word to my parents, only telling a dear friend about my flight, who advised me to be more cautious. He was right, but I didn't listen." She did not mention that her dear friend was now her husband or that their love affair was one that came late in life and lay deeply in their commitment to each other as well as their recognition of each other's individual needs. Elspeth wondered if this was something the young woman with her could understand. "It was several years before I could acknowledge my mistake and heal the wound that I imposed on my parents by not telling them. They are still loving and forgiving, but our relationship after that was different."

"But they let you go!" Christiana cried.

"I gave them no choice."

"Did they forbid you?"

"No, they simply didn't know about Alistair until the deed was done. I think my point is, however, not how much harm I must have imposed on my parents by my rash action, but what harm I did to myself. The first years in Hollywood were indeed a dream. I was a young and unformed Scottish girl. Hollywood signified glamour, mixing with the rich and famous, my task being to see that my husband had all the support he needed for his career. But along the way I forgot that I was a human being with my own emotions, intelligence, education, and in need of my own separate existence. Hollywood didn't offer that to me, and had I listened to my friend, I would have seen that before I ran off and got married without any real consideration of what that meant for me personally."

"What are you suggesting, Ms Duff? That loving Harald is a fantasy?"

"I have no idea if it is or isn't, but I think you don't know either. I don't mean to be oppositional. Rather, I hope I can be supportive in your decision, but I wonder how much you have thought about your own future, and just not Harald, although he seems an admirable and lovable person, and no doubt will make a good husband."

Christiana lowered her head and then looked up defiantly.

"You seem to be putting him down."

"Not at all. I don't know him, and I don't know you, but I do know there are great disparities in your backgrounds and, if you do marry, you'll have to work them out to the satisfaction of both of you. It may take time, but you probably will both be happier in the long run if you do so. I know you can't approach your parents about this; their minds seem to be set. Because I want to help you all, I only ask that you take some time to consider all the ramifications of your decision."

As Elspeth spoke, the princess sat very still. She took a sip of her tea but did not seem to taste it, for all its fineness. Then she put her mug down, stood up and walked to the French doors without saying anything.

Elspeth waited, drinking her tea and nibbling at a biscuit, while considering her next words.

"Love, the real kind, lasts forever, or should. If it's rushed, it can be fleeting. I feel that you marrying Harald could be a good thing for you both. He seems serious and he obviously is in love with you. But, Princess," Elspeth said using the title judiciously, "he has grown up in a protected environment, more protected than yours. He's been exposed to court life through his employment with your father and because of his chosen field of study, understands the traditions of your country, but at heart he's a scholar and the son of scholars. Oxford traditions are as strong as royal ones and almost as ancient. You two are going to have to work out how you can come together happily."

Christiana turned back to Elspeth. "Do you think we can?"

"If you truly love him, if he is not just an escape from your life, if you can find a way to live with him and love him and still be who *you* are, you'll be able to work it out, but it won't be easy."

"Did you and your husband work it out?"

"No, which is still hurtful for our children."

"Why are you being so candid?"

Elspeth answered from her heart, although she had not intended to do so. "Because, unexpectedly, I care, for you, for Harald, and for your parents. I don't want you to make the mistakes I did. My infatuation with my first husband was a way for me to run away, not to have the life I really wanted. I hope you don't make the same mistake."

"And your second husband?"

"I fought the consequences of loving him for a long time. Even when I agreed to marry him, I was clear about my own needs, but I'm older, and know myself better, and I have no doubts about my feelings for him."

"Does he accept that?"

Elspeth could not hide the smile that crossed her face and her heart. "Yes, of that I'm sure," she said and then added with a cock of her eyebrow, "Almost."

Christiana laughed. "I like you. Ms Duff, and I do trust you. I want to go back to Harald now, but I'll consider what you've said. May we talk again tomorrow? It's been a long day."

"Of course. Call me. Mary has my mobile number. With your concurrence, however, I want to talk with your parents tonight and tell them you are safe."

"Just tell them I'm OK. Please don't mention anything else about us."

"Agreed," Elspeth said and shook Christiana's hand.

26

A thunderstorm passed in the night rousing Elspeth. The drumbeat of the rainfall on the roof and windows increased her wakefulness. Elspeth pounded her pillow in frustration and wished Richard were there. Well after the showers had passed, she sat up, knowing she would not get to back to sleep easily. Her mind whirled over the last few days and her pressing need to find the murderer. There was so little to go on, and so many of the clues reverted back to Princess Honorée. Elspeth felt trapped. She decided to concentrate on any facts that would implicate someone else. It could have been the rain that made her think of the fire sprinklers, but that matter had been lost with all the other activity since Martin Hagen's body had been found. 'Why didn't the fire sprinkler work?' That had been one of her first questions, and the answer to it seemed to imply that someone with more knowledge of such things than Princess Honorée had tampered with the fire sprinklers in Room 17. Elspeth realised that she knew little about such systems, apart from their presence in all Kennington hotel rooms, so rather than struggling to get back to sleep, she rose, found her laptop and brought it into bed with her. What she needed was a primer in fire suppression systems. Google brought up multiple sites, and she began to scroll down them, hoping to find something simple enough to be comprehensible in the middle of the night but technical enough for her to understand why the sprinkler heads in Martin Hagen's room had malfunctioned. On her third hit, she found the answer. Satisfied, she discarded her laptop, rearranged her covers, and puffed up her pillows.

Sleep still did not come, despite her re-arranging her pillows several times. Finally, she gave up in frustration and rose from bed. The question of the failure of the fire sprinklers would not go away. From her new knowledge, limited though it was, she had to infer that something had stopped the fusible links from breaking, thus preventing the sprinkler heads from dropping and opening the water line to it. If the murderer had any idea of how fire sprinklers worked, wedging something beside the link so they would not break would be child's play. If Martin Hagen was already dead, the murderer would have had the opportunity to climb up on a chair or table, insert a stiff object next to the link, and then push the table or chair back into position before starting the fire. Would the police think of this? If not, would the fire department? If she were to prove the princess's innocence, she needed to find out if the fire sprinkler heads in the bedroom and bathroom had been tampered with. She checked the clock at her bedside, which read 3:57.

Finding the clothes she had worn the day before, she pulled them on, splashed water on her face and drew a comb through her hair. She opened her door to the hotel garden and saw it was still raining, though gently now. She turned back to get her windcheater. She rummaged in her handbag and found a small LCD torch. She also took a compact with a hand mirror and put it in her pocket. They were hardly the tools of a practiced sleuth, but Elspeth expected that they would arouse little attention if she were interrupted in her task. She found her master key card at the bottom of her handbag and added it to her collection. This was the best she could do on short notice.

The darkness and rain made the possibility on anyone being in the garden doubtful. Low lights lit the path, allowing guests to trace their way to their rooms late at night, but otherwise the path was dark. Because she knew the way to Room 17, she went quickly along the path. When she arrived, however, yellow and black tape was still strung across the door, but it was marked 'construction 'and not 'fire zone'. She looked about and saw no one was minding the door, but she was loath to lift the tape and enter the room. Hoping the beach entrance to the room would not be taped off, she made her way through the kitchen. Two of the early morning bakers were there, but otherwise it was deserted. She waved at them and found her way out to the loading area. Skirting the rubbish bins, she walked down the access drive and veered off towards the back of the smokers' wing. The night breeze had fallen, and the only sound was the steady rhythm of the waves. She let her eyes get accustomed to the darkness and made her way along the pathway. Her only concession to the lack of light was a quick flash of her torch on the faceplate that identified Room 17. Even in the dark, she could see that the exterior wall had already been re-painted, and no external sign of the fire remained visible. Before inserting her master key card, she made a quick surveillance, but no one was about. Now she hoped her card would work. Thankfully, it did.

The Kennington maintenance crew had been at work. The interior of the room still smelled acrid, but by the beam of her torch, she could see that the burnt husks of furniture and scraps of the carpet were no longer there. The lath and plaster had been removed from the ceiling and from two of the walls. A stepladder leaned against one of the intact walls, and a partly filled dustbin stood by another. She shone her torch on the ceiling. The sprinkler pipe hung at a rakish angle as one of the support wires had been broken. She waited for her night vision to improve and eventually was able to move about the room without her torch, even though the windows had been blocked out with brown translucent paper. She pulled the ladder to the centre of the room, set its lock and flashed her torch briefly to determine the exact location of the sprinkler head. Slowly she climbed up, rung by rung, hoping the ladder would prove tall enough to allow her to see the sprinkler pipes clearly. She reached the second highest rung and began to despair, but by stretching her arms she was able to throw her light directly at the sprinkler head. As she suspected, a nail was wedged by the plug that released the water, although the fusible link had melted. At least her theory had been correct. Her self-congratulations were short-lived, however, when a blazing light flooded the room, and someone shouted, "Freeze! Put your hands above your head!" There was no doubt about the authority behind the voice.

She reached up for the pipe to steady herself, but in doing so, dislodged it, and it fell noisily to the floor. Still hanging onto it, she swung as if on a jungle vine to the floor. The pipe broke and water began to spew from one end. "Damn", Elspeth said out loud. She struggled to her feet and put up her hands as commanded. The spray of water slowly drenched her clothes and hair. She moved out of the water's path but not before she had lost all her dignity and most of her pride. The beacon of light followed her.

"Police," the harsh voice said. "Who are you and why are you here?"

"Elspeth Duff, hotel security," she said mustering as much presence as a woman drowned in water could. "I saw a light and came to investigate."

"Why, Ms Duff, or should I say Lady Munro, were you on the ladder?" the all too familiar voice of DCI Hart asked, "and why were you examining the fire sprinkler pipe?"

Elspeth wiped the water from her face and tried to think of an appropriate answer. None came. She walked toward the torchlight with as much decorum as she could, considering her wet clothes and hair, and, as she did so she shielded her eyes. "There's something I want you to see, Chief Inspector," she said, "but first someone will have to turn off the water. Will you send one of your men to the front desk, and they will get the night-time repair man. I suggest we go outside while we wait."

A policewoman with the chief inspector turned off the beacon of light and shone her smaller torch at the floor. Elspeth blinked several times to adjust her vision to the brightness.

"I suggest, Ms Duff, that you come with me. I need to question you about what you were doing here and why you were up on the ladder. I'm in the midst of another case and was called by one of my men when he saw your light. I must be on my way, but PC Clayton will take you to your rooms. Please dress in dry clothes, and then she will accompany you to the police station. I'll see you there in about an hour, assuming I clear up this other matter."

"But, Chief Inspector. . ." she began.

"Ms Duff, I've given you more than enough latitude and if it were not from pressure from above, I'd have kept you in jail. As it is, I'll merely question you. I hope you have a good reason for being here. Clayton, take her now, don't let her out of your sight or earshot and see that she is in my office within an hour."

Police Constable Clayton was a younger woman in a dark blue police uniform, with stout police shoes, drawn-back hair, and a serious face. Under other circumstances she might be described as pretty but her face was grim. She took Elspeth's arm firmly. "This way, madam. You'll have to show me where you are staying."

Elspeth took her along the path and through the patio door to her rooms. She had left the lamp burning by her bed but switched on the overhead halogen spotlights when they entered her suite. The officer drew back her breath. "Wow! This looks like a Hollywood movie set," she said before containing herself. "Are you actually living here?"

Elspeth smiled at the delight of the uninitiated when first seeing the extent of luxury at the Kennington hotels. It might be the first and last time the constable would ever experience it.

"I'm not a guest. I'm staying here as part of my assignment with the security office for the hotels."

"How much does this cost a night?"

"More than you or I could ever pay. I always appreciate that my job lets me stay in rooms like this. But, have a seat. I would dearly love to shower and wash out my hair. Let me order coffee for you and some fresh scones, which they make at this time of the morning. I'll order some for us."

"I'm not supposed to let you out of my sight."

"Then come into the bedroom. I'll leave the bathroom door open if you like."

"Yes, ma'am."

Elspeth picked up the phone and called room service. A sleepy voice answered and promised the coffee and scones shortly.

Constable Clayton followed Elspeth into the bedroom and then to the walk-in wardrobe.

"Are these clothes all yours?" she asked.

"Yes, I need to dress for many different occasions in my job as a security advisor and therefore have to bring them all with me."

"Security?" the younger woman said. "How did you get your job?"

"Many years ago I started out as an officer like you but at Scotland Yard." Elspeth did not add that she had read law at Cambridge, or that in the intervening years, she had dabbled in private detection in Southern California. Nor did she mention she had a wealthy friend in Hollywood who had introduced her to the world of Kennington hotels, and this had eventually led to her position in the Kennington Organisation. The constable would probably never rise above detective sergeant, if she were lucky. Elspeth did not want to raise false hopes, but she felt she might get more leniency, or at least privacy in her bath, if the officer felt a bond with her. "But I went into private security after that. I was lucky to get this job."

"You sure were. It beats the police station," PC Clayton said wistfully.

"I know the chief inspector said you were not supposed to take your eyes off of me, but would you settle for my having my shower in private but talking to you the whole time, or singing? I think you may prefer the former. Besides there's no window in the bathroom, only a large skylight." Elspeth did not add that if you used the spa at night you could sink back and enjoy the stars, which she had demonstrated to her husband several nights before.

Before PC Clayton answered, there was a ring at the door and Elspeth, watched by the policewoman, let in room service. The trolley, as always, was arranged in Kennington style, even at this early hour, with flowers and freshly cut fruit as well as the scones and a large urn of coffee. Elspeth signed the chit and let the sleepy attendant go.

"Help yourself, Constable. I'll get on with my shower. As she stepped into the steaming glass cubicle she called out, "How do you like the scones? Try the lemon ones. They're my favourite."

A contented sigh of pleasure came from the bedroom. "I've never tasted scones like these before. They melt in your mouth."

"Good, aren't they, especially when they are still warm from the oven. How's our time going?"

"We still have forty minutes. It's only about ten minutes to the station by car. Let me know when you're ready, and I'll call one. There's no sense waiting for one when there might be another thunderstorm."

"I agree with you. I'll be out in a minute but will need a bit of time to dress and attend to my face and hair."

Once finished, Elspeth came into the sitting room and poured herself a cup of coffee.

"Have you had any sleep, constable? It seems to me that when I was in the police force, I always felt tired." Elspeth did not tell her that this was equally true in private security. She thought back, and in her present assignment she was unsure how many nights ago she had slept through the night. She longed for her bed in London and a reprieve from her current responsibilities. Lord Kennington couldn't deny her three or four days off when she returned to London, certainly not after the last few days. PC Clayton was probably never granted this privilege.

PC Clayton said. "Since we have time, I'd love another cup of coffee and some of that fruit."

"Help yourself, please. There is no sense for it to go to waste. We can take the extra scones with us if you'd like to share them with the others."

The policewoman's face broke into a grin. "May I take them home to my family? They don't often get treats like this."

"Only if I'm cleared of bribing you," Elspeth laughed.

PC Clayton took out her mobile and rang for a car. Because no one was likely to be in the lobby at such an early hour, Elspeth suggested it come to the front of the hotel.

As she was leaving the room, Elspeth saw her book and reading glasses sitting on the table by her bed. "Constable, since I may have a wait in the Chief Inspector's office, do you mind if I take my book and spectacles?"

The policewoman nodded assent. Elspeth called room service for a box and had the scones and the remainder of the fruit packaged in it. When they walked to the front door together, Elspeth hoped no blackmailers were lurking in the lobby; for the hotel to have three blackmailers in one week would be excessive.

They sat on the hard, wooden chairs in the corridor outside of DCI Hart's office. PC Clayton kept eyeing the box and finally Elspeth suggested that there were still a number of scones inside and one less would hardly be noticed. She looked at Elspeth shyly and opened the box. Elspeth suppressed a grin and turned to her book. She took the envelope that Richard had put there to mark her place and was about to tuck it into the back cover of the book when she saw it was addressed to her. In large, rambling letters the name 'Elspeth' was written on the front and embellished with a flourish. Elspeth frowned. She ripped open the envelope. An equally sloppy signature and another flourish revealed the sender of the note was 'Dorothy'. In her sleep-deprived state, it took Elspeth a moment to make out that the sender was Dorothy Ayers. The note was simple:

> *Dear Elspeth,*
> *How delightful to meet you here in Bermuda and have such a lovely dinner together with you. Do visit East Sussex soon and bring Sir Richard with you.*
> *With hope of seeing you soon.*
>
> > *Yours,*
> > *Dorothy*

Elspeth stared at the letter. Its sprawling letters and the way she formed the letter *S* were distinctive, and Elspeth realised she seen this handwriting recently. But where? In the hotel register? No, that was all done by computer these days. She looked again at the message, mystified.

She leaned back against the hard slats of her chair. Where, where, where? She looked across at the constable, who had finished her scone and who had her eyes closed contentedly. Elspeth lowered her head and tried to concentrate on the note, but she was getting nowhere when the door opened and DCI Hart came through the door.

"Clayton!" he barked.

The policewoman came to full attention, spilling the box to the floor. The box spun round, but the top did not come lose and its contents remained intact. Elspeth reached over and recovered the box, which she put on the chair next to her.

"Chief Inspector, PC Clayton has been diligent," Elspeth said. "Please don't chastise her on my account. We're all rather short on sleep."

"You are dismissed, Clayton!"

"Yes, sir."

"Here, take the rest of your breakfast," Elspeth said.

"Give the box to me," DCI Hart demanded.

"It's left over from our coffee earlier, Chief Inspector. Is there any harm with her putting it out in duty room?" Elspeth asked.

The Chief Inspector opened the box.

"Have one," Elspeth said. "They're from the hotel."

He eyed her, but hunger must have overcome discipline. He took one and shoved the box back at the policewoman, who withdrew with a quick glance of thanks to Elspeth.

Perhaps the sweetness of the scone, which DCI Hart tasted as if he were testing for poison, softened him.

"Come in to my office, Ms Duff, and explain yourself."

Elspeth followed obediently, clutching her book, Dorothy's note, and her reading glasses.

After licking his lips and fingers clean, he motioned Elspeth to a chair.

"Now tell me why you were examining the fire sprinkler system last night by stealth with your small torch," he said.

Elspeth settled herself with poise and raised her chin.

"I didn't have a bigger one and the lights in the room no longer worked," she said. "I had to know why the sprinklers hadn't engaged when the fire started, and report back to Lord Kennington in London."

"Didn't you think we'd thought of the same thing and that the room had been sealed so that the evidence would not be tampered with?"

"The sprinkler *had* been tampered with—before the fire."

"We photographed everything extensively, and don't need your interference. Bermuda may only be a British overseas territory, but our police methods are not backward."

"I'm not implying that they are," Elspeth said, "but I'm responsible for hotel security. I can't abrogate that responsibility, however much you may fault me."

"Do you frequently interfere in police investigations?"

"No, I am usually asked to assist in them."

"Are you implying we have hindered you from doing so?"

"I'm not, Chief Inspector. You may have reasons to suspect my complicity in the murders, particularly regarding the contents of the safety deposit box and the blackmailer's attempt to extort money for his hotel fees from me. It wasn't terribly clever on his part to reveal why he was at the hotel."

"Now, Ms Duff, do you have a way to clear

yourself of committing these crimes?"

Elspeth's mind raced and an idea came to her. "Chief Inspector, may I see the contents of the safety deposit box again?"

"For what reason?" he asked.

"I want to see the letter that was with the newspaper clippings. I have an idea but can't be sure of it until I see the letter."

The DCI picked up his phone and asked that the evidence be brought in. A clerk responded after several minutes and brought in the sealed plastic bag.

Thanking her, the chief inspector brought out a pair of surgical gloves. He undid the seal on the plastic bag and drew out its contents. He found the letter that she had requested to see.

Tell me how much you want. I will meet you by the stature of the bear in Paddington Station at three on Tuesday and will bring the money to you, it said. The configuration of the *S* matched those in Dorothy's note to Elspeth.

"Inspector, I know who the murderer is." She pulled Dorothy's note from her book. "You'll need to complete the investigation. I'm sure the authorities in the UK will assist you."

DCI Hart glowered at Elspeth. "Explain yourself," he demanded.

Elspeth did so. "In the hotel business, particular in high end hotels, we always have to deal with those unpleasant people whose object is to prey on our other guests, most of whom are rich or famous or both. Martin Hagen came under our radar about seven years ago. In fact it was I who reported him to the security office. I didn't realise at the time that he was a blackmailer, but one of the older women at one of our hotels in London reported that he was paying inordinate attention to her and she felt uncomfortable. I'd just begun to work for Lord Kennington, and he sent me to the hotel to investigate. Martin Hagen was that man. As I told you earlier, he approached me when I first arrived in in Bermuda, probably because he assumed I had come to investigate his activities. When he confronted me, it was obvious that he knew who I was. In fact, I think he and his accomplice, Lilianne Balfour, set me up. Their chief objective was Dorothy Ayers, but Martin Hagen knew me and probably wanted to, how shall I put it, divert my attention from his real victim."

"Can you prove that?"

"Only partially, Chief Inspector. I'll leave the proof to you, but I can assist you in apprehending Martin Hagen and Lilianne Balfour's real murderer. Here's the letter she sent to me. I'm sure your handwriting experts can match the writing with the note in the safety deposit box."

"Is this your only evidence," DCI Hart asked.

"I can testify, if you like, that Mrs Ayers told me she was going to buy a hat that matched the one on the tapes. Besides she is a tall woman, taller than me, and could have more easily put the nail in the fire sprinkler head than I. Undoubtedly when you trace the gun, you'll find it was owned by Mrs Ayers. I'm certain you can carry on from here, and you have my full cooperation."

27

Elspeth felt she was becoming far too familiar with the road from the police station back to the hotel. By the time she left the chief inspector, dawn had come and gone, and a cloudless day was breaking. Elspeth drew her jacket more securely across her shoulders. She was grateful that DCI Hart had returned her passport, but not without an admonishment for her to stay out of trouble and not to interfere with the ongoing investigation. She also was instructed to let him know when she was leaving Bermuda. Having promised all these things, she waited for his thanks for solving his case for him, but none came. So be it. Perhaps he was still annoyed that Richard had pulled strings to get her out of jail.

When she arrived back at the hotel, it was close to eight o'clock. She went back to her suite and checked the voice mail on her mobile, which had three messages. Scrolling down, she saw that one was from Richard, the second from Eric Kennington, and the third from a blocked number, which she assumed belonged to Mary or Christiana. She listened to her husband's message first. It was loving but filled with concern. She quickly texted back: "Cnt tlk now. Wll cll u soon, explain. Lv, E." He hated such brevity, but she knew she could make it up to him later.

Next, she called the unknown number and Mary answered.

"Can you meet us at the ice cream shop in half an hour?"

"Make it nine o'clock. If I'm late, I'll be there as

quickly as possible," Elspeth said, not knowing what result the next phone call might bring about. "But give me a number where I can reach you in case I'm delayed."

Mary complied.

Elspeth held her breath as she dialled Lord Kennington's private number. He answered immediately, and from the gruffness in his voice, Elspeth knew he was not in a receptive mood.

"Elspeth, I had a call from the prince, and he's not pleased."

Elspeth swallowed; she hoped not too audibly. "In what way?"

"He told me his wife is quite upset."

"Did he say why?"

"You tell me."

Elspeth tried to imagine what might have agitated the princess. The possibilities were numerous, particularly since their last meeting had ended on a somewhat hostile note.

"Eric," she said, "Give me the chance of seeing Princess Honorée this morning. I expect she's concerned about the murders, but this morning I met the police and told them I discovered who the murderer is. It's is up to the police to prove it, but there's enough irrefutable evidence to make me certain. If I explain this to the princess, I hope she'll be relieved."

"Why should she be relieved?"

Elspeth had not told her employer about the princess's involvement in the blackmail and decided that she no longer needed to.

"Everyone who knows about the murders is a bit on edge."

"Now tell me Elspeth what you have not told me so far. Why did the princess know about the murders? I thought I had told you to keep them under wraps."

I put my foot in that one, Elspeth thought; now she had to think fast. "Very few people do know. However, I had to warn the royal party about the possibility of the press finding out about them being at the hotel. I urged everyone in the bungalow to be particularly cautious and to stay out of sight."

Eric Kennington seemed to accept her explanation although it was an impromptu prevarication.

"Now tell me about the murders. Certainly you ought to have rung me before."

"I've just come back from the police station," she said without explaining the early hour. She hoped he was too impatient to calculate the time difference between London and Bermuda. "Almost certainly Martin Hagen and his cohort Lilianne Belfort were blackmailing a guest by the name of Dorothy Ayers. The police found the evidence that Martin Hagen was using to extort money from her in his safety deposit box at the hotel, and I was able to match the handwriting on a note in the box with that in a letter Mrs Ayers had written to me. Unfortunately she's the mother of one of my daughter's closest friends in East Sussex. It won't be easy to tell Lizzie. It's a task I don't relish."

"I want all the details when you return to London."

"Certainly, Eric," Elspeth said, but she knew that the detail of the lost brooch would remain a secret between her and the princess. Eric Kennington did not need to know, nor did Richard. Confidences between women went back many ages, and Elspeth had no intention of breaking the tradition. "I hope to be back in London in two days' time."

"Call and let me know exactly when. I have a busy schedule."

Elspeth knew from the past that he would clear time to see her, especially regarding something as important as hiding from the public two murders at one of his hotels.

"I will" she said and rang off.

It was now fifteen minutes past eight. Elspeth debated whether it was too early to call the bungalow, but she needed at least to talk to Hope, if not the others as well. She rang through, and Greta von Fricken answered the phone and confirmed that Hope was up. Hope came on the line shortly afterwards.

"Hope, can you come the back way to my rooms?" Elspeth asked. "I'll meet you outside the patio gate."

"Now?"

"Please. It's important."

"I'll make excuses."

"Thanks."

Hope Tilden arrived shortly afterwards with a quizzical look on her face. "Is this regarding Mary and Christie, or Honor?"

"All three. I've ordered coffee and a light breakfast. Will you join me?"

"It will be my pleasure, as long as you explain yourself."

"I've contacted Mary and am meeting her and Christiana later today."

"That's wonderful news!"

"Hope, what have I done to alienate your sister?"

"Honor is very touchy when she thinks something has happened that will damage her standing with the prince. She has given him a fortune, which he did not have before, and a child, but beyond that royals by marriage, especially commoners, have a much higher standard to meet than true royals. Surely you can appreciate that. I sense there's something between you two that has caused her all this anxiety. I don't want to know what it is, but I feel you need to deal with her directly."

"You're absolutely right. I do. I'd like to meet her later, away from the bungalow. She may not want to see me, but tell her that the police have discovered who the murderer is, and I want to explain to her how they did so. It may put her mind at ease."

"They have? That is a relief. No one we know, I suppose."

"No, you wouldn't, but the person was being blackmailed by the murder victims." Elspeth was careful to leave her information gender neutral.

"Will the identity of the murderer become public?"

"Not if Lord Kennington has anything to do with it. Murder doesn't create good publicity. Hope, I have one more request. Do I remember correctly that you told me that Princess Christiana has an income of her own?"

"Yes, from my grandfather. He may have been a German aristocrat, but he believed women should have enough money not to become 'chattels' to their husbands, his word not mine. His thinking was quite forward-looking in his day. Both Honor and I were given a settlement at eighteen, long before each of us inherited our full share of our grandfather's wealth. Certainly having financial independence made it easier for me to flaunt convention and marry Francis. I sometimes wonder that, if I had been poor, I'd have taken the risk. In hindsight, my marriage to him has given me more happiness than anything else in my life, except perhaps Mary. I don't think my sister can say that."

"More's the pity," Elspeth said, "but I need to be certain before I go to see Christiana that she can, if she chooses, live without financial reliance on the palace."

"She definitely can. It won't be the luxurious life in her family's castle, but she won't suffer any hardship."

"Hope, what is your take on Christiana's feelings for Harald? Does she really love him or is he the object of a dream that she imagines to be real?"

"Both."

"Both?"

"I suspect that Christiana, despite her defiance of her parents, really wants to have a purpose in life. She has always admired Mary's drive and dedication to her field, even though Mary has none of Christiana's social advantages. Certainly Christiana is as bright as Mary and, given a chance, could succeed in her own right. I've heard Christiana speak often of the environmental movement and her concern for the future of this earth. I can envision her taking up the cause, perhaps studying ecology at Oxford and becoming a spokesperson for environmental issues in her own country, in the UK, or beyond. Her rank would help her. How would this mesh with her romantic feelings for Harald? I don't know, but as the wife of an Oxford don and perhaps as an Oxford scholar herself, she would carry greater weight than merely being a frivolous princess from a small kingdom. My fondest dream is that she'll realise her full potential."

"Will you help her?"

"With all my heart."

"And Princess Honorée and Prince Michael?"

"Despite their hostility, Elspeth, I think they would prefer my solution over Christie becoming a member of the jet set and wasting away her life."

"Can you persuade them?"

"I can try. After the affair with Ali Ayan, the alternative would be a relief. I might be able to convince them that it will enhance the stature of the monarchy, as monarchies are less and less in favour these days."

"Thank you. You've given me an idea for when I meet Princess Christiana. I'll try to convince her to see you and her parents."

"How can we thank you? Is this part of your usual job?"

"No, not at all, but somehow I've been personally touched by your situation. Perhaps that's why your sister was so hostile yesterday evening. I must have overstepped my boundaries in her eyes."

"Not in mine," Hope said. "Let me talk to Honor before you see her again."

Elspeth made her way towards the ice cream shop, where Princess Christiana was waiting for her. She was no longer in the tracksuit but was dressed in jeans, a t-shirt saying 'Save the Whales', and the trainers she had worn the day before. Her hair blew free of the baseball cap which she was holding in her hand. Christiana waved, and Elspeth waved back.

"Have you had anything to eat?" Elspeth asked as she joined Christiana.

"Some wretched coffee at the station," the princess said.

"Are Mary and Harald nearby?"

Christiana smiled "They're inside."

"Then, with your concurrence, let's join them. Perhaps I can persuade you all to come back to my rooms at the hotel, and we'll have a breakfast that is quite suitable for a princess and her entourage."

Christiana laughed. "I'm in need of one," she said. "The digs where we are staying are short on ambiance and lean in the larder. I'm starving."

Elspeth took Christiana's arm and they walked companionably inside. They found Mary and Harald on high stools around an infinitesimal round table, finishing ice cream cones. Christiana went up and hugged Harald, and then gave Mary a pat on her arm.

"We've been invited to a proper meal in Ms Duff's rooms. She promises if we sneak in the back we won't be seen."

Elspeth's promise was not quite correct, as they encountered an elderly couple walking with their dog on the beach, but the two of them were more involved with the miniature canine than the gaggle of young people surrounding Elspeth.

Once inside, Elspeth suggested that the three of them retreat to the bedroom and use the bathing facilities if they so choose. If their 'digs' lacked amenities, a Kennington hotel bathroom would enchant them. In any case, she needed to clear them from the room when room service came with the breakfast. After ordering, she heard their whoops of glee over the plumbing facilities and the thickness of the abundant towels. Elspeth had the room service attendant set up a table and put the food on warming trays on the sideboard. She made no mention to the waiter why this was the third breakfast she had ordered in the space of a few hours. He was trained not to question the behaviour of guests and staff visiting from London, but Elspeth expected he might make a comment when back in the kitchen, although this was strictly against hotel policy.

Mary and Christiana emerged first, both freshly scrubbed as children might be after a bath. Mary's hair, being shortly cropped and curly, had been rubbed dry. Christiana had hers wrapped in a towel. They explained that Harald, in gentlemanly fashion, had offered to go last and would join them shortly. As Elspeth was dispensing coffee, she assured them the food would far surpass that at their lodgings. Soon Harald emerged, now closely shaven and smelling of the hotel aftershave. Elspeth disliked scent on a man, but Lord Kennington's choice of male cosmetics was the least offensive she had ever encountered. His new scent obviously pleased the princess who rose and told him so with a kiss on his cheek. Elspeth smiled at young love and hoped Christiana and Harald had found the real thing. All three, Mary, Harald and Christiana, filled their plates with eggs, bacon, sausages, kippers, tomatoes, mushrooms, hot rolls and fresh fruit. Elspeth contented herself with a cup of coffee and remembered the days of filling her plate with all the niceties of a Scottish breakfast without the least thought of its effect on her figure.

Elspeth let them settle into their meal before she spoke of the issue uppermost in her mind. She felt rather like a mother hen and carefully avoided starting her conversation with 'my dears' in the mode of Peter Rabbit's mother.

"You all must be aware of how much worry you have caused Prince Michael and Princess Honorée. Mary, the reason I was a bit late this morning was that I spoke to your mother beforehand. I usually don't take any personal interest in the people I deal with at the hotels, but I told your mother that this time I feel differently. I may have imposed my own personal life experience inappropriately on what has happened here. Lord Kennington will be unhappy if he hears this, as will my husband, but I can't leave you all hanging in the balance."

Elspeth did not expect Harald to speak first, but he did.

"Ms Duff, but for you, we would have found a way to leave Bermuda by now. Can you offer us any hope in persuading the prince and princess that we are serious?"

"A glimmer, or perhaps a great deal more. I'm not sure. I think you need to trust Mary's mother. She has agreed to step in as your spokesperson."

"In what way?" Christiana asked.

"I think she should explain. Mary, do you feel comfortable calling her?"

"Sure. Mother and I have always been able to talk."

Christiana sighed. "Lucky you."

"Come on, Christie. Your parents aren't that bad."

"Yes, they are. Let's see what happens. I predict a roadblock."

"I don't," said Elspeth.

Christiana turned to her. "Why?" she asked.

"After breakfast, I need to speak to you alone, Princess, and I will explain. I can't predict what your mother and father may say to you, but I think I can give you something that will ease the way."

She let them finish their meal, including a second helping for Harald Wade and another serving from the fruit bowl for the young women. When it became clear they were replete, Elspeth repeated her request to see Christiana alone. Mary and Harald bowed out gracefully and told Christiana they would see her back at their lodgings.

"Now, Ms Duff," Christiana said, for the first time sounding like a royal, "what's so important that you can't tell the others?"

Elspeth rose and went into the bedroom. When she returned, she held a small packet wrapped in tissue paper. "I want to give you this," she said.

The princess looked puzzled and slowly opened the packet as if it contained an unwanted birthday present. Elspeth watched her as she drew out the brooch.

"Do you recognise it?" Elspeth asked.

Christiana examined it carefully. Elspeth suspected that Christiana was trying to place the brooch and then, after recognising it, seemed perplexed as to why Elspeth had it in her possession.

"Where did you get this?" she said, her voice unsteady.

"So you do remember it."

"It belongs to my mother by way of the royal treasury. In a fit of anger, I took it from her jewellery collection."

"And sold it," Elspeth said.

Christiana nodded. "But that doesn't answer my question. Where did you get this?"

Elspeth skirted the question. "Your mother knows, and it will be up to her to tell you. It has caused a great deal of trouble since you last saw it, both to your mother and to the relationship between your parents. Princess, I'm giving it to you because I have no desire to keep it and because it belongs to your family. Your mother found out that you took it to the jeweller, but she doesn't understand why. Your father knows none of this. In fact, he insisted that insurance cover its loss after your mother admitted it was missing."

"Who recovered it?"

"I did, but under unfortunate circumstances. Your mother won't be able to justify its reappearance to your father without implicating you. She would have to tell your father that she knew why the brooch was missing and that he had committed a . . . what shall I call it . . . an act of fraud in asking for the insurance money."

"Why are you giving it to me?"

"I spent a great deal of time last night trying to figure out what best to do with it. I'd thought of giving it to your aunt, but I don't think she knew any of the circumstances, and I didn't want to tell her what had happened. Instead I thought it best to give it to you."

"What am I to do with it?"

"I can think of two things. When you return to your family's residence in London or to the royal palace, you may hide it there in a very obscure place and then miraculously discover it. But on second thoughts, the best solution might be that you give it to your mother, say you had forgotten about it, and only recently found it among your other jewellery. I think that solution would satisfy your father, even if your mother knows the truth."

"Do you think she'll cover for me?"

"You know the dynamics of your family far better than I do. I'll let you pick which one of the two options, or perhaps find another one."

"You are asking me to lie then?"

"The choice is yours."

Christiana frowned down at the brooch. "I never much liked it," she said, "but it is, or was, a favourite of Father's mother, the queen. I think Mamma wore it for her sake."

"I see," said Elspeth neutrally. "I may be overstepping my boundaries, but why did you take it?"

"To spite my parents, I suppose, although it now seems a foolish thing to have done. They were being hard-headed about Harald. I've regretted taking the brooch ever since, but you still haven't told me how you acquired it."

"I'll let your mother do that, and I'll always keep your secret. I've shared it with no one and never will."

"Do you think my mother will see me?"

"I'll be speaking to her shortly and will ask. I'll tell her what has just passed between us. Princess, trust your aunt and Mary. They're strong people who have been highly successful at bucking the status quo and making a great success of it, and, they both are on your side."

Christiana looked down at the brooch and folded it in her palm. She looked back up at Elspeth, who saw tears in her eyes.

"I think I should thank you but I don't know how."

Elspeth smiled. "I'll be satisfied if I hear you've discovered who you really are, what you want to be and then acted on it."

Elspeth dreaded her next interview. After the tension that had riddled her last private meeting with

Princess Honorée, Elspeth did not know what to expect as she walked towards the bungalow. She wished she could have support from Hope, but she also knew Christiana would have a greater chance of success with her parents if they did not think that Elspeth had orchestrated her return to grace. Princess Honorée was waiting for her by the gate, her large hat in hand.

"Shall we walk on the beach?" It was a royal command disguised as an invitation.

Elspeth had come unprepared for the cloudless day. She felt she was getting more sun than she wished, but, hatless, she accompanied the princess to the beach.

"I was rude last night, Ms Duff. After you left, I regretted what I had said. You see, I thought you suspected me of being involved in the murders."

"Did your sister tell you that the police have information that points to the real identity of the murderer?"

"Indeed, and it made me even more be sorry for my words last night. Hope said she suspected you might have been involved with discovering who that killer was."

"I did supply some evidence, but now it is up to the police to confirm what I found and to arrest the culprit. Unfortunately the suspect, who was a guest at the hotel, has returned home to England, and the police here will need to cooperate with the police there to catch . . ." Elspeth almost said 'her' but then switched to the grammatically incorrect but gender neutral 'them'."

The princess followed suit. "Were they being blackmailed?"

"Yes. The papers in the safety deposit box were damning."

The princess stopped and turned to Elspeth. "You took the brooch from the safety deposit box, I know. Was that terribly honest?"

"Not really," Elspeth admitted, "but blackmail

isn't terribly honest either. The brooch was yours, and, in retrospect, I'm glad it was not in the box when the police examined its contents. It's best that they don't know your presence at the hotel or the purpose of it."

"Do you still have it, the brooch I mean?"
"No, Princess, I gave it to your daughter this morning, and also gave her several suggestions on how she might return it to you openly and without raising questions from your husband. Your daughter is a fine person, and I predict that one day she will make you proud of her. But I don't want to interfere any further. I know I've gone beyond my job responsibilities already."

The princess did not speak but took Elspeth's arm and walked with her across the sand to the rocky point which jutted out into the ocean.

"Perhaps you did overstep your boundaries, but you have given my family a good deal of hope. We came to Bermuda with none. I want to thank you."

Elspeth reddened with pleasure and not from the sun. "The Americans, I think," she said, "have a better reply than we British, although we now commonly use it. You're welcome."

Epilogue

"I don't understand, Mummy, why you were involved at all." Elspeth's daughter, Lizzie, was noticeably upset. "Surely you have better things to do than going about getting the mother of one of my best friends charged with murder."

The two of them stood facing each other in the drawing room of Elspeth's Kensington flat. Lizzie had not taken off her coat since her arrival, nor had she accepted a cup of tea from her mother.

"Lizzie, I couldn't ignore the facts."

Her daughter gnashed her teeth and stared hostilely at Elspeth. "Why do you continue in that beastly job of yours? Certainly Daddy left you well enough off that you don't have to work at all, and Richard would be delighted if you stopped running around the world and settled in to be his wife."

Elspeth knew there was no reasoning with her daughter when she was in this mood, and she answered honestly. "Not even you, Lizzie, could see me taking Lady Marjorie's place."

"I think you love meddling in other people's lives. You always have."

Elspeth tried to stay calm. "I don't consider it meddling. My job is to find out when things go awry at the hotels. Unfortunately in Bermuda I recognised the truth too late. I'm sorry it hurt your friend."

Lizzie wasn't consoled. "Do you know what you did to Olivia's life?"

"It was her mother who should have thought of that. I did nothing other than report what I had discovered," Elspeth said. She did not attempt to tell Lizzie the complexities of the situation in Bermuda.

"You could have said nothing."

"That's never an option when murders have been committed. Seriously, Lizzie, I had to speak up. Two people, and a baby earlier, are dead, and Olivia's mother undoubtedly killed them. I found undeniable proof of the last two murders. I can appreciate how hard this is for Olivia, but I can't avoid my obligation to the law, and I can't lie to the police about a murderer when I know her identity."

Lizzie threw her body down on to one of the white sofas in front of the gas fire and wrapped her coat more closely around her body, although Elspeth's flat was warm.

"What am I to say to Olivia? 'So sorry, my mother helped put yours in prison, probably for life, and in doing so ruined your life and your family's forever as well?' She's my close friend and neighbour, and her children play with the twins every day." The twins were Elspeth's grandchildren, now approaching three years old.

"That isn't exactly how it is, Lizzie. Would you like me to come to East Sussex and speak to Olivia?"

"What could you possibly say?"

Elspeth had no idea how to answer, because there were no healing words. "I could tell her the circumstances," she finally managed.

Lizzie dismissed her mother with an exaggerated shrug, and then drew her arms more tightly around her body.

"What is Olivia to say to her children? 'Sorry, but your grandmother is in prison and probably will never get out. She's a murderer, and a triple one at that'."

Elspeth swallowed. "Lizzie, she *is* a murderer. Olivia will have to accept it and cope as best she can.

You can help her survive it."

"How do you suppose I could do that?"

"Continue to be a good friend. Olivia hasn't changed. She'll need support in a society where people love scandal. We British always have, but eventually it will die down. Hold Olivia close right now; she will need you. And, eventually the worst of it will fade."

Lizzie looked defiant. "How can I explain your part? You'll be testifying at the trial, won't you?"

"I'll have to. I gave the police the evidence that established the final link between the murder victims and Dorothy Ayers."

Lizzie scoffed. "So you will be the star witness, your name spread all over the gutter press."

"As you may suspect, the Kennington Organisation will do everything possible to have the trial heard *in camera*. There are no guarantees, but both Eric Kennington and Richard have connections. If we are fortunate, the news won't spread beyond Bermuda."

"Can you be sure of this?"

"No, of course not. The media, when they want to be, can be insidious, but Dorothy Ayers's earlier crime has long since been forgotten. We can try to make sure it is not brought up again. Lizzie, don't ever desert your friend and don't condemn me for what I had to do. Neither will serve you well."

"I think you shouldn't come to East Sussex again. How could I face Olivia if you were there?" Lizzie growled.

Elspeth blanched at the prospect. The punishment of not seeing her grandchildren go from toddlers to children, cut deeply, as Lizzie must have intended it to do. But Elspeth hoped she knew her daughter well enough to know that the threat would pass.

"We can talk about that later. It might be better if you bring the children here or that we can meet in

Malta or in Scotland, for a while anyway. Please, Lizzie, don't cut me off because Olivia's mother, by her wilful actions, cut her off. You know I love you and wouldn't do anything to hurt you if there were any possible way I could avoid it."

Lizzie's tears spilled over her cheeks, and she wiped them with the back of her hand the way a child would. "Then why don't you leave your bloody job before you hurt more people!" It was uncharacteristic of Lizzie to swear, and this resonated deeply within Elspeth. She pulled a clean handkerchief from her pocket and offered it to her daughter.

"Is it all the bloody perks? All the posh living? All the high and mighty Ms Duff with her elegant clothing and superior airs? This expensive flat? Your reverse snobbery at rejecting the title Richard gave you? Mummy, I never thought I would find you so despicable. Your values are so empty!"

Bile filled Elspeth's mouth and her heart wrenched. She thought of all she might have done better when raising Lizzie and how she might have been able to repair the gap that had always tacitly existed between them. Until now, Elspeth had granted the independence her daughter had asked for since childhood, but now she wondered if that distancing had closed doors of intimacy that could not now be reopened. Elspeth remembered her own parents and the freedom they had given her, and also their constant love. Had she offered the same to Lizzie? It seemed not. As Olivia would need time to accustom herself to her mother's crimes, Elspeth knew it would take time for her relationship with Lizzie to heal, but her heart was heavy. She did not like her daughter's condemnations but did not know how to refute them. The truth, she thought, will not always set you free.

Author's Notes and Appreciation

A Blackmailer in Bermuda was written in 2006, but for many reasons I was not able to visit Bermuda until twelve years later. The people, the places, the colours, the vegetation, and the climate exceeded all my expectations, although I had done extensive research before going there.

So many thanks are due to the people who helped me there. The staff of the Fairmont Southampton (Princess) Hotel, particularly at the concierge desk and beach club, assisted me throughout my stay there. My excellent tour guide Edwina Lambert taxied me across Bermuda in my attempts to find the locations I had used in the book, even places not open to the public. Ryan Amaral, caretaker at The Old House, showed me around the extensive grounds of this beautiful estate, which I chose for the fictitious location of the Kensington Bermuda. Police Constable Kimberley Spring gave me a tour of the police station and jail and explained the arrest and charge procedures there. Aaron Denkins, Divisional Officer/Fire Protection Officer at the fire station in Hamilton, told me about the services provided by the Bermuda Fire and Rescue Service. Amazingly he had witnessed three murders similar to the one I describe in the book. My apologies to them all if I have altered their information in error or modified it to fit my plot. Readers familiar with Bermuda will note that I have disguised several of the places used in the book as I did not get permission to use their names.

The greatest appreciation goes to Alice Roberts,

my editor, who picked up numerous mistakes in my manuscript and adapted the book into British English, and to Beverly Mar who gave the book a final proofread.

I could not write and publish any book without the support of Ian Crew, who constantly encourages me to go forward.

Ann Crew is a former architect and now full-time mystery writer who travels the world with her iPad, camera, and sketchbook gathering material for the Elspeth Duff mysteries. She lives near Vancouver, BC.

Visit *anncrew.com* for more.

CPSIA information can be obtained
at www.ICGtesting.com
Printed in the USA
FSHW021625221219
65367FS